"You ~~think~~ ... ~~...~~ , too."

"When did I ever say so?" she replied.

"Each time you gazed at him. I, on the other hand, while aggravating and opinionated, am not a bore nor a coxcomb." To prove his point, his strong arms swept around her shoulders and his mouth descended to plant a resounding kiss on her lips.

Caught by surprise, Rosalind felt herself responding to the embrace with a fervor that left them both breathless.

"Do you always conduct your flirtations in so brazen a manner?" she asked.

He held her off for a moment. "Flirtation? My good woman, I am making you a declaration, if you would but notice."

Other Fawcett Books
by Clarice Peters:

THE FALSE BETROTHAL

SAMANTHA

THEA

ROSALIND

CLARICE PETERS

FAWCETT CREST • NEW YORK

for Jeremy

A Fawcett Crest Book
Published by Ballantine Books
Copyright © 1985 by Clarice Peters

Library of Congress Catalog Card Number: 85-62788

ISBN: 0-449-20872-9

Manufactured in the United States of America

First Edition: December 1985

Chapter One

From the window of the sitting room overlooking Berkeley Square a pair of gray eyes avidly scanned the street below. Lady Manning was not in the habit of staring out of windows as a rule, but her scrutiny continued unchecked until a certain high-perched phaeton turned the corner from Hill Street and stopped on the flagway below. Dropping the rose-colored curtains lest she be caught spying, she quickly crossed the room toward a tray of sherry glasses.

Like most matrons saddled with a bachelor son, Lady Manning desired nothing more than to see him happily wed, with a nursery full of children for her to spoil. This state of mind was induced somewhat by the occasion of her own wedding two months previous after nearly a decade of widowhood. If she at three and fifty had found happiness and love, there was no earthly reason that Alastair at two and thirty should not.

Lady Manning was not in the habit of ringing a peal over her son on account of one scrape or another. Up to now—and this was the early March of 1817—she had kept her wishes concerning his marital state to herself, but she had determined just this once to give him a nudge in the direction of Miss Rosalind McHenry, a young lady she had met during her wedding trip to the Continent.

On first meeting Miss McHenry at a very boring ball in Vienna, Lady Manning had felt instinctively that here was the very wife for her Alastair. Indeed, if she had sketched a spouse for her son she could not have been more on the mark. Miss McHenry was beautiful without being flashy, good-humored, and blessed with a *joie de vivre* that could only attract. Although at three and twenty Miss McHenry could not be considered in the first flush of her girlhood, Lady Manning did not view this as an insurmountable obstacle.

She had spent part of her wedding trip confiding as much to her new lord, perfectly convinced that Alastair had only to meet Miss McHenry to settle once and for all the issue of his marriage.

As befitted a new and indulgent bridegroom, Lord Manning listened to these confidences with only half an ear, rousing himself at the necessary intervals to murmur, "Very true, my love," and contenting himself with the belief that once they had returned to London, his wife would dwell no longer on the charming Miss McHenry. Fate, however, dictated otherwise.

The two had not been in London more than three days before Lady Manning discovered through an old bosom bow, Lady Haversham, that Miss McHenry, far from being a Vienna resident as previously thought, was herself in London for the Season. Lady Manning was not prone to superstition as a rule, but the match did seem fated, and she threw caution to the wind, deciding the time had come to take a hand in her son's affairs. Only now, with Alastair's tall, elegant, fair-haired figure looming in the doorway, she was suddenly beset with doubts concerning the path she had embraced.

"How now, Mama," Eberhart said, coming in with a smile. "That can't be sherry I spy on your tray, can it?"

"Of course it is, you absurd boy," she retorted. "It came all the way from France at quite horrid cost. And no matter what propriety dictates a lady to drink, I'd rather sherry than that vile concoction they call ratafia!"

Chuckling, he stooped to kiss her powdered cheek and allowed her to draw him down next to her on the crocodile-legged couch.

"Where is my new stepfather?" he inquired.

"At White's," she answered, pouring the sherry. "All this moving is driving him to distraction. Two months ago it seemed like the merest trifle to combine two households into one, but now that we are involved in the task it's more difficult than either of us imagined." Her head of guinea curls bobbed as she spoke.

The earl laughed. For one enduring the rigors of moving, his mother looked quite her usual fashionable self in a French cambric morning dress augmented by a sable fraise.

"Travel must agree with you, Mama. You look radiant, and you are sporting a new fraise, I see. Quite charming. From Paris, I trust? And this sherry is devilishly good. I shall tell Harry so when next I see him. Where did you come upon it? I would have thought the Frenchies would drink it up rather than part with it."

"We found it in a remote inn near Dijon," his mother replied, shuddering at the memory. "Harry can provide the full particulars if you are interested."

"Every gentleman is interested in sherry such as this, Mama," he said, taking another judicious sip, giving her the opportunity to observe him more closely.

Any other mother would have felt her bosom swell with pride at the sight of the tall figure on the couch next to her, but Lady Manning felt only a growing vexation. It was a pity that Alastair was so handsome. Had he been a little uglier—a trifle stoopbacked perhaps, or saddled with a temporary wart or two—he might cease to be so nice in his requirements concerning a wife. She sipped her sherry, gathering her courage to the sticking point.

"Alastair," she said, recklessly interrupting his pointed remarks on the dubious merits of English sherry. "I wish to have a word with you about marriage."

His brow lifted a fraction of an inch. "About marriage, Mama? Oh dear, I do hope that after a mere two months you haven't had a sudden change of heart. We have not had a bill of divorcement in the family, and divorce is always alleged to be such a sticky business. Of course, if Manning won't do, he won't do—"

"I am not speaking about my marriage to Manning!" his mother expostulated.

"That's a relief," Eberhart said, crossing an elegantly shod foot over his knee. "One has only to think of the ready he wasted on those wedding gifts for you. Pretty lavish, if you ask my opinion. And did you ever find a place for that swan?''

"I persuaded him to return it to wherever he found it," Lady Manning said distractedly. "And I do wish you would stop talking about my marriage to Harry and attend to what I am saying."

"I believe for once I may be ahead of you, Mama," he said, putting his sherry down next to hers on the ormolu table. His gray eyes met hers. "Confess, were you not thinking it high time I took a leg shackle?"

"Well, yes," she admitted, taken aback by his acute grasp of the situation: but then Alastair had always been a precocious child. "It's not that freakish a notion."

"Certainly not," he agreed, a twinkle in his eyes. "What a sordid old world this would be if people didn't marry. Livelier no doubt, but definitely more sordid. You may not have known it, Mama, but I have been thinking of marriage myself, particularly during the last month. But it didn't seem proper to broach the topic to you until I had settled it in my own mind."

Lady Manning was jolted. Never in her wildest dreams, as she would later divulge to Lady Haversham, had she dared hope that Alastair would speak sensibly about marriage—particularly his own.

"Well, my dear, I am heartily glad to hear that," she said, picking up her sherry glass and wondering how best to launch into a recital of the many charms of one Rosalind McHenry, late of Vienna and now of London.

"I've also settled on the female, Mama," Alastair went on. "A Miss McHenry."

Lady Manning uttered a shriek and spilled her sherry down her fraise.

"Miss McHenry, did you say?" she gasped finally.

The earl, handing her his handkerchief, looked mildly alarmed at such a reaction from his usually sedate parent.

"Yes, a charming lady, Mama. Young, perhaps, but that is all to the good, for then I can school her as to what a husband likes and dislikes in a wife."

At any other time his mother would have taken issue with such a maddeningly male point of view, but she was too occupied now in drying her fraise and struggling with her own incredulity. That Alastair should talk of marriage was one thing, improbable though it was, but for him to single out Miss McHenry from all the females in the world was nothing short of miraculous.

"I daresay you are in shock," Eberhart said, taking her silence for continued disbelief. "After all, you no sooner clap your eyes on me than I present you—metaphorically speaking, of course—with a daughter-in-law. But once you've met her, I'm sure you shall see she is the very one for me!"

"Alastair, are you roasting me?" she demanded. "Or," she added, her gray eyes narrowing in sudden suspicion, "have you been speaking with Harry?"

Her son drew back, a look of puzzlement discernible in his eyes. "Speak to Harry? Whatever for?"

"Oh, pray don't think me a shatterbrain," she implored, on the verge of spilling more of her sherry. He prudently removed it from her grasp. "But this is such a coincidence! And if I live to be a hundred—which I really don't want, for only think how hagged I shall look at such an age—I don't think I shall see its like again. When I think how I asked you by today especially to warn you against your growing predilection for the single state."

"And I stole a march on you?" he quizzed.

"More than you can imagine. And Miss McHenry. I wager a monkey Harry won't believe me when I tell him. I vow it's almost enough to make me believe in gypsy fortune telling."

"Is my stepfather acquainted somehow with Miss McHenry, Mama?" Alastair asked, still befogged by his mother's remarks.

"We both are!" Lady Manning said with an emphatic bob of her head. "Our acquaintance is very recent. We met in Vienna. She had half the gentlemen there languishing at her feet."

Eberhart smiled, not displeased by such a scene.

"I'm not surprised," he told her. "She is a charming creature. So quiet and unassuming, with the disposition of a lamb."

Lady Manning, seated on the Egyptian couch, bolted upright at these words.

"The disposition of a lamb?" she asked incredulously. Such a description did not reconcile with her image of the vivacious Miss McHenry she had met in Vienna.

"Is that what you wish in a wife, Alastair?"

The earl glanced up, mildly surprised. "Certainly, Mama. I'll tolerate no histrionics in my home. A wife should know her place."

"As should a husband," Lady Manning murmured in a challenging tone.

His smile acknowledged the hit. "I have every hope that Miss McHenry shall fill that position to perfection. She's green, as I've said. I wouldn't put her much beyond sixteen or seventeen."

"Sixteen or seventeen? Stuff and nonsense!" Lady Manning crowed. "Alastair, my dear. I know you've never frequented Almack's the way others have nor been thick in the petticoat line, and that has saved me considerable discomfort, for nothing is more disagreeable than to have a rake for a son. But surely even you must know how to judge the age of a female. Sixteen or seventeen indeed!"

His mother's scornful laugh caused the earl to frown. "I'm quite certain of my facts, Mama. Her father mentioned it to me when we spoke."

Lady Manning went rigid. "Her father? What father? From what I know of things, he died at least ten years ago." A sinking sensation spread in her chest. "Alastair, we are speaking of Rosalind McHenry, aren't we?"

The earl recoiled. "Rosalind McHenry? Who the devil is she?"

"Then she isn't . . . Aren't you planning to marry her?"

"I certainly hope not, for I don't even know such a female," her son declared. He fortified himself with a pinch of snuff. "I see where the confusion lies. There must be any number of McHenrys floating about the kingdom. My Miss

McHenry is called Felicity, a pretty name, don't you agree?''

"Yes, very," Lady Manning murmured, still absorbing the fatal news that her son meant to marry some other Miss McHenry. "Pray, how did you ever meet her?"

"Actually," he divulged, "I haven't."

"You haven't met her, Alastair?" his mother asked incredulously.

For once the usually unflappable earl appeared discomfited.

"I know it sounds odd, Mama, but I've spoken to her father."

"But, Alastair, if you've never met her, how do you know she is the wife you desire?" she asked with as much practicality as she could muster.

Her words had an effect on her son. He paused and rubbed his chin ruefully for a moment. "Well, I've made inquiries. And I've seen her once or twice in the street," he went on, noticing that his mother did not appear impressed by these words, "and she is pretty enough. And Fergus speaks highly of her," he added.

Lady Manning plummeted the depths of her memory, which was not as shockingly bad as her son's. "Fergus?" she murmured, then the light dawned. "Do you mean your secretary? Alastair, you didn't send Mr. Fairweather forth to find you a wife!"

Eberhart's eyes twinkled at the notion of his staid secretary engaged in such a task.

"No, I did not," he assured his mother. "And Fergus has no knowledge of his responsibility. He came back to London after a visit to his family in Warwickshire. He happened to mention meeting a charming, quiet, well-mannered chit by the name of Felicity McHenry. I had been thinking of marriage, and Fergus spoke so highly of her I started inquiries of my own."

"What was she doing in Warwickshire?"

"Going to school, I believe."

Lady Manning's eyes remained riveted on the handsome

face next to her. "Is that all you know?" she expostulated. "That she attended school in Warwickshire?"

"No, of course not. I know more. Her family is respectable. Her father has fallen on hard times because of his gaming habits. Nothing new in that! She's been kept at school most of her years. I'm sure you'll agree nothing could be better. She won't have had time yet to learn any bad habits that I must break her of."

His mother uttered a despairing sound.

"I know that sounds abominable," he went on. "But can you really blame me? Most of the ladies nowadays are the hurly-burly sort. I don't want that in a wife. I've spoken to Felicity's father and he looks favorably on the match. But you don't look so pleased, Mama."

"Of course I'm pleased," Lady Manning lied, swiftly gathering her wits about her, having by now correctly identified to her own satisfaction the unknown Felicity Mc-Henry as being the young lady in the charge of Miss Rosalind McHenry back in Vienna. How vexatious that Alastair should have fallen in love with the wrong Miss McHenry.

Or had he? Certainly he had spoken of her civilly and courteously, but with nary a hint of a gentleman in the throes of a grand passion. Indeed, he might have been informing her of a new purchase from Tattersall's for all the emotion he displayed. And knowing the range of emotion in her son, this was a surprise.

"Alastair," she said, determined to settle this point to her own satisfaction, "do you have a *tendre* for Felicity McHenry?"

Her son, admiring a new landscape by Mr. Constable, turned around now to stare at her. "*Tendre*, Mama? Good God, no. What put such an addled notion into your pretty head?"

"You plan to offer for the chit," she pointed out.

"Yes, but that's marriage, not love," he said, drawing what he hoped was a firm line between the two.

His mother made no effort to press him further during his visit with her, for while no love existed between the two, there still might be a chance—albeit a slim one—for *her* Miss McHenry.

At no time did Rosalind McHenry take the slightest pleasure in seeing her profligate older brother, Gerald, gracing her establishment on Green Street. And this morning was no exception.

"If it's a loan you wish, the answer is no," she said briskly as she sailed into the ivory saloon, her raven curls flowing from under an azure riding cap. She had been expecting the arrival of the Viscount Coppleton, one of her admirers.

"I am not here to borrow money," Gerald retorted.

Rosalind's violet eyes widened in surprise as they focused on her brother's pudgy figure sprawled in her Etruscan armed chair.

"What have you come for, if not money?" she asked, unable to think of any other motive for his visit. Relations between the two of them had always been cool, in large measure because of his habits of gaming and his belief that her fortune, left to her by an aunt, ought to have passed to him.

He answered her question with one of his own. "Where's Felicity?"

Rosalind's astonishment grew. Never had she known Gerald to betray the slightest interest in Felicity. Indeed, she could not even remember when he had last inquired after his daughter's health and interests. His query now and the smug look he shot her made her distinctly uneasy.

She managed to mask her emotions, replying that Felicity was out strolling with Anna, her maid.

"Why do you ask?"

Gerald's self-satisfied smile spread across his pendulous cheeks. "Because I've received an offer for her."

This announcement caused the color to drain from his sister's face and afforded him several moments of intoxicating bliss. It was just like Rosalind to think that she possessed all the wits in the family.

"An offer for Felicity?" Rosalind could not believe her ears. "You can't be thinking of marriage for the girl."

"Of course I'm thinking of marriage."

Unable to keep still, Rosalind was striding the length of the room. "But she's just a child!" She turned back to her brother. "She's been at school all these years except for the last weeks when I took her with me to Vienna. She's not even out yet."

"So much the better," Gerald replied, opening his snuff-box. "It will spare me the expense of a Season for her."

"Spare *you* the expense!" Rosalind uttered scornfully. Had there been a season for Felicity, Rosalind would have borne the expense and not Gerald.

"You've never spared Felicity a moment's attention before this. Why all the sudden interest?" she demanded, determined to get to the root of things.

"I'm mending my ways."

Rosalind was flabbergasted. "Mending your ways? Don't pitch that gammon at me. You've been a profligate and a wastrel since I was ten. You can't have changed your colors now."

This harsh but accurate indictment of Mr. Gerald McHenry's character left the recipient unmoved.

"Whatever you think of me, Rosalind," he said, settling back more comfortably into his chair, "Felicity is my daughter. And a father has every right to see to a daughter's future. As for my new interest in her . . ." He paused and shrugged. "That should be obvious. The chit's growing up."

"But why marriage now?"

"And why not marriage?" he countered. "Every female's future lies in marriage, even though yours doesn't seem to. And perhaps," he added with a sly look, "that's why you don't fancy the idea of her marriage. Could be you're envious, Rosalind."

"Don't be absurd, Gerald," she declared, grinding the heels of her riding boots into her precious Wilton.

"Wouldn't be the first female to feel that way," Gerald went on, oblivious to her words. "Here's your niece making a brilliant match, and she's not even out. And you've been out how many seasons? I ain't saying you haven't had offers, but you'll wind up an ape leader if you're not careful!''

"Thank you for your concern, Gerald," Rosalind said frigidly, "but I still wish to know why you are doing this now. You hardly fit the role of any matchmaker of my acquaintance. And you may save that twaddle about your fatherly interest in Felicity. You haven't seen her more than three times in the years she's been away at school since Chloe's death. So why are you doing this?''

"Because I want to, blast it!" he snapped, his jowls working furiously. "Lud, Rosalind, it's not as though she won't be happy in the marriage. You ain't even heard who the chit is marrying.''

"I don't need to," she said with a glare. "If he's one of your cronies, the match is doomed from the start.''

Her words brought him bounding up from the chair. "That's what you think, is it? By Jove, you are so full of yourself. Well, just think of my having Eberhart as a son-in-law. An earl, mind you. What think you of that?!''

Rosalind gaped at her brother, for once bereft of speech. She had no real acquaintance with the earl, but she knew his position in Society.

"Now I know you're bosky," she said, gathering her wits together. "Eberhart doesn't run in your circles or mine. He's very high in the instep.''

"It's him, just the same," Gerald replied. "And don't think I went running after him. 'Twas the other way around. You could have floored me at White's one night when he came up to ask if I was the father of Felicity McHenry. Seems he had heard much about her beauty and gentle nature.''

"But why should a nonpareil like Eberhart wish to marry Felicity?" Rosalind inquired.

Gerald shrugged. "He's of an age to marry. He must be at least thirty. He wants a proper, well-bred girl like Felicity. I never thought such good fortune would fall my way.''

"*Your* way?''

Gerald colored slightly under the suspicious gaze of those violet eyes.

"Why, yes," he said. "Do you know how rich he is? Richer than Golden Ball, or so they say."

Rosalind's eyes were riveted on her brother's face. What she saw there did not augur well for Felicity's future.

"Settlement, is that it, Gerald? Eberhart is going to settle those monstrous debts of yours before you will agree to the match with Felicity."

"And what if he does?" her brother retorted. "You don't realize the obligations a man is under."

"You would have no such obligations if you ceased your gaming. That's what caused Chloe to go into a decline and die."

"Oh, bother Chloe," Gerald said, waving away this memory of his late unlamented wife.

"I thought you were in the funds when I went off to Vienna."

Mr. McHenry let out a snort of disgust. "Good God, one of my horses came in. But that can't erase years and years of debts."

"And Eberhart has agreed to settle those debts. But I have a better plan. Why not simply sell Felicity into bondage in America to get the money?"

"I am doing nothing wrong," Gerald said stiffly, the sting in her words causing him to lash out at her. "Besides, the marriage might be a happy one. Felicity has as good a chance at happiness as any other female embarking on matrimony. Perhaps better than most, if you don't go spoiling it by turning her against the earl. He's a first-rate catch. One of the prizes on the marriage mart. Felicity will be happy as long as you keep your tongue still."

Rosalind was spared the necessity of answering this, which held, she was bound to admit, some particle of truth, by the entrance of Felicity herself. She stopped abruptly at the threshold, seeing the hostilities underway between her aunt and father.

"I'm sorry, Aunt Rosalind," she said softly. "I didn't know Papa was here."

"Come in, child, come in," Gerald said heartily, perhaps too heartily, for Felicity, who could remember receiving nothing but curt orders from him to be silent or to go away, looked completely baffled.

Rosalind gave her a reassuring smile and stretched out a hand. Felicity clasped it at once. There could be no denying the beauty of young Felicity McHenry. Her crown of golden hair fell in soft ringlets to her shoulders, framing a rosy complexion and lustrous blue eyes. Rosalind sighed involuntarily. Her marriage to the wrong man would be like leading a lamb to the slaughter. How could Gerald do such a thing?

"I've just been telling your aunt some good news," Mr. McHenry said. "Very good news indeed."

"Is that so, Papa?" Felicity asked softly. "How exciting."

"Yes, er . . ." Gerald glanced hopefully over at his sister. "Rosalind, would you like to tell her the news?"

"I wouldn't dream of usurping your station, Gerald," she said demurely.

"Botheration!" he exploded. "I don't see why you shall make a Cheltenham tragedy of things." He turned abruptly to his daughter. "Felicity, I've been telling your aunt that Lord Eberhart wishes to marry you, and that I've given my consent to the match."

Having gotten that off his chest, he turned to fix a baleful eye on Rosalind.

"I told you there was nothing to make a fuss over. The chit's going to be a countess. Better than any storybook could be, ain't that so, Felicity?"

Felicity, however, could not furnish a suitable reply, for she had turned chalk-white at her father's words and sunk down to the floor in a heap.

"Good God!" he exclaimed.

"She's fainted," Rosalind said, feeling for the pulse in her niece's wrist. Assured that the heart was still beating, she dug into her reticule and waved a vinaigrette vigorously under the girl's nose. A terrifying moment passed before the eyelids fluttered open.

"Excitement, that's all it is," Gerald said, hovering nervously in the background. "She'll be recovered by Friday, won't she, Rosalind?"

"Probably," Rosalind said, continuing her ministrations. "But why should you be so concerned that she recovers by Friday? What happens then?"

"Eberhart is giving a party," he replied quickly. "He'll expect Felicity there. And you'll be receiving an invitation as well."

"How civil of him and you," his sister answered. "But I beg you to consider me excused. Wild horses wouldn't drag me to any such thing!"

Chapter Two

As his young bride-to-be was being revived at Green Street, Eberhart entered his establishment in St. James Square. Catching sight of his secretary hard at work in a back office, he crooked his finger, beckoning him to the library.

Mr. Fergus Fairweather had been wrestling with the bills for Quarter Day and quickly took advantage of this break in his routine.

"I trust you found her ladyship in good health, sir?" he asked in the library.

"In excellent health, Fergus," his employer replied. "By the by, remind me to ask my stepfather for the name and address of an inn in Dijon."

He waved his secretary into one of the two Trafalgar chairs the library boasted and took the other himself.

"An inn in Dijon," Fergus repeated. "To be sure I shall remember to remind you." His lean face creased into a frown. "Are you planning a trip across the Channel, sir?"

The earl smiled. "No, I am not. I have no liking for being jolted all over the sea. I'm thinking instead of the excellent sherry I enjoyed at my mother's."

"I see, sir," Fergus replied, obviously not seeing at all but too well-bred to admit it.

Eberhart smiled again, genuinely amused. "You always do. Indeed, Fergus, I sometimes wonder how I ever contrived without you. To think I owe it all to your aversion to medicine."

A faint blush spread on the secretary's cheeks. Mr. Fairweather had served the earl for nearly two years to the mutual satisfaction of both. Before taking this post he had been encouraged toward the study of medicine, following in the footsteps of several of his uncles. A certain indisposition to the sight of blood, however, forestalled him from the successful pursuit of this path, which made Eberhart's offer of employment a salvation for a young man just down from Oxford. Fergus, now five and twenty, was a prudent, sober young man, an excellent addition to anyone's staff.

"Now then, Fergus," Eberhart said, "I have a task to set in front of you. I warn you, it shall be difficult."

Fergus glanced up eagerly. His day thus far had held nothing more promising than the computation of sums owed to the chandler's.

"I intend to give a small party Friday evening. You will find the guest list on my desk." The earl waved a languid hand toward the mahogany escritoire. "Dispatch the necessary invitations, order the menu, flowers, musicians. You'll do it up proper."

"Yes, sir, of course," Fergus said. He was at the desk, scanning the guest list. His green eyes flicked rapidly over the names, stopping with a jolt when they happened on one particular name.

"Oh, I shall want you at the party, too, Fergus," the earl added.

"Very good, sir," his secretary said woodenly. He gave his head a shake. "Sir, I couldn't help noticing a name on the list."

The earl was meticulously examining a speck of lint on the knee of his pantaloons. "Which one?"

"The McHenrys, sir. They're not among your usual acquaintances."

"I know, Fergus, and in point of fact I shan't bother to hide my intentions from you. I plan to marry Miss Felicity McHenry."

"What?!" Fergus ejaculated, and then, becoming aware that the earl was glancing oddly at him, quickly composed himself. "I mean, it's very sudden, sir."

"Not as sudden as you think. And you had a hand in it."

Fergus appeared staggered. "I, sir? I don't recall."

" 'Twas your mentioning Miss Felicity some time ago which prompted me to make inquiries of my own. And I must say, Fergus, she more than lived up to your words. Young, charming, gentle-mannered, exactly what I desire in a wife.''

He rose, and with another indulgent admonition that his secretary mustn't work too hard, he left the bookroom, leaving Mr. Fairweather to pursue the preparations for the Friday evening ball.

But for once the secretary's usual industry flagged. Miss Felicity McHenry to marry the earl? That sweet, innocent, charming child! Not that his lordship was a hardened rake! But still, it had to be a dreadful mistake!

Although wild horses might not have induced Rosalind to attend Eberhart's ball, a certain mulish young relation could and did do so.

Nothing, or so declared the younger Miss McHenry, would induce her to attend the affair without her aunt close at hand. Rosalind herself was not convinced that she would be of much assistance to Felicity, for with each day that passed she found Gerald's scheme more abominable. She even thought of telling Felicity his true motives for the match but decided ultimately against it. What would be the use of upsetting Felicity further?

Toward Eberhart her feelings were less charitable. She had never met him, but only a hardened rake would offer marriage to a child he had never met, and her imagination quickly sketched him a veritable Bluebeard with a penchant for young girls. Matrimonial plum or not, he would find her turning him a cold shoulder.

By Friday, however, Rosalind succumbed to Felicity's tears and entreaties and gave her reluctant agreement to attend Eberhart's soiree. She donned an azure ball gown from her wardrobe, a new purchase from Paris which she still found a trifle daring, as it was off one shoulder.

She sat back before her mirror and allowed Juliette, her maid, to dress her hair in a half crown of ringlets. By the time the hair had been done and a pearl necklace, an heirloom from her mother, had been clasped about her throat it was nearly a quarter past seven. Hastily she entered Felicity's room. Eberhart's dinner was set for eight o'clock, and Gerald had warned repeatedly that his grace was a high stickler for punctuality.

Rosalind wrinkled up her nose now, wishing that she could tell Eberhart exactly what he might do with his precious punctuality.

"My dear, are you ready?" she asked Felicity. "I fear Gerald shall be in hysterics if we are another minute late."

"Oh yes, Aunt," Felicity replied, turning around. Rosalind's smile deepened. Felicity truly was in her best looks this evening in an exquisite pink satin that showed off her youth. Damask roses were entwined in the blond hair. Eberhart would have to be blind not to want her.

Together they hurried down the stairs, Felicity struggling with a Paisley shawl, a new purchase. When she was halfway down the stairs, her feet became entangled in the shawl.

"Look out!" Rosalind cried, and she reached out a hand to steady the girl. As she did she felt her own dress rip.

"Oh, no!" Felicity exclaimed, glancing down at the portion of her aunt's gown that lay beneath her shoes. "Your gown, Aunt Rosalind. I am so sorry."

"It is of no importance," Rosalind said, although her heart sank. The tear could not possibly be mended in time. She would have to change her gown. Returning to her bedchamber, she swiftly stripped off the Paris gown.

"Miss Rosalind?" Her abigail looked startled to see her.

"I'm changing my gown, Juliette. It's torn. I don't have time to explain. Let's find something else to wear."

"But you don't have anything else," Juliette exclaimed, opening the wardrobe. "Remember, Fanchon said there would be a delay completing the fittings you ordered. And you didn't press her, for the season wasn't underway. And the rest of your older ball gowns are on their way from Vienna. The only things we have here are at least a year old."

The best of these turned out to be a saffron-yellow dress that she had worn only once, and with good reason. It made her look hideously sallow. The style of flounced hems was now *de trop*. But it would have to do.

"Oh, Miss Rosalind," Juliette wailed.

Rosalind flinched involuntarily. She had never liked the style of flounced hems, and now she knew why. She consoled herself and assured her servant that it was Felicity's night and not hers.

"I daresay no one shall pay me a jot of attention."

By the time Rosalind descended the stairs to find Felicity, now *sans* shawl, pacing anxiously below, twenty minutes had passed.

"Aunt Rosalind, are you wearing that?!"

"I know, I look hideous," Rosalind said cheerfully. "But no one shall pay me a moment's attention."

"But your other gown looked so lovely, and this one—"

"Makes me out a dreadful dowd," Rosalind agreed. "But all my other gowns are still in Vienna. It was too stupid of me to take them there for such a short stay. And I only hope they haven't been lost. Meanwhile I must make the best of this. And now we must fly. Gerald will be livid if we are any later."

The two ladies were, however, destined to be even more tardy. As they stepped out the door, Rosalind was stunned to see her carriage standing with one horse missing, an absence that her butler quickly explained was due to the appearance of a spot on the foreleg of one of the pair, necessitating a replacement.

By the time the new horse was hitched and they were off, a full hour had passed. Rosalind sank back against the velvet squabs, knowing full well what Gerald would say. He had offered her his escort to the party, but nothing would induce her to share his carriage.

"I still don't see why the earl wishes to marry me," Felicity complained as their vehicle clattered noisily over the cobblestones.

"You have only to gaze in a mirror to see why," Rosalind replied. "You are lovely by any standards, and charming and well-bred."

"But so are you, and he hasn't offered for you!" Felicity said naïvely.

Rosalind's eyes twinkled. "Ah well, there is no accounting for tastes in gentlemen. Perhaps the earl prefers blondes."

"I wish you wouldn't jest," Felicity said, pouting a little. "And I wish I knew when he saw me. I'm sure I never saw him. I should remember meeting an earl."

"Who is to say precisely how you caught his eye?" Rosalind replied with a smile. "These things do happen."

"I wish this evening were over," Felicity said, wringing her hands. "I shall do something stupid. I just know it."

Rosalind gazed over at Felicity. In the shafts of moonlight that fell through the window she could see the agitation in the young face next to her.

"Do calm yourself, my dear. I've never seen you in such a twitter."

"That's because I've never had to marry an earl before," Felicity replied. "And why must I, Aunt Rosalind? I didn't ask Papa to arrange this brilliant match. If he must marry me off, why didn't he choose someone else? Someone like . . ."

"Someone like whom, my dear?" Rosalind asked as Felicity's voice trailed off.

The younger woman hunched a shoulder. "I don't know. Just someone besides an earl."

"There is no need to hold all earls in such aversion," Rosalind replied. "You shall undoubtedly meet a few earls before your time in London ends and shall undoubtedly be thought freakish if you take every one of them into a dislike, not to mention what you may think of a marquis or duke. And there is no need for fear. I shall be with you."

"Yes, I know," Felicity murmured gratefully. "No harm can come to me when I am with you."

A silence engulfed them as the carriage moved steadily on, stopping finally at the stately town residence that was the home of Eberhart whenever he was in London. Rosalind had set her mind against the earl, but even she could not dispute the tasteful elegance of the Roman entranceway, the chandeliers glittering with a thousand candles, and the strains drifting down from what must be the music room.

She mounted the stairs with Felicity, aware that the rest of the guests had by this hour finished with their dinner and gathered into the music room for entertainment. Knowing that she and Felicity would be the target of all eyes, she found herself wishing that she might be wearing her Parisian gown. Absurd notion, all in all.

She squared her shoulders, adjured herself not to be a ninnyhammer, and waited as the footman opened the door to the music room. A young lady, no doubt one of Eberhart's relations, sat playing the pianoforte in a dull, lackluster manner. This was unfortunate, since the audience, which had been bored to tears, had a welcome diversion in the latecomers now entering.

Much speculation had risen from their absence. Mr. Gerald McHenry had gone so far as to mutter aloud that he wouldn't put it past Rosalind to kidnap Felicity now that freedom from his debts lay within his grasp.

Had Eberhart been privy to these confidences he would have thought McHenry foxed. He was, however, considerably annoyed that the female he was planning to offer for had not appeared at the appointed hour to meet his mother and assembled guests.

He had attempted to carry on in his usual unflappable manner, but even he could not scotch the tittle-tattle that swept the rooms. Dinner had gone on as scheduled, but the earl's mood was black, and he barely tasted the French delicacies prepared by his chef, or heard the nervous pleasantries directed to him by his guests.

Lady Manning, ably assisted by Mr. Fairweather, had carried on with some semblance of cordiality, but even they were afflicted with the liveliest curiosity about the absent ladies.

Now, with his attention mercifully removed from the abominable piano playing of his cousin Amelia, Eberhart swiveled his head toward the open door. He recognized Felicity at once, and his mouth softened involuntarily at her beguilingly simple dress and the rosebuds in her hair. She looked like an enchanting fairy princess.

Unfortunately, the same could not be said of her companion, wearing the most outmoded gown Eberhart had ever laid eyes on, one that no self-respecting lady of fashion would appear in.

Through his quizzing glass the earl noticed that the newcomer was not without some pleasing attributes. Her head of raven curls was distinctive enough, and her figure lithe and graceful. Her most intriguing feature by far, however, was a pair of violet eyes, the color startling him almost as much as their expression: a look of out-and-out hostility.

Rather nettled and determined to freeze such ill-mannered behavior—for no one threw him dagger looks in his own residence—he put down his glass and turned his attention back to Amelia, who was punishing the piano. Miss Rosalind McHenry, for it was undoubtedly she making such a tardy appearance, could stand there for all eternity as far as he was concerned.

Chapter Three

Eberhart's manners might have failed him, but not so Lady Manning's. Observing by the pugnacious look suffusing her son's face that he was in a mood, and recalling all too vividly the altercations that look had heralded in the past, she decided to act quickly. Why Miss McHenry should arrive so late and wearing such a dowdy dress was certainly a matter that teased her own curiosity, but she was sure there must be a good explanation.

Conscious of the silence that had fallen over the room as Amelia ceased her fingering at the keyboard, Lady Manning clapped her hands, sparking a polite round of applause.

"My dear, that was just splendid," she said, going to Amelia. "And just the thing to put us all in the mood for dancing. Now we must all go to the ballroom." She threw a supplicating glance at Fergus, who, because of his employer's own notable lack of interest in the newcomers, rose nobly to the occasion and succeeded in ushering out the majority of the guests.

That task behind her, Lady Manning turned to the two late arrivals, only to find them being quizzed by Mr. McHenry.

"I should have known you'd play such a hoydenish trick on me, Rosalind!" Gerald muttered.

"Oh, Gerald! Don't be a nodcock."

"The humiliation of it all," he said as his jowls worked furiously. "I shan't be able to look at any of these people in the eye tomorrow."

"Hardly a portentous matter," she replied. "You haven't clapped eyes on any of them before tonight or I'll go bail."

"Don't scold Aunt Rosalind, Papa," Felicity interjected. "She wasn't to blame. It's my fault we are late, on account of my wretched shawl."

"Shawl? What shawl?" Gerald demanded. "Ain't even wearing one."

The skirmish ended at the approach of Lord and Lady Manning. Gerald, directing a quelling look from under his heavy lids, was forestalled from performing the introductions by Lady Manning herself, who engulfed his sister in the folds of her seawater-green satin.

"My dear Miss McHenry. How glorious to see you again! When did you arrive from Vienna? You must tell me all about your trip."

"Indeed, ma'am, I am delighted to see you," Rosalind replied, a trifle stunned to see her acquaintance from Vienna in the London music room. "And you, sir, as well!" Her smile included the bluff figure of Lord Manning.

"You remember Lady Manning, don't you, Felicity?" Rosalind went on. "And you must allow me to present my brother!"

"We have already met," Lady Manning replied, reserving her own dubious opinion of Mr. McHenry. But every family must have its black sheep. "But you have not met my son, Alastair," she told Rosalind. "That is he wearing that disagreeable frown. He always does that when he is on his high ropes. Pay it no mind."

"I shan't, but why should he be in the hips, ma'am?"

"Rosalind," Gerald hissed in her ear. "Don't be a nitwit. It's Eberhart she's talking about."

"Eberhart!" Rosalind's eyes widened. "Is Eberhart the dear Alastair you talked so much of in Vienna, ma'am?"

"Yes," Lady Manning divulged with a sunny smile. "And you needn't be frightened of him. He shan't bite, I do assure you. If only he would not frown so. It makes him look like an old man of seventy, and he only has thirty-two in his dish!"

Rosalind scarcely heard her. To discover that Lady Manning's son should be Eberhart was the outside of enough.

She had known his mother only by her new title of Lady Manning and had never connected her to her son.

It was too late for recriminations, however, for she was being led by her friend over to the stony-faced gentleman glaring at them. He was tall, but not of such a height as to cause a roundness of his shoulders, a pair certainly wide enough to suit any tailor's demands. His swallow-tailed coat, white frilled shirt, and intricate cravat suited him to perfection.

At first glance one might have taken him for a fop because of that head of curly blond hair and that upturned nose, legacies from his mother, but there was no mistaking the muscles that rippled under the silk stockings.

Lady Manning had spoken of her son's delightful sense of the ridiculous and his true gentleness of spirit. But she must, Rosalind reasoned, have been speaking from the perspective of blind mother love. There was nothing remotely gentle in the brittle gray eyes staring at her. And his mouth was unmistakably haughty.

Despite his being Lady Manning's son, Rosalind would move heaven and earth to keep Felicity out of his clutches.

"Alastair." Lady Manning spoke first, well aware that she was skating on very thin ice. "You have not greeted your guests, Miss Rosalind McHenry and Miss Felicity Mc-Henry."

"No, Mama," he replied. "You stole a march on me there." He nodded curtly at Rosalind and directed a brief smile at Felicity. "Enchanted."

Lady Manning nearly succumbed to the urge to box her beloved son in the ears.

"I trust your groom had difficulty finding Saint James Square?" he asked Rosalind.

She was confused by his question. "Why, no, sir. What makes you say that?"

"Because of the late hour," he said pointedly.

She had been about to apologize for their belated arrival, but his words put her back up.

Lady Manning, doing her best to stem the impending battle, interrupted to remind Eberhart that he had wished to dance with Felicity. The earl, no slow top, recognized his mother's motives, but he broached no objection to this suggestion. Smiling at Felicity, he offered his arm. Felicity, swallowing her fright, allowed him to sweep her out of the music room.

"A charming pair, don't you think?" Gerald asked gleefully.

Lady Manning, absorbed in her own thoughts, jerked her head up.

"Yes, yes, charming." She gave her head a brisk shake and took hold of Rosalind, leading her toward the ballroom. "My dear, how have you been?"

"Quite well, ma'am," Rosalind replied. "And I know we are dreadfully late, and I do apologize for it. And perhaps I ought to have said so to your son as well, but—"

"It is that mulish look on his face," Lady Manning said with an understanding sigh. "But you shan't starve. We'll have supper later." The two ladies had entered the ballroom, which glittered with flowers and lights, and Rosalind found her attention drawn against her will to Eberhart, who was dancing with Felicity.

"They do seem well paired, do they not?"

Lady Manning's opinion was echoed by almost everyone in the ballroom. Eberhart and Felicity appeared to win universal favor. The only ones who might have thrown a spanner in the works were Rosalind and Fergus, who watched the dance with tormented eyes.

"You must dance, too, Miss McHenry," Lady Manning announced. Casting her eye about the room, she produced a partner in a trice, remarking that Mr. Fairweather had a great love of dance.

Fergus paled at this overgenerous estimate of his skills, but Rosalind accepted him good-humoredly. It took her only a few moments to realize that Lady Manning had overstated Fergus's prowess in a ballroom, but she did not really repine. He was a sensible, sober young man in spite of being the earl's secretary.

She ought to have taken Fergus in a dislike, but his manner was so calm and pleasant, so different from his autocratic employer, that she felt sorry for him toiling in Eberhart's household.

"Have you worked for the earl long?" she asked.

"For nearly two years," Fergus replied.

"Do you plan on remaining with him?"

"I don't know. Lately I have been thinking of the diplomatic field. My uncle once offered me assistance. I wasn't keen on it. Now I am. But the thing is, I'm not sure he would consent to sponsor me. And he lives in Brussels."

"I have been to Brussels on numerous occasions," Rosalind said. "Pray, what is your uncle's name?"

"Mr. Osgood Fairweather."

"A most worthy gentleman," Rosalind exclaimed. "I know his wife well. By all means you should pursue the matter with him."

"Do you think so?" Fergus asked, brightening for the first time that evening. "I hesitated to put myself forward by writing to him."

"I'm sure he shall enjoy hearing from you. I am well acquainted with his wife. Would you like me to write to her, telling her—indirectly, of course—of your interest?"

"That's very civil of you, Miss McHenry!" Fergus said, stunned at such generosity from a perfect stranger.

Rosalind cut short his thanks. "I can't think of anything I'd enjoy more than helping you escape from Eberhart's employ."

The gratitude on Fergus's face vanished, replaced by dismay. "Miss McHenry, you mustn't think I don't like serving the earl. And as for my escaping from him, you are quite mistaken. He doesn't beat me, you know!"

"I wouldn't put it past him to try, and you needn't try and convince me differently, Mr. Fairweather," Rosalind said, casting an eye across the room to where the earl was dancing with Felicity. "I am well aware that to work for such an arrogant, high-handed person must be penance of the highest order."

While Fergus strove to correct this mistaken notion during the remainder of their dance, his employer was involved with his own problems with Felicity. At first he had failed to find any problem at all in his first opportunity to observe her close at hand. Her beauty and demeanor were up to his most exacting standards. In fact, she seemed lovelier than he remembered. She was exactly what he had ordered: quiet, shy, and beautiful. But he did find himself wishing to heaven that she would speak now and then of her own volition.

Not that she was completely mute. Every question of his elicited an answer. But her responses were of the "Yes, my lord" and "No, my lord" order of things. It was enough to drive him to the wall, and he wondered if her aunt had put her up to it solely to vex him.

Felicity might not have possessed great wit, but she was aware that the dance was not going as splendidly as one might have wished. Any other female dancing with such a prime masculine specimen—so elegantly dressed as to rival Mr. Brummel himself in his prime—would have been cast in alt. But she felt only dread at making a fatal miscue. A shudder shook her at the memory of the thunderous look that he had shot at Rosalind in the music room. Had he unleashed such a glare on her she knew she would have been reduced to jelly.

Although the eyes smiled down at her now, the earl could not fully mask his exasperation, and Felicity was relieved when the ordeal of dancing with him was finally ended.

Lady Manning intercepted them as they were going off, saying with a soft smile that Lord Manning had desired a chance to dance with the young lady. Her spouse had, in fact, been about to desert his wife and retire to the cardroom with his cronies, but observing the keen message in her eyes, he offered his arm to Felicity, who was only too glad to put distance between herself and the earl.

"Skittish creature, isn't she?" Eberhart remarked.

"It's her youth," Lady Manning replied, fanning herself lightly with an ivory-handled fan. "But she is pretty, well-mannered and soft-spoken."

"Perhaps too soft-spoken."

Something in his voice prompted a wild hope to leap in Lady Manning's breast.

"Alastair, you haven't changed your mind, have you?" she asked.

"No! Only perhaps we should encourage her to speak up more. I shouldn't wonder if that dreadful aunt of hers has bullied her unmercifully."

Lady Manning was aghast at such slander. "Alastair, don't be absurd," she said tartly. "I've never seen anyone as devoted to Felicity as her aunt. She paid for the child's schooling herself. And I can't tell you the number of times in Vienna when she took considerable pains to introduce Felicity about."

"I'm sure she did, Mama," Eberhart said skeptically.

"I wish you would not talk like that," Lady Manning admonished. "If only you would get to know Rosalind. You would find her charming."

The earl laughed. "The day I find that woman delightful is the day I shall eat my high-crowned beaver felt, the new one from Mr. Locke!"

"Don't be impossible," Lady Manning implored. "You are planning to marry into the family, remember. You must be civil to Rosalind." She poked him with her fan. "There she is sitting with Fergus. Go over and ask her to dance."

The earl recoiled visibly from such a command. "I'd sooner stand up with a baboon!"

Lady Manning's temper began to fray. "She is Felicity's nearest female relation here. And since you are planning to marry Felicity—"

"Oh, very well," Eberhart said, giving ground none too graciously. "But just to please you, Mama."

He moved across the ballroom, stopping now and then to speak to those who approached and finding little pleasure in the prospect of dancing with Rosalind. Nevertheless, he stopped in front of her and extended a languid hand her way.

"I wonder, Miss McHenry, if you would honor me with this dance."

The invitation had been a request, but the earl's tone made it more of a command. The possibility of a refusal never once crossed his mind. On those few occasions when he danced in public, his partners had been overcome with pleasure and gratitude. He saw no reason not to expect the same now.

He had, however, reckoned without Rosalind's own sense of pride. To be asked to dance was one thing, and had the invitation been civil she might have accepted; but to be virtually ordered to the floor in so toplofty a manner was unconscionable. She had no wish to suffer through a dance with so disagreeable a partner.

"Did you hear me, Miss McHenry?" Eberhart asked impatiently, wondering if she could be deaf in addition to her other flaws.

"Oh, yes," Rosalind affirmed now. "But the thing is, I wouldn't."

His hand dropped to his side. "Wouldn't what?"

"Wouldn't like to dance with you," she elaborated. "I'm convinced it is so much more comfortable to dance with those of one's liking. And I don't think either of us likes the other. Speaking frankly, it's more congenial not to dance with someone in a thunderous mood."

"I am not in a thunderous mood," the earl denied as his color gave the lie to his words.

"Then I should hate to see you when you are," she replied. "And I don't believe you wanted to dance with me. Your mother foisted the task on you. So it would save us both botheration if we didn't dance, don't you think?"

"What I think, Miss McHenry, would be better not expressed in public," the earl muttered as he turned on his heel and stalked away, leaving everyone avidly observing the encounter with the impression that the unthinkable had happened. Eberhart had asked Miss McHenry to stand up with him and had been refused!

Chapter Four

"Are you trying to see me in a poorhouse?" Gerald demanded the next morning at Green Street.

His sister, looking remarkably composed in a cream-colored cambric, paused as she dipped her nose into a steaming mug of hot chocolate.

"Of course not, Gerald. I'd much prefer a debtor's prison."

He flung up his hands, incensed at her levity. "I should throttle you!"

"I shouldn't try that," she said, her eyes glinting sharply. "And instead of blaming me for all your troubles, you ought to look to your own predilection for cards, drink, and horses."

He flushed scarlet. "Cards or not, I had the chance to turn my luck at last. You are spoiling things deliberately! Causing an uproar at Eberhart's last night. I've never seen the like!"

"An uproar?" Rosalind licked her lips, savoring the sweet sensation on her tongue. "I explained about the delay."

"I don't mean that, although it was quite bad enough. But did you have to refuse him the dance? You've not a particle of sense. I've said that before. I don't think Eberhart's stood up with more than half a dozen females in all his years. And what must you do? Insult him!"

"Fiddle-faddle!" Rosalind replied. "Nearly every gentleman gets turned down for a dance at some time. I did it quite civilly. You have only to ask Mr. Fairweather, who witnessed it all. And if the earl shall make a Cheltenham tragedy over such a trifle, that is his doing, not mine. And I don't know why you must toady to him, or why you want him to marry Felicity. But then," she went on, allowing him no chance to respond to these charges, "actually you needn't bother to explain. The magic word 'settlements' beckons, does it not?"

"Yes," Gerald said with some bitterness. "Unless you spoil things. I will be free of my debts and Felicity shall be established in a brilliant marriage."

"Ah, yes, you mustn't forget dear Felicity."

Her rebuke stung. "You act as though I were selling her into slavery."

"It amounts to the same thing as far as I can see."

"Do me a favor, Rosalind. Keep away from Eberhart. When you and he get together the sparks fly."

Rosalind was happy enough to grant her brother this favor, for it was apparent that the earl and she shared no great liking for each other's company. And Gerald, satisfied, departed, leaving her to enjoy the remainder of her breakfast. She was halfway through a basket of fresh strawberries when Felicity came in, looking a trifle hagged from the previous night's doings.

"Good morning, Aunt Rosalind," she said with a wan attempt at a smile.

Rosalind kissed her on the cheek. "Good morning. I see you are feeling the effects of your first ball. Have a little chocolate. It will bring the color back to your cheeks. There was no necessity to rise so early. I would have sent someone up with a tray."

"I wanted to come down," Felicity said, sitting in the chair next to Rosalind. "I thought I heard Papa's voice."

"Fortunately his visit was brief," Rosalind told her.

"Did he come to scold you?"

"Among other things. But do let's not talk about Gerald. The day is too fine for that. Have you seen the sun? What do you think of a trip to Madame Fanchon's this morning? She has promised to have those ball gowns ready for us soon. And after that dismal appearance I made last night I fear I must press her to complete the new gowns as soon as possible.''

''Yes, of course, if you like. . . .'' Felicity said pensively, pushing her fork about her plate. Finally she gave up all pretense and began to cry.

''Good gracious, what is the matter?'' Rosalind asked, alarmed. She cupped Felicity's chin in her hand. ''Are you ill? They say the influenza is raging about the town. Perhaps some of Eberhart's guests last night—''

''It's not the influenza.'' Felicity managed to choke out the words.

''Then did you wish to do something besides our visit to Fanchon? If so, there is no need for tears. I'll see her myself.''

''It's not Fanchon,'' Felicity said thickly. ''It's the earl.''

''Ah.'' Rosalind sat back in her chair, watching as Felicity wiped her eyes with a handkerchief. ''What did he do?'' A sudden fear swept through her. ''Felicity, he didn't perhaps try to kiss you last night, did he?''

''Oh, no,'' Felicity denied with a vigorous shake of her head. ''He did nothing I could take exception to. He was quite civil all in all, asking how I liked London and where we had gone in Vienna. But I'm sure he thought me hopelessly insipid, for I barely uttered a word or two in reply.'' A shadow fell over her face. ''I could tell he was vexed, because that look would come into his eyes. You know the one I mean?''

''His lord-of-the-manor look?'' Rosalind quizzed.

''Yes, exactly!'' Felicity exclaimed. ''And all last night in bed I thought of how it would be to be married to such a man and—'' She broke off into a new flood of tears.

''No wonder you are crying,'' Rosalind soothed. ''But my dear, Eberhart had ample reason to be annoyed last night, although certainly not with you. And it is normal to feel some hesitation, since you have scarcely met him. There will be time for you to become fully acquainted.''

''I don't need to be fully acquainted,'' Felicity said, repressing a shudder. ''He frightens me.''

Rosalind took another sip of her chocolate. Nerves were

one thing, and a bride might by the time her wedding day approached have gotten over a bout with nerves, but fear was something else. And of course the child would be frightened of Eberhart.

"Felicity, there is no real need to be frightened of Eberhart. I know he looks very grand and stern, and he is an earl; but so was your great-grandfather!"

Felicity found no comfort in her lineage. "He has a frightful temper," she pointed out.

"Yes," Rosalind acknowledged. "But when he rages at you, you must simply learn to rage back."

Felicity paled. "Aunt Rosalind, I could never do that!"

This, Rosalind was bound to admit, was only too true. Felicity's nature was true to her name. Always quiet and shy, she would burst into tears if anyone addressed a harsh word to her. Marriage to Eberhart would be an eternal vale of tears.

"Well, then," Rosalind said briskly, "there is only one thing left to do."

"What?" Felicity asked eagerly.

"Refuse him when he makes his offer."

"Refuse Eberhart?" Felicity asked, a stricken look in her eyes.

Rosalind nodded. "You have been telling me he has you in a quake. Do you mean you'd rather marry him now?"

"Oh, no!" Felicity said unhesitantly. "But can I really refuse an earl?"

"Why not? He may be an earl, but he can't force you to marry you against your will."

"But it will be so unpleasant to refuse him," Felicity said. "If he became so intractable when you refused him one dance, what shall he do if I refuse an offer of marriage?"

This was, as Rosalind admitted, a good point. "But however disagreeable he becomes, that will be better than marriage to him. You shall simply have to screw your courage to the sticking point and tell him so."

Felicity chewed on her lip. "Perhaps he won't go so far as to offer for me."

"Perhaps not," Rosalind agreed. "You could discourage him."

Felicity glanced up. "Discourage him how?"

Rosalind laid down her fork. "From what Gerald has told me, Eberhart wants a quiet, well-behaved young lady for a wife. So if you started to act hoydenishly, he might—"

"Oh, Aunt Rosalind!" Felicity looked appalled. "I couldn't do that."

"No, I don't suppose you could," Rosalind said with some regret. "Well, then you shall just have to act cold and uncaring when you are with him. He shall deduce you have no interest in him and may not even attempt to pop the question. However, he seems to be of so blockish a temperament that you might have to hint him quite obviously away."

Felicity digested this advice. "But what will Papa say? He's gone to such trouble over the match."

"You are not to spare a moment's thought on Gerald," Rosalind said tartly.

Felicity's eyes turned curious. "Why?"

Rosalind sighed. "I didn't wish to say it earlier, because I didn't want to prejudice you against the match. But I suppose now that you have decided against Eberhart there is no harm in divulging the truth. Gerald wanted the match for you because Eberhart agreed to settle all those debts your father has accumulated."

"What?" Felicity exclaimed. She had turned quite pale.

"It's quite reprehensible," Rosalind agreed. "I told Gerald what I thought of such a plan. I would have told you earlier, but while the possibility existed that you might grow to like Eberhart, I was obliged to keep my tongue still. So you see, you are under no obligation to either the earl or Gerald."

She looked up, expecting to see relief on Felicity's face, but instead the girl looked dismayed.

"My dear, there is no need to look so unhappy! Haven't you been listening? You shan't have to marry Eberhart."

"But I must now, if what you've told me is true."

Rosalind gaped at her. "Felicity, don't be a shatterbrain.

You told me not five minutes ago that just dancing with the earl put you into a quake!''

"Yes, but that was before I knew poor Papa was depending on me! If I don't marry Eberhart he'll never get out from his mountain of debt. I must marry the earl, Aunt Rosalind. I owe it to Papa.''

Had it been humanly possible Rosalind would have soundly boxed her own ears. She should have remembered Felicity's sense of family.

"You have helped Papa before, Aunt Rosalind,'' Felicity went on. "I haven't. I have often thought that if he got out from his debts he might be a new man.''

"That is a farrago of nonsense,'' Rosalind said. "I have known Gerald considerably longer than you. You can't marry Eberhart merely because of your father.''

"But I must,'' Felicity said, looking tortured. "Only think how Papa is always outrunning his creditors or hanging on your sleeve. And I know you have helped him all you can in the past. But now I have the chance to help him. And I must. It's all any daughter could do.''

"And what of your own life with Eberhart as a husband?'' Rosalind queried.

Felicity's face turned ashen, but she went on. "Some sacrifices must be made.''

Mr. Fairweather walked down the length of the hall that led to his office, carrying a sheaf of papers he yearned to lay in front of the earl. But this was not an opportune time. His lordship, by the vivid account of his valet, Tymes, had awakened in a foul temper, rendered even more peevish by that servant's offer of assistance in dressing, an offer that had been rejected out of hand.

When Eberhart finally emerged from his dressing room an hour later, he prepared to depart for Gentleman Jack's.

"Gentleman Jack's, sir?'' Hedges, his butler, inquired. "Begging your lordship's pardon, but it's not your usual hour with him.''

"Yes, I know. But I'd liefer spend it with Jackson than run someone down with my carriage.'' He paused as he picked up his hat and gloves. His negligent gaze flickered on Fergus, who had emerged from his office. "I don't suppose you would know the streets Miss Rosalind McHenry might be in the habit of crossing, would you, Fergus?"

"No, indeed not, sir," Fergus replied.

The earl lifted an eyebrow. "Don't look so shocked, my boy. It was merely an idea."

And one that bore considerable merit, in his humble estimation. He took up the reins of his phaeton, and his team of Welshbreds set off. His evening's acquaintance with Miss McHenry was enough to sour him on the entire female sex. What in thunderation did his mother see in such a female?

He was still musing about this strange lapse in Lady Manning's usually fine judgment when his vehicle halted in front of Jackson's boxing saloon. Soon thoughts of science and the love of a good mill banished from his head all thoughts of haughty females.

An hour of sport took the edge off his bad temper, and when he took up the reins again he decided to stop in on the Berry Brothers and look over their mixture of snuff. While doing so, he found himself accosted by Mr. William Wilding, an old friend, who had come in to peruse the new selection of teas from India.

"Capital stuff, my dear Alastair," Mr. Wilding said affably. He was a stocky gentleman with a square face and a universally good temper that won him a host of friends. "Bit of a Chinese blend too, or I'll go bail." He held a jar out to the earl to sniff. "What are you seeking?"

"Snuff."

"Well, you don't want that mixture!" Wilding said as he laid aside the tea. "Much too dry, for one thing, and that"—he pointed his malacca cane at another bag—"is much too wet. I tried some of it only the other day."

Eberhart bent over and inhaled a pinch. "It seems decent enough to me."

"My dear Alastair!"

The earl laughed. "If you feel so strongly on the matter, William, you choose the mixture for me."

He stood aside, amused, as Wilding, who fancied himself

as great an authority on snuff as on tea, began a judicious discussion with Mr. George Berry among the pots and jars in the shop. After exhaustive argument on the properties of each jar, Mr. Wilding finally selected an assortment to be mixed in careful proportion according to his own personal recipe and dispatched later to St. James Square.

"Obliged to you, William," Eberhart said as they left the shop together.

"The merest of trifles, Alastair," Wilding said, waving off his thanks. "If by some odd quirk you don't care for it, you may give it to me."

The earl chuckled and promised to do that.

"What are you doing about so early in the day?" Wilding asked as they tipped their hats at two ladies who passed.

"I had some business at Gentleman Jack's."

"Ah, yes. Nothing like a good mill to clear the old cobwebs. And speaking of mills, they say you are about to take a leg shackle. Any truth to that prattle?"

Eberhart shrugged. "I had thoughts along those lines."

"Second thoughts now, perchance?"

The earl stopped and stared into his friend's innocent face.

"What makes you say that, William?"

"Nothing. Although some might say you would profit more from a good dancing master than a pugilist!"

Eberhart's frown turned into a glare. "Whom have you been speaking to, William?"

Mr. Wilding held up his hands in protest. "No names, Alastair, please. And you needn't fly into the boughs at me. I couldn't help it if I was forced to miss your ball last evening, and the quizzes would wish to fill me in." He laughed. "It appears Miss McHenry doesn't wish you in her family."

The earl climbed into his carriage. "We shall see about that, William," he replied grimly. "We shall see about that!"

He drove off, but instead of turning the carriage in at St. James Square he continued down the Strand over Ludgate Hill toward the offices of Messrs. Rundell and Bridges. Loath though he had been to admit it, he had been having second thoughts about his impending alliance with Felicity.

But he would be blue deviled if Rosalind McHenry would queer his game so easily.

Thus far he had nothing against Felicity herself except for a certain shyness, which he was sure he could coax her out of.

And besides, he told himself as he prepared to enter the jeweler's shop, Miss Rosalind McHenry would soon learn that what Eberhart set his mind to having he would have, and no ragmannered female would prevent him from having it!

44

When several young ladies have already made good their
claims upon your time...

When in full sight, resplendent in her usual elegant at-
tire...

Chapter Five

Although Eberhart was not among Rosalind's avowed admirers, other prominent gentlemen were. Chief among these
was Viscount Coppleton, known to his intimates as Waldo.
The viscount, a red-haired gentleman with none of the temper that usually went along with that coloring, had offered
for Rosalind no less than five times in the past and would
simply not be discouraged by her refusals.

In any other gentleman this might have evidenced a
blockish temperament, but in the viscount it merely bespoke
his supreme confidence that in the end Rosalind would see
the merits of an alliance with him and accept his offer.

Rosalind found him a convenient companion whenever
the dictates of Society necessitated the presence of a male,
and when she discovered Monday morning that Eberhart
had invited Felicity for a drive in the Park, she pressed
Waldo into service that same afternoon.

The viscount had been agreeable enough. This was an opportunity to show off his new pair of Welshbreds, but once
his vehicle entered the Park, Rosalind seemed to lose interest in him. Even the possibility of meeting his mother later
that week won no glimmer of interest from her.

"I say, Rosalind, are you listening to me?" he demanded, looking into the face under the beribboned bonnet.
For someone who had wished to be seen in the Park she
seemed oblivious to everyone there.

Rosalind, gazing into Waldo's vacuous eyes, felt a momentary pang of guilt.

"Yes, Waldo. To be sure I was listening to you," she
said quickly. "You were telling me about your new pair of

Welshbreds. Quite a capital buy, all in all. I only hope they didn't cost you too dearly.''

"Not at all," he said, restored to his usual good humor as he took the carriage along the path leading to the Serpentine. "Foster sold them to me. I got the better part of the bargain since he was hard-pressed for cash. But I was not speaking about my horses just now, my dear, but about my mother and sister."

Rosalind was astounded. "Your mother and sister, Waldo? Pray, when did they become interested in horses?''

"Horses? Nothing of the sort," the viscount said, thrown off stride by such a remark. "They're coming to London next week. Don't you remember my telling you? I'll be taking them about, probably to Somerset House. Mama is quite anxious to see the exhibit there, and she is quite eager to meet you before she returns to Kent. She's staying only a se'ennight.''

"I don't know if I shall be able to meet her," Rosalind said, recoiling at the very thought of the viscountess. Waldo was a pet, but she hoped he wouldn't use his mother's visit for yet another offer. She grew weary of refusing him. He always looked so stricken, as a puppy might after being struck by a beloved master, and she was sometimes—in her weakened moments—tempted to just accept Waldo and have done with it.

"Oh, you must come with us to Somerset House," he suggested now. "It shall be ever so much fun.''

The hopeful expression in his eyes reminded Rosalind again of a puppy she had once owned.

"Of course I shall. So good of you to invite me.''

Waldo beamed and patted her hand with one of his damp palms. "I just know they shall love you.''

While Rosalind sat absorbed in dubious thoughts of the viscount's mother, another vehicle was clattering down the road leading into the entrance of the Park and joining the crush of carriages. For Felicity McHenry the customary fashionable hour in the Park held no pleasure, only a dread that had been building ever since she had received the earl's invitation.

Shuddering a little, she stole a look at the undeniably handsome visage next to her. The brittle smile in those eyes froze her to the marrow. But why did it? Other females they had met in the Park showed not the least amount of awe of the earl. They spoke to him quite easily, and some, she was shocked to discover, had even flirted with him. Would that she could do the same.

"You are very quiet this afternoon, Miss McHenry," Eberhart said, jolting her from her reverie. She pressed her gloved hands together to still their shaking.

"Oh, no, my lord!"

He smiled. "I hesitate to contradict so charming a creature, but you are very quiet." His smile turned to a puzzled frown. "I hope I am not in your black books."

"Why, no!" Felicity exclaimed. "What put such an idea into your mind?"

He shrugged. "That aunt of yours has no great love of me."

"Yes, I know," Felicity acknowledged before blushing furiously. "I didn't mean—"

Eberhart gave a hollow laugh. "I am well aware of what your aunt thinks of me. Her opinion, however, is of no great import."

Hearing a bitter note in the earl's voice, Felicity held her tongue, not sure whether she should answer or not. Fortunately a diversion occurred just then in the appearance of Mr. Peter Thorpe on his latest mount, a high-spirited Arabian, which carried him down the path in full view of the passersby.

The earl chuckled aloud at the struggling rider. A fine horse, but it lacked the proper temperament for the city, or perhaps it was the rider who lacked the temperament. He cast an oblique look at his young companion.

"Do you ride, Miss McHenry?"

"A little, my lord."

"Good. We must ride together sometime. You shall permit me to mount you. I have a second hack who is gentle but spirited. I should count it a great favor if you would exercise her."

Although only an indifferent rider, Felicity realized that the earl was making her a generous offer. She could do little except to stammer out her thanks and wonder why the idea of riding under his scrutiny should fill her with such gloom.

He was so daunting and imperious. Nothing at all like that nice Mr. Fairweather, with whom she had danced Friday night and whom she remembered meeting once before in Warwickshire. In Mr. Fairweather's unalarming company she felt thoroughly at ease and not quite so insipid. Sighing, she twisted the strings of her reticule about a finger. Why couldn't Eberhart be more like his secretary?

Happily for his own self-esteem, Eberhart was unacquainted with Felicity's thinking. To be compared—unfavorably at that!—with another gentleman, particularly his own secretary, would not have set well in his dish.

Reassured that Mr. Thorpe was in no danger of suffering a broken neck, Eberhart started his team forward again, driving the phaeton deftly away from the most congested areas and toward the quiet path that led to the Serpentine.

He felt rather pleased with himself, and had no fault to find with Felicity. True, she still spoke very little, but with some coaxing she might cease to be so tongue-tied. And her reticence was not such a flaw when he remembered the prattle boxes who had talked his ear off in the past. And the fact that she rode was capital news.

His carriage rolled on, and soon the lake beckoned, peaceful and beautiful, the perfect spot to present Felicity with the gift he had selected at Rundell's. With this in mind he halted the carriage, a move that sparked a mild outcry from Felicity.

"Don't be alarmed," he soothed. "I thought we might admire the lake together, and you might be persuaded to open this."

He had produced a small jeweler's box from the folds of his great multicolored driving cape.

"Open it," he said as she showed no sign of doing anything except stare at it.

Automatically, Felicity obeyed. She was immediately struck by the dazzling sight of a bracelet with twelve perfectly matched rubies and twelve equally flawless diamonds.

The earl watched with a smile, waiting for some display of delight from her. He was thunderstruck when she thrust the bracelet back in its box, shoved the cover on it, pushed it at him, and began to bawl into a handkerchief embroidered in red and gold, her favorite colors.

"Good God, Miss McHenry," he ejaculated, alarmed at her transformation into a watering pot. "What is the matter? Do you have some dislike of rubies? If you'd rather have sapphires, I'm sure I can oblige you. Rundell told me he had a new shipment from the Indies just in. Star sapphires, they were."

Felicity remained mute, her shoulders quaking.

"Just take another look at the bracelet," the earl suggested.

"What are you doing to my niece?" an outraged voice hissed from behind them.

Turning, Eberhart gazed over his shoulder to discover Rosalind and Waldo. He had been so absorbed with Felicity that he had failed to hear the other carriage approach.

Having received no response from the earl, who appeared stunned at her question, Rosalind turned to Felicity.

"Felicity, my dear, what has he done to you?"

Her niece, however, was in no condition to do anything except cry, which she now did in earnest. Rather annoyed at finding himself in the midst of a scene, Eberhart declared acidly that he had done nothing whatever to Felicity.

"I am a gentleman, Miss McHenry," he said, glaring balefully at Rosalind.

She answered his look with a dagger look of her own.

"If so, why is she crying?"

"Because . . . How the devil should I know?" the earl exploded. "And don't think you can lay the blame for this at my door! I haven't done a thing. And I shan't be treated as though I put her into a quake by misbehaving!"

At this, Waldo, a mute witness to the proceedings, murmured a deprecating sound lest he be called upon to take up the cudgels in Rosalind's defense, an action that might well lead to the grim possibility of meeting Eberhart at dawn at Paddington Green.

Since Waldo was a poor shot and the earl's prowess with a pistol was regarded by the habitués of Manton's as nothing short of uncanny, his qualms were justified. But Rosalind did not need any help in fighting her battles. From the first moment she had laid eyes on Eberhart she had taken him in a hearty dislike, and now to find him browbeating a poor lamb like Felicity!

"Browbeating!" The earl controlled his temper when she put this charge to him. "My dear Miss McHenry, you are indulging in a fit of melodrama, not surprising in a female of your temperament."

She stiffened. "My temperament? Pray, what do you mean?"

He gazed down his nose at her. "On the two occasions we have met, I have observed that you are notoriously prone to whim, think nothing of propriety, and leap to conclusions!"

"I don't need to leap to any conclusion to deduce that you have terrified my niece!" Rosalind retorted. "And do leave my temperament out of this."

"Willingly," he said, pushing back his high-crowned beaver. "But I shan't have you point the finger at me. All I did to Miss Felicity was to present her with a small token of my esteem."

"What token?" she asked skeptically.

Mutely, he handed her the jeweler's box. Rosalind, her curiosity piqued, opened it and stared dumbfounded at the dazzling array of jewels. The bracelet was stunning.

"Good heavens, these stones are exquisite," she said in real admiration.

"I'm glad they meet with your approval," the earl said acidly. "Miss Felicity, however, found them wanting."

"Oh, I didn't find them wanting, sir," Felicity said at last, her voice quivering. "It's just that I'm not worthy of them."

"That's a new excuse. I doubt there are any females worthy of these jewels, but you are probably the only one in Christendom who would say so." He looked down at her still-tearful countenance and smiled gently. "Come now, wouldn't you like to try it on?"

"No," she cried, shrinking back against her seat.

His jaw clamped shut. What in heaven ailed the chit?

"Do you have some aversion to jewelry?" he asked politely.

"Oh, do stop hounding her," Rosalind said, out of patience with both the earl and her niece. "Can't you see that she is not feeling the thing?"

"Indeed, ma'am, I am fully aware of that. Her tears are evidence enough."

"Then stop interrogating her," Rosalind ordered. "Since she is not fit to accompany you for the duration of the drive, Viscount Coppleton and I shall see her home. If you would kindly help her down from your phaeton."

"I have yet to desert any companion in need," the earl declared, making no move to obey Rosalind's command. "And I am fully capable of escorting Miss Felicity back to Green Street. Perhaps it will reassure you if I divulge that I have no further trinkets to present that might spark another show of the vapors. And now, Miss McHenry, if you don't mind, I suggest we move on. Our little tête-à-tête is causing considerable interest, which I for one can do without!"

Made aware by this remark that the four of them were the target of curious eyes, Rosalind did not press the point, but she did give Waldo explicit instructions to keep the earl's phaeton in view as they drove from the Park back to Green Street.

Chapter Six

Mrs. Withers looked up in quick concern as Rosalind emerged from Felicity's bedchamber, carrying a dinner tray.

"Is she feeling more the thing, Miss?" the stout housekeeper asked, a worried look on her genial face.

"I don't know, Mrs. Withers," Rosalind said truthfully as she relinquished the tray and headed for her own bedchamber.

Her temples throbbed, and her heart felt heavy. Felicity had by now recovered sufficiently to pour out all manner of contradictory confidences to her aunt. She respected Eberhart. She feared him. His gift had cast her into transports. It had dashed her hopes. She could never marry such a man. She must marry him.

Suspecting that Felicity was teetering on the edge of hysteria, Rosalind persuaded her to drink some laudanum to soothe her frayed nerves. Now alone, she reflected ruefully on the muddle they had landed in.

There was no way around the truth. Felicity had behaved like a perfect wet goose in the Park. She had no earthly reason to fly into a pet over the ruby and diamond bracelet, the likes of which Rosalind had never seen before. Felicity's reaction was yet more proof of her youth and how ill-suited she was to the earl. The match must be stopped.

Rosalind sat down on her bed, trying desperately to think of a way out of their dilemma. She knew Gerald too well to suppose that he would turn down Eberhart's offer. And Felicity was too timid to do the deed herself. So it was up to Rosalind to find a way to scotch the match.

* * *

Over at Manton's shooting gallery the earl was engrossed in thoughts of his own, ones that caused him to miss the bull's-eye twice, more than enough to bestir a ripple of interest among the intimates of that establishment.

" 'Pon my soul, Alastair, that's not like you," William Wilding clucked as he clapped his friend on the shoulder.

"What's not like me?" Eberhart asked, taking aim at the target again and firing.

"Missed again," William observed, rubbing his nose with a slender forefinger. "It appears to me that your mind ain't on your shooting. Fortunate you don't have a duel brewing on the morrow."

"What brings you here, William?" Eberhart asked, putting down the pistol and scowling. "I thought you deplored pistols and preferred swords."

"It is rather old-fashioned of me," Wilding said, owning to this prejudice. "But there's more skill involved in a successful thrust or parry than in just pointing a pistol and firing away." He shot the earl a quizzical look. "I shouldn't worry too much about the sudden deterioration of your skill with a pistol. Cupid probably had something to do with it."

Eberhart had donned his coat, and he eyed his friend now with considerable loathing.

"It never ceases to amaze me how you hear so much!"

Mr. Wilding laughed. "A gentleman never gossips. But what can he do if others persist in gossiping to him? And," he reminded his friend, "it did take place at the fashionable hour in the Park. You'd best conduct your quarrels indoors as most civilized folk do."

"I hadn't intended to find myself in the midst of a quarrel," Eberhart remarked. "At the time I merely wished a quiet drive with a lovely lady. That shows you what a paperskull I am."

Wilding chuckled. "You've no luck with the McHenry females, it seems. First the aunt won't dance with you. Then the niece fights shy in the Park. And I am devilishly curious to find out what Miss McHenry said when she came upon the two of you together!"

Eberhart's lip curled at the memory. "She tried to give

me a set-down. Preposterous female. There wasn't anything to rake me over the coals about. Queerest female I've ever met!''

"The aunt or the niece?" Wilding asked, a trifle confused.

"The aunt. Nothing confusing about the niece, not that I knew she was such a watering pot."

Mr. Wilding gave his friend an encouraging pat on the back.

"The path to true love has always been rocky, Alastair."

"When did you turn philosopher, William?"

"The same day you turned suitor," he retorted. "And if you mean to cast aspersions on my philosophizing it appears that I'd make a better job of it as philosopher than you've done thus far as suitor!" He laughed. "Only think of all the ladies who have lain in wait so long for you to throw them the handkerchief."

"Frankly, William, I find your observations a bore."

Mr. Wilding was not offended. "Courtship has a way of making a man testy."

"I am not testy!" the earl said irritably.

Still chuckling, Wilding drew him out the door. "Of course you're not. Let's go to White's. A game of whist shall take your mind off your troubles."

"I don't have any troubles. And though I'm obliged to you for the offer, I am promised to my mother for dinner."

The invitation to dine had been issued some days previous by Lady Manning, but by the time her son put in his appearance at her Berkeley Square residence, the whole of the afternoon's escapade in the Park had reached her ear, put there by the Countess Montgomery, who had the story straight from her daughter, who had viewed Felicity's tears firsthand.

Ordinarily Lady Manning did not listen to *on dits* concerning her son, but when the matter involved not only Alastair but also Rosalind and Felicity, she was all ears.

Greeting Eberhart that evening, she wondered if the story could have been a hoax. Nothing in the smiling face gave the slightest clue that he had suffered a rebuff. For the first part of the evening she managed to keep her curiosity in check, assisted by Lord Manning, who had had his own ear bent during the afternoon by Lady Manning's many confused schemes to rid her son of his infatuation with Felicity. Lord Manning was dotingly fond of his new wife, but he rather thought there was no need for either of them to thrust their oars into what didn't concern them.

Over a dinner consisting of boiled eels, fresh asparagus, and a leg of the tenderest spring lamb, the earl learned that the newlyweds' moving woes were finally behind them. Lady Manning had summoned up her courage to ask her butler if he wouldn't like to be pensioned off, anticipating a frightful row.

"Only to be flabbergasted," she said now, "when he replied he'd like that very much."

"It seems he'd stayed on only because we had need of him," Lord Manning added. "All the while he wished to live with his daughter in Yorkshire."

As they ate, the earl continued to listen with interest to his mother's recitations of the many sights and sounds the two had encountered on the Continent, including a vivid description of the barbarous manners of the French.

"Come now, Mama," Eberhart teased as they relaxed over a bottle of claret. "They can't be so barbarous if they make claret like this." He turned to Manning. "You must tell me the name of that inn in Dijon, sir. First sherry and now claret!"

"Gladly, but you shan't find any more bottles," Manning replied, his mustache twitching slightly in a jovial smile. "Bought the lot up. I knew if I didn't, you would!"

His stepson laughed. "There is one thing to be said for France. She produces excellent wine. And her countryside is said to be pretty as well."

"I suppose it is," Lady Manning admitted grudgingly. "And yet, of all the sights the Alps were the most spectacular. You must go there yourself, Alastair, and see them."

"Perhaps I shall on my wedding trip," he said lightly.

"If a ride in the Park induces Miss Felicity to hysteria,

Alastair, I should think twice before I brought her face to face with the Alps!'' his mother said without thinking.

Eberhart put down his glass of claret. "I see the quizzes have been busy. I had hoped they would spare you the story."

"Well, they didn't," Lady Manning said frankly. "And I don't believe that you would put any female into a quake. That much of a coxcomb you are not!"

He grinned. "Thank you, Mama. But I'm much afraid that's what I did do to young Felicity, unintentionally it goes without saying. She turned missish, and before I could endeavor to ask what might be plaguing her she had burst into tears."

"Quite a surprise," Lord Manning said from his comfortable vantage point of sixty years.

"It quite bowled me over, sir," Eberhart acknowledged.

His mother reclaimed his wandering attention with a wave of her hand.

"She is so young. Alastair, I hope you didn't perchance try to make love to her in the carriage!"

The earl cocked an eyebrow. "Really, Mama!"

"Then why the attack of vapors?" she asked exasperatedly. "Or was that mere exaggeration?"

"I wish it were," he replied. "She wept. How she wept. An inexhaustible flow."

"Perhaps she was crying from happiness," Manning said, discomfited by any female tears, even those he was not obliged to witness.

Eberhart laughed. "I might delude myself into thinking they were from happiness, but I'm not such a nodcock. Odd to have a bracelet from Rundell's elicit such a response."

"And yet you seem rather composed about the entire affair," his mother said, amazed that he should take such a calm view of the matter.

"What ought I to do, Mama?" he countered. "Rant and rave? I'll admit to being tempted to do that, particularly when that harebrained aunt of hers bungled onto the scene with that idiot Coppleton and practically accused me of taking a whip to Felicity."

A pained expression came into Lady Manning's eyes. The hope that had been rising in her breast was dashed down again.

"Do you mean you are still planning to offer for Felicity? After that scene in the Park?"

"I am willing to overlook a few mistakes," the earl told her. "Don't you agree, sir?" He looked over at his stepfather, who was savoring the claret. "One should overlook certain flaws in the person one marries."

Lord Manning cast a wary eye in the direction of his new spouse and made a strangled sound before taking refuge again in his glass.

"Why do you object to my marriage, Mama?" Eberhart asked.

Lady Manning decided it was time to open her budget completely.

"Perhaps it is not just skittishness that affects Felicity," she said gently.

The earl frowned. "Then what lies behind her curious behavior?"

His mother laid a hand on his wrist. "Perhaps, Alastair, she might not wish the match."

Eberhart was astonished. Whatever private notions he had entertained about Felicity had not included this unlikely thought.

"Don't be absurd, Mama," he said now. "Of course the chit wishes the match. That is understood."

His mother gazed at him for a long moment. "Are you so certain?"

He felt a pang of doubt. "Well, it stands to reason. I don't wish to be boastful, but I am alleged to be quite a catch, am I not?"

"A matrimonial prize of the first water," she agreed. "But perhaps to someone as green as Felicity you might not be in her style."

"Mama," the earl expostulated, "can you be serious? Lady Jersey once told me I was going to waste as a bachelor. Pray, what do you detect wrong with me?"

"Nothing at all, my love," Lady Manning said hastily.

"Perhaps it's the cut of my coat," he teased. "Not one of Weston's finer efforts."

"Now, Alastair! You know perfectly well that your coat is exquisite."

"Then it must be my looks," he continued in a rallying tone. "More than enough to put a female into fright?"

"No, not your looks," his mother said thoughtfully, "but perhaps your manner."

The teasing light vanished from his eyes.

"I have been told my form of address was unexceptional! Mrs. Drummond Burrel herself once told me I was the soul of civility. And you know what a high stickler she is!"

"Yes, but all the same, Alastair, when you are in the boughs a most daunting expression comes into your face. It glowers. That might cause a green girl like Felicity to think you uncivil."

"A glowering look, Mama?" Eberhart stared. "I confess I am not always the most placid of fellows, but am I such an ogre? Surely you exaggerate."

"Well, I must own that once or twice even I have been somewhat daunted by it. Not that you would do anything to me. But all the same, it does give one pause."

Her son scoffed at such an idiotish notion, and Lord Manning wisely changed the topic to the more agreeable one of horses. Later, however, as the earl drove back to St. James Square, he pondered his mother's words. He had not given Felicity's wishes much importance. Indeed, he had assumed that any female would wish to marry him. But did she or didn't she?

Although Eberhart had eschewed the various comforts and diversions to be found that evening at White's, Mr. Gerald McHenry had not. He had arrived at the club in the early evening, hoping that this night would herald the start of a lucky streak. Unhappily, his luck ran true to form: appallingly bad, a fact he blamed with characteristic venom on his sister, who had had, he was certain, a hand in his daughter's freakish behavior earlier that day in the Park.

"Blasted chit will spoil everything," he complained now

to Mr. Gideon Dankley, who had been with him throughout the play at the green baize tables and was now standing him a glass of claret. Mr. Dankley was fifty years of age, lean and spare, with a purse he kept locked and to himself. Rumor had it that he had ties to trade, but no one knew this for certain.

His birth had been modest, and his standing in society would have been just as slight were it not for his purse, which won him entree into certain select circles, including White's.

"Is it the lovely Felicity you are speaking of?" Mr. Dankley asked now.

"Felicity? Bless me, no! It's that shatterbrained sister of mine," Gerald replied. "It's goose to guineas she said something to Felicity that caused her to fly into a pet with Eberhart today. Wouldn't be surprised if this puts an end to my understanding with him. Man of his standing wouldn't care to be made a cake of by a schoolroom miss, and in public, too! It's dished me."

Mr. Dankley patted his mouth with a bony hand. "Why is that?"

Gerald stared gloomily into his glass. "You've seen my luck at the tables tonight?"

Mr. Dankley nodded, not unsympathetically. "If I were you, I'd quit. Whist ain't your game."

"Nothing is my game," Gerald said with a snort. His fingernails drummed lightly on the table. "Sometimes I think the only answer is to emigrate to America. They say a man can make a fortune there easily enough."

"Perhaps so, but it's such an uncomfortable journey to endure."

Gerald gave a mirthless laugh. "If Felicity loses Eberhart I may have to emigrate, long journey or not. I can't stave off my creditors forever."

His companion permitted himself a small smile. "Premature, my good McHenry. The earl may not be your daughter's only suitor."

"Eh? What do you mean?" Gerald asked.

"If Eberhart should bow out, I can think of someone else who might take his place as husband to your Felicity."

"He'd have to be well pursed."

Mr. Dankley smiled again. "He is."

"Well, who, man? Tell me!"

"Me."

McHenry stared. "You're bosky."

Mr. Dankley smiled. "I have seen your Felicity once or twice, and I think we would suit. A young wife would look after me in my dotage. And," he added with a shrewd look at Gerald, "I would be more than willing to make whatever settlements you desire."

The frown faded from Gerald's pendulous cheeks. "Settlements, did you say?" he inquired as he took Dankley's measure. "I never took you for the marrying kind, but by all means let's have a drop more of this fine claret and discuss the matter further!"

Chapter Seven

Fergus approached the earl's bedchamber door with all the trepidation appropriate to the eleven o'clock hour registering on the great grandfather clock in the hall. As a rule the earl was rendered testy by any disturbance prior to noon. But the communication Fergus carried in his hands seemed to demand Eberhart's immediate attention.

Hedges had placed the missive on Fergus's desk only moments before, reporting with a meaningful look that Miss McHenry had requested that the earl receive it at once.

It would have been simple enough to dispatch a footman with it, but some inner devil drove Fergus to do the deed himself. His eyes fell on the cream-colored paper he grasped tightly between thumb and forefinger. It bore every appearance of a love note. His heart grew heavy. What would be his fate as Eberhart's secretary with Felicity installed as countess? That thought nearly caused him to turn back down the stairs. But it was too late.

Eberhart, applying the last touch to his cravat, had just emerged from his chamber. "Fergus, what are you doing up and about? I do hope that's not a bill from Locke's in your hand."

"No, indeed, sir," Fergus replied, "it's a private communication that just arrived for you."

Eberhart cocked his eyebrow at his secretary. Was it his imagination, or did his secretary look paler than usual?

"A private communication, you say?" he asked as he turned the note over. "I don't recognize the hand, but it looks suspiciously female."

"I believe Hedges said that Miss McHenry's footman delivered it,'' Fergus said woodenly, torn between the desire to quit the room and the urge to know just what Felicity had written the earl.

"Felicity, is it?'' Eberhart said, unaware of Fergus's turmoil. He was not himself displeased to get a letter from Felicity. In all likelihood it would be a note of apology. Smiling, he broke the seal with a quick twist of his thumb. A second later his smile vanished.

"What abominable cheek!'' he ejaculated.

Astounded at such a display of violence, Fergus looked across in bewilderment.

"Not bad news, I hope, sir.''

"It's not from Miss Felicity. It's from that dratted aunt of hers. Here, read it yourself.''

"Oh, really, sir, I couldn't,'' Fergus demurred.

"Then I shall do so for you. 'Dear Lord Eberhart, I should be obliged if you would be at Somerset House tomorrow at eleven in the morning. I have something vital I must discuss concerning your future and Felicity's. Rosalind McHenry.' Interfering chit.'' The earl looked up. "Whom does she think she is ordering about in this fashion?''

Fergus coughed. "Begging your lordship's pardon, but if you do marry Miss Felicity, that shall make her your aunt, so to speak. And you would be her nephew.''

"Good God, Fergus, you are right!'' the earl said grimly. "And if I were less stouthearted, that would cause me to turn cat in the pan.'' He crushed the note in his hand. "What can she want? And why Somerset House?''

"Do you intend to go, then?'' Fergus asked, unable to repress his curiosity.

The earl nodded. "Far be it from me to disobey any future aunt's summons. But it will be the very last summons she ever dares to issue to me. And I shall take pains to tell her so tomorrow.'' He turned to his secretary, recalling another matter. "I meant to ask, Fergus, about that inn in Dijon my stepfather stumbled across. He told me there was no claret or sherry left in the cellar, but one never does know what an innkeeper shall hoard. Can you see to it? Write a small letter of inquiry.''

"Yes, sir, I shall," Fergus said distractedly.

The earl gazed at him with some concern. "Fergus, you seem rather preoccupied. I hope I haven't been working you to death. If so, you have only to say the word."

"Oh, sir! Overworked! You are jesting."

"You haven't received bad news from home, I hope?" Eberhart asked kindly.

Fergus shook his head. "No, indeed. And now if you will excuse me, I shall see to that letter to Dijon."

Mr. Fairweather parted company with the earl at the bottom of the stairs. But half an hour later the sheaf of paper on his desk was still blank, and when he did at last apply his quill to paper it was not a landlord in Dijon he addressed but his uncle in Brussels.

Twenty-four hours later, Rosalind, squashed between the personages of Viscount Coppleton and his stout mama, greeted with relief the edifice of Somerset House. The carriage ride from Green Street had seemed endless. The conversation was punctuated with repeated references to people she didn't know. But it could have been worse. Waldo's sister might have been with them instead of prostrate in her bedchamber with a migraine.

"Not that I would ever desert a child in need," the viscountess said, leaning over to address Rosalind, a move that caused their carriage to lurch precariously to one side. "But Waldo insisted I meet you."

"And we're obliged that you could, Mama," Waldo said with a merry smile.

"I do hope that Mary will feel better," Rosalind said.

"Oh, I have no doubt about that," Waldo replied. "I don't see why she must be so invalidish."

"Your sister is not invalidish." Lady Coppleton exercised her maternal privilege to scold her son. "She has a delicate constitution, as you do." She eyed Rosalind for a moment. "Both my children take after me."

"So I notice, ma'am," Rosalind murmured, leaning back against the velvet squabs and musing on the uncanny resemblance between Waldo and his mother. While Waldo was not as stout as his mother, nor of her age or sex, he did bear a remarkable similarity, with the same aquiline nose, squarish jaw, thin lips, and red hair. The viscountess's hair, however, Rosalind had no doubt, had been helped by artful coloring.

Fortunately her impulse to dwell on the similarities between mother and son came to an abrupt conclusion as they reached Somerset House. Waldo helped his mother down from the carriage while Rosalind looked anxiously about for Eberhart. But the earl was nowhere in sight.

She frowned, uncertain how to proceed. She didn't know how to detach herself from Waldo and his mother and search for Eberhart. Fortunately Lady Coppleton proved an ally. She pressed her son into service to discuss each and every painting in the rooms, enabling Rosalind to trail behind until she had lost sight of her companions. Then she retraced her steps to the entrance. By now the hour was well past eleven. Where was Eberhart? How vexatious if he came later or not at all!

Just as these doubts assailed her, Eberhart came out of one of the side rooms, looming in the hallway, his wide shoulders filling the entire breadth.

"There you are, and late!" he accused, advancing and looking, she had to admit, quite striking in his biscuit pantaloons and gleaming Hessians.

"I, late?" she asked, stung. "I have been here for the past ten minutes. You are the tardy one."

"I was here precisely at eleven," the earl said thickly. "I took a turn in the rooms, thinking you might have gone ahead." He made an impatient gesture with a glove. "Now, what is all this about?"

His blunt query unnerved Rosalind momentarily. She had decided that the only way to make certain that Felicity did not do something goosish, such as marry Eberhart, was to prevent the offer from ever being issued. That meant applying to the earl himself, unpleasant though such a task must be. She gazed at him now, the trace of hauteur discernible in his eyes, wondering how to proceed.

"I daresay you thought my note odd," she said at last.

"By no means," he drawled adroitly, admiring almost against his will the blue walking dress and matching pelisse she wore. "I thought the note very much like you. But why the need for so clandestine a meeting? A civil request asking me to call at Green Street would have sufficed."

"No, it wouldn't have," she countered. "Felicity might have gotten wind of it. I couldn't risk her knowing. Today, as it happens, she took herself off to Hookam's in search of something to read. But I had no way of foretelling that. And since I was promised to Waldo and his mama today at Somerset House, I thought you and I could contrive to meet her. And do you think we might walk?"

The earl had followed this tortuous commentary with unusual patience, but at her last question he looked at her as though she were daft.

"Walk? Walk where?"

"Anywhere in the rooms," she said. "Just in case Waldo should reappear." A faint flush stained her cheeks. "He might jump to conclusions. That might be awkward for you."

"I feel sure I could withstand any onslaught the viscount might wish to unleash," Eberhart said dryly.

"Oh, he wouldn't dare attack you. It's just that it would be awkward. His mother is here, too. It might appear more ordinary if we say we met by chance."

"I have already walked through the rooms once, but if you wish it . . ." He followed her into the opposite room, unoccupied save for several dour portraits on the wall. "Now, what is this all about, Miss McHenry?"

Her eyes searched his for an appraising moment. His expression was unreadable, but she thought she detected curiosity behind the lazy lids. She decided to take her fences in a rush.

"Lord Eberhart, you intend to offer for Felicity, don't you?"

The earl extracted a snuffbox from the pocket of his great coat. "I was not planning to offer her *carte blanche*, ma'am."

"No, of course. But she is very young, you must realize.

Scarcely out of a schoolroom. Indeed, she has not even enjoyed one Season!''

He frowned as he inhaled a pinch of snuff. ''It was not my intention to deprive Miss Felicity of the joys of a first Season. And there is no reason she must forgo them. We shall become engaged during the Season, and the wedding will follow later. That will give her time to enjoy everything. Will that do?''

''No, it would only make things worse. Like slow torture!''

''Torture?'' Eberhart snapped the lid of the snuffbox down. To have one's impending betrothal spoken of as torture was effrontery of the highest order.

''Oh, dear.'' Rosalind had observed the anger kindling in his eyes. ''You have that look on your face as though you were about to eat someone alive. It would be me, I daresay.''

''You needn't worry, Miss McHenry. I do not profess to cannibalism. And for all that you appear undaunted.''

''Well, that's because you couldn't do anything to me. Not really,'' she pointed out. ''And I consider hysteria and vapors poor weapons, don't you?''

''*Au contraire*. In the hands of most females they are more dangerous than either pistol or sword. Miss Felicity proved that only the other day.''

His words put Rosalind once more on the defensive. ''Felicity's really not vaporish,'' she said, ''even though it might appear that way. Oh, what a muddle all this is. I don't know what else to tell you, except perhaps just straight out. Felicity doesn't wish to marry you.''

Her words, reminiscent of his mother's on the same topic, took Eberhart by surprise.

''If so,'' he said carefully, ''she has only to tell me so herself. I shall drop my suit.''

''Yes, but she can't. Or rather, she won't!''

''Has she been struck dumb since last I saw her?''

Rosalind was not amused. ''Eberhart, do be sensible. How could an obliging child like Felicity possibly turn you down?''

"The same way you did at my dinner!"

"Good heavens!" Her eyes widened. "Are you still holding that dance against me? I assure you I shall dance with you any time you like hereafter. And pray do not lead me off onto a tangent. Felicity does not wish your attentions."

He stared down at her for a long moment. "Does she know you're here?" he asked at last.

"Well, no. She wouldn't like it."

He threw his hands up to the ceiling. "Miss McHenry, I am wholly at sea. On the one hand you tell me that Miss McHenry would consider any betrothal between herself and me as a fate worse than death. On the other hand you tell me that if I did inquire into this situation she would deny everything. Is this the heart of the matter or isn't it?"

Rosalind was obliged to admit that all in all he had managed to put his finger on the problem.

"It makes a good story, I must own," he said.

Her head snapped up. "Story? I assure you I speak the truth."

"We shall have to ask Miss Felicity that. If she dislikes the match, she need only say so. I shall heed her wishes. I have no desire to take a martyr for a wife. Matrimony is difficult enough."

"But she won't say no," Rosalind said. "Haven't you been listening to me?"

"Indeed I have. For reasons that fully escape me you want to scotch the match between Felicity and myself."

She stared at him for a long moment. "You don't believe me!" she said, dumbfounded.

He smiled. "I don't doubt your desire to end my courtship of Miss Felicity. But does it stem from true concern, as you maintain, or from something else?"

Rosalind drew herself up.

"You have been frank with me," Eberhart continued before she could unleash the lightning bolts building in her eyes. "Allow me to do the same with you. You are some years Felicity's senior and have been out for several Seasons. You consider your niece a green girl and yet she has attracted the attentions of an earl. Even the most affectionate of aunts would find her feathers ruffled somewhat by such an occurrence.''

Rosalind eyed him with acute distaste. "That would depend on the earl," she said witheringly.

Eberhart absorbed this blow with a slight bow. "If Miss Felicity is set against the marriage, why doesn't she inform her father? He has only to tell me the matter is as you put it and I shall withdraw. Presumably he can speak!''

"Oh, pray don't mention Gerald. It's his fault Felicity is embroiled in such a scrape to begin with. He's never paid any attention to her. But now he's willing to sell her to anyone to pay off his debts!''

These words uttered in the white heat of passion brought a frigid look to the earl's face.

"You paint a charming picture of me as a slave master," he said, putting on his gloves.

Rosalind knew that she had gone too far. "I beg pardon. I didn't mean . . .''

"You have been too free with what you mean," he said coldly. "I take no interest in slaves. My sole intention was to find myself a wife.'' And with that he turned on his heel and stalked away, almost colliding with Lady Coppleton's broad bosom.

" 'Pon my word, was that Eberhart?'' Waldo asked after the earl had extricated himself from the viscountess and stormed away.

"Yes, Waldo," Rosalind said. "That was Eberhart.''

"What was he doing here?'' Waldo asked curiously.

"Admiring the paintings, of course," she muttered in a voice that was, for her, oddly muted.

All the way back to Green Street Rosalind endured an orgy of self-reproach. What could she have been thinking of? Of all the baconbrained plans in the world!

An involuntary sigh sparked a flurry of questions from Lady Coppleton, whose shrewd eyes had already diagnosed Rosalind's lachrymal mood as symptomatic of the influenza raging in the city.

To add to Rosalind's discomfiture, Waldo saw her to the

door of her residence and seized the opportunity to issue another of his tedious proposals. How could he do such a thing
with his mother waiting in the barouche?

"Waldo," she implored, "I do wish you would not keep
asking me. I hate to say no."

"Then say yes. Mama shall be so pleased."

This comment nearly sparked a fit of giggles in Rosalind,
who would have wagered a monkey that the viscountess
would have an entirely different reaction to news of her
son's impending nuptials.

She managed to fob him off now by issuing a gentle but
firm refusal to his offer and pointing out that the viscountess, blessed, as she had put it, with a delicate constitution,
might be taken with an inflammation of the lungs if he
tarried any longer, which had the desired effect of sending
him guiltily back to the barouche.

Chapter Eight

After dispatching Waldo into the waiting arms of his mama, Rosalind withdrew to her own sitting room. She did not regret having divulged the truth about Felicity's feelings to Eberhart, but she supposed that she had bungled the matter somewhat.

She thought at first of writing him a letter of apology, but banished the idea almost at once. Any further communication from her to the earl would undoubtedly end up in his fireplace.

Self-rebuke was not one of Rosalind's customary habits. Qualms of self-censure she regarded as a waste of time, but today she acknowledged to the portrait of her mother on the wall that her tongue had run on carriage wheels. True, Eberhart was odiously starched up, but she should have been more diplomatic, even though he had scarcely endeared himself to her by implying that envy of Felicity was her true motive.

On the whole she felt listless and worn down by her morning's activities, a mood not remedied when she found Felicity weeping quietly on the library couch.

"My dear child," she exclaimed at once from the doorway. "Whatever is the matter?"

"Oh, nothing really, Aunt Rosalind," Felicity said, blotting her tears with a handkerchief. "It is just this new novel I am reading by Walter Scott. It is all about love. It makes me want to cry."

"So I see. But do stop it," Rosalind implored. "Your face will get blotched." She picked up the offending book and turned it over with a dubious eye. The cover looked innocent enough. "Did you purchase this at Hookam's?"

Felicity shook her head, still drying her eyes. "No, Mr. Fairweather gave it to me."

"Mr. Fairweather? Do you mean the earl's secretary?"

Felicity nodded, smoothing the ends of the handkerchief lightly with a hand. "He was at Hookam's, too. Do you know he is the most prodigious reader? He has read all of Virgil and a good part of Ovid in the original Latin."

"A heroic undertaking," Rosalind agreed, most impressed. "Is Walter Scott one of his favorites?"

"I'm not sure," Felicity said, sobering somewhat. "He asked me what type of books I read, and when I said romances, he recommended this one to me."

"How civil of him. He certainly is an obliging young man. I wonder if he still plans to go on to Brussels."

Felicity dropped the book that Rosalind had given back to her. "Brussels?" she exclaimed now. "Pray, what would he do there, Aunt Rosalind?"

"Help his uncle in the diplomatic field, I believe," Rosalind said absently. She stooped to pick up the book for Felicity. "He mentioned it to me in passing the night of Eberhart's ball. But don't breathe a word of it to anyone, for I'm sure he doesn't wish the earl to get wind of his plans."

"But if Mr. Fairweather goes to Brussels he shan't be with the earl when Eberhart and I . . ." Felicity's voice trailed off.

"No," Rosalind agreed. "But there is no need to tease yourself. Eberhart might not offer for you. Or perhaps someone more charming and wealthier might."

"Such as?" Felicity sent her an inquiring look.

"Well, I don't know precisely," Rosalind replied, "but that possibility always exists, doesn't it?"

And on that optimistic note she left Felicity in the library and turned her attention to the various household tasks that Mrs. Withers had laid in front of her, which included approving all the menus for the weeks to come.

Someone wealthier and more charming than Eberhart. Her own words teased her as she tried to listen to Mrs. Withers's litany of complaints against an underfootman caught intoxicated for the second time in as many weeks.

"And he's only been with us a fortnight," Mrs. Withers exclaimed, making plain what she thought of such a fellow. "Do you wish to speak to him, Miss? Or shall I dismiss him?"

"Whatever you think best," Rosalind said idly.

"I'd dismiss him," Mrs. Withers said frankly. "I wouldn't have taken him on except that he was brother to one of the upstairs maids."

After approving the dismissal of the footman, Rosalind continued to sit alone at her desk, staring at the sheaf of bills in front of her. But after perusing a few, she pushed them aside. This was not the time to think of such things, not when she felt the answer to their troubles was brewing in the recesses of her mind.

Her excitement grew as she pondered the problem. What had started as a wild scheme grew more rational as she turned it over in her mind. If she hadn't scared Eberhart off, he would undoubtedly offer for Felicity soon, and that would never do.

But perhaps she could supply him with some competitors for Felicity's hand. Competitors who were just as wealthy as he—precious few were wealthier!—and kindlier of temperament. And here she felt on more certain ground. Surely almost anyone else would be better-tempered. If Felicity fell in love with one of them Gerald might be persuaded to let her marry him instead of the earl, particularly if the settlements were made.

Quickly Rosalind retired to her bedchamber to draw up a list of eligibles and to make plans for a small soiree on Friday evening where Felicity might meet them all.

"Fergus, if you were a female, would you marry me?" Eberhart asked, striding into the secretary's office, his driving cloak still gathered at his shoulders.

Mr. Fairweather was astounded at so unprecedented a question.

"Well," Eberhart prompted. "Would you or not?"

"I'm not sure I understand you, sir," Fergus said.

Eberhart sat on the edge of the desk. "It's a simple enough question, Fergus. Let's say you were a female and you saw me as I appear in front of you today. Would you think marriage to me a fortunate or unfortunate occurrence?"

"I'd consider it fortunate, sir."

"That's what I thought, too."

Fergus looked into the pensive face. "Begging your pardon, sir, but what makes you ask such a thing?"

"My visit to Somerset House with Miss McHenry," Eberhart said with a grim smile. "Would you believe the chit had the utter cheek to suggest Felicity might not wish to marry me?"

"She *doesn't*?" Fergus exclaimed, unable to suppress a hopeful note in his own voice. "I mean," he said as the earl looked at him curiously, "how disappointing for you."

Eberhart's lips tightened. "Disappointment is only half of it. I feel more anger than disappointment."

"Anger at Miss Felicity?" Fergus asked cautiously.

The earl shook his head. "No, at the aunt. Drat the woman. First she tells me Felicity would view any match to me as slow death, and then she insists that were I to ask the chit myself she would never get up the gumption to confess to anything so missish."

"Quite vexing, I agree, sir," Fergus said.

"Oh, her real barbs didn't hit their mark till later," the earl said bitterly. "According to the aunt, Miss Felicity is being married off on account of her father's debts. That is the sole reason he agreed to the match. It's deuced insulting, and I don't care for the match if Felicity is opposed to it." He sighed and got up from the desk. "I should never have thought of getting hitched at all. I thought it would be so simple. It's turned into a Pandora's box."

At this, Fergus, whose hopes had been rekindled by the account of the earl's meeting with Rosalind as well as by his own encounter with Felicity at Hookam's, ventured to ask if this meant the earl would not be offering for Felicity.

"I don't know what it means," Eberhart said truthfully. "But I do hope I've seen the last of her infernal aunt!"

He then left the office and was informed by Hedges that Mr. Wilding had called some twenty minutes earlier.

"Wilding?" Eberhart tried to think what his friend might have wanted. "I can't quite remember."

"I believe your lordship was promised to him for an engagement at Tattersall's," his butler said helpfully.

The earl grimaced. "You are right. What did you tell William?"

"That you had been unavoidably detained but that you would see him at Tattersall's later if at all possible. I hope that was satisfactory, sir."

Eberhart clapped him on the shoulder. "I don't know how I could contrive without you, Hedges," he said, and went out the door, thinking that the day might be salvageable. At least horses with Wilding was infinitely more agreeable than paintings with Miss McHenry. Not, he told himself with a laugh, that he could recall any of the paintings he had seen at Somerset House.

Tattersall's that day bustled with its usual activity of buyers out for bargains and sellers wishing to get the better of any visiting greenhorn. Eberhart found several acquaintances amid the buyers at the auction, but there was no sign of Wilding until he investigated the farther stalls.

Mr. Wilding stood, elegantly dressed, his quizzing glass in hand, looking over a deplorably shortboned creature.

"His father was an Arabian," the seller said.

"Indeed?" Mr. Wilding looked impressed.

Eberhart shook his head as he stepped forward. "If you buy that nag, William, you shall be laughed out of White's."

Wilding swiveled his craggy head at the sound of the earl's voice.

"Hallo, Alastair. You took your time about coming."

"My apologies. I was unavoidably detained."

"You sound suspiciously like a butler, do you know that?"

Eberhart chuckled. "Look here, William, you're not seriously contemplating buying that horse, are you?"

"What's wrong with it?" Mr. Wilding demanded, turning his attention back to the four-legged creature in front of them. "I think it a capital buy. This man here has been telling me that she's hardly been ridden at all. And wait till I tell you the price!"

"Whatever price you pay would be too dear," the earl drawled. "As for what is wrong with her, one would do better to ask what was right with her. But for a start, the neck is much too short for the body, its left hind leg shows signs of ulceration, and the coat is dull."

Mr. Wilding stood back, properly impressed by this catalog of flaws. "Well, what does strike your fancy hereabouts? I'm determined to buy something!"

Since Wilding insisted that the earl choose a horse for him, Eberhart followed him through the rest of the stalls. The pickings were slim, but within the hour he had produced a very nice bay.

"Not shortboned, either," he told his friend. "And not dagger cheap, but the good things in life rarely are. And if you were willing to waste the ready on that first nag—"

"Say no more!" Mr. Wilding commanded. "The bay it shall be." He completed the purchase and gave the order for the horse to be sent around to his residence. That accomplished, the two men strolled on. "I wonder what I shall name it."

"Why not Caesar or Zeus?"

"Good heavens, no!" Mr. Wilding looked appalled. "Can you imagine sitting on a horse possessed of such a name?" He gave a shudder that ended with a yawn.

"A late night?" the earl asked sympathetically.

Wilding nodded. "Very late. Cardroom was devilishly busy."

"I hope you won."

His friend shook his head sadly. "That hope is in vain. But"—he brightened—"neither did I lose. And that is half the battle."

The earl kicked a small stone with the toe of his boot.

"Tell me, William, are you perchance acquainted with Mr. Gerald McHenry's habits of gaming?"

"Hasn't but one habit, Alastair, and that's losing," his friend replied. "I'm all for a man who ain't afraid to lose. But he presses his luck, and most of it is bad. In Dun Territory, they say, and has been there for considerable time."

"How is it that his sister seems well pursed?"

"Ah, that is another story. She inherited a tidy competence from a female relation. Her brother has traded on that fortune and her credit more than a few times. She's helped him time after time, but the prattle boxes say that she's finally lost her patience and won't part with a groat more. I can't blame her, really. Besides, she doesn't have enough to pay off all his debts. An ugly customer, that Gerald McHenry," he said, before remembering the ties his friend had to that family.

"Sorry, Alastair. I'd forgotten he's to be your father-in-law."

"That was my intention," the earl admitted, rubbing the nose of a passing horse. "What manner of man is McHenry, William?"

His friend stopped in his tracks and pushed back his high-crowned beaver felt. "Good gracious, Alastair, you'd know that better than me. You're marrying the daughter, aren't you?" He gazed into his friend's troubled eyes. "Don't tell me the wags were right for once!"

"What wags?" Eberhart asked, frowning.

Mr. Wilding made a face. "Sir Thomas Spalding and Lord Monmouth. They've wagered that you won't marry the McHenry chit after all. It's even been recorded in the betting book at White's."

"Devil!" the earl ejaculated. "Damned impudent pups."

"It's this younger generation," Mr. Wilding informed him with a sigh. "Such a want of dash about them. All they seem to do is sit near the bow window at the club and comment rudely on the passersby. But why the interest in McHenry now?"

Eberhart shrugged. "I've had occasion to speak to his sister. Something she said made me wonder about him."

"Are you worried that he'll hang on your sleeve once you've wed his daughter?"

"Something like that," the earl agreed, and he decided to view Mr. Gerald McHenry in action at the green baize tables at the next opportunity.

Chapter Nine

Two days later Fergus perused his morning mail and was thunderstruck to discover an invitation from Rosalind. His thoughts immediately raced to the inevitable conclusion that Hedges must have put the invitation in the wrong pile on his desk. It must surely belong to the earl. But as he turned it over, he read his own name across the front of the invitation and not the earl's.

Feeling a trifle lightheaded he laid the invitation down on his desk, wondering what had prompted it, and then, more avidly, whether he should accept or not.

Could Felicity have had anything to do with it? he wondered, rising now to pace the length of his narrow office. A wild hope bloomed within. Perhaps the Walter Scott had caused her to view him in a new light.

Paying no heed to certain underfootmen who shot him curious looks as they passed in the hallway, Fergus continued to pace away his morning, torn between accepting the invitation—and thus seeing his beloved Felicity again—and refusing—and sparing his heart further trial.

Stopping abruptly in mid-stride, he slapped one fist into the palm of the other hand. Why shouldn't he go to the ball? For once he decided to follow the dictates of his heart. He had a right to some social diversion, and his birth, while not as high as some, was every bit as respectable as most.

Dashing out of his office, he encountered Eberhart just about to set out for Mr. Baverstock, his banker, and he quickly broached the issue of his absence Friday evening.

"Good gracious, Fergus, you are my secretary, not my lackey," the earl exclaimed. "Your evenings are to do with as you like. As long as you don't wind up in some sluicery, I shan't complain.'' He picked up his malacca cane, chuckling at the idea of his staid secretary in such straits.

Feeling quite happy, Fergus returned to his office and settled back to work in anticipation of the Friday evening to come and the pleasure of perhaps dancing with Felicity.

Promptly at eight o'clock on Friday evening Fergus arrived at Green Street. No one seeing his slender form augmented in the swallow-tailed coat, frilled shirt, and plain but correctly tied cravat would have picked him out as not belonging to Rosalind's original list of eligibles, a list that included such worthies as Major Winchester, Lord Ebbing, Mr. Peter Maxwell, and Lord Barry, all men of fortune and equable temperament.

Lord Ebbing, however, within five minutes of greeting Rosalind proved himself to be incorrigibly horse-mad, and Mr. Maxwell, sporting a cravat of the most vivid violet, was a dandy, Rosalind was obliged to deduce. But these were not fatal flaws. And she hoped that Felicity might find herself in love with someone by evening's end.

When Fergus entered, a feeling of foreboding swept through Rosalind. Felicity, garbed in a gown of lime-green silk, had been oblivious to the care with which Lord Barry was detailing his beloved estates in Yorkshire, and, wearing a particularly sweet smile, she wafted over to greet Mr. Fairweather.

Rosalind, swathed in a white spider gauze, managed to fob off Lord Barry on one of Felicity's friends and then bustled over to greet Fergus as well. She had wondered at her niece's insistence that he be included in the gathering, and now, as she watched the exchange of glances between the two, her heart beat a frantic warning.

Mr. Fairweather was still the slender, sober young man she had met a few weeks ago, but his visage was transfixed now with an expression of blinding admiration as his eyes remained riveted on Felicity.

''Good evening, Mr. Fairweather,'' Rosalind said.

The secretary started. ''Oh, good evening, Miss McHenry. I'm so obliged to you for your invitation.''

"Aunt Rosalind," Felicity interrupted, "Mr. Fairweather has asked me to stand up with him for the quadrille after dinner. I may, mayn't I?"

"Yes, of course," Rosalind said, observing the glow of pleasure on Fergus's cheeks. "But I do think for now that Lord Barry is anxious to tell you more about his estate in Yorkshire."

Felicity wrinkled her nose. "Oh, Aunt Rosalind, must I?"

"Yes. I shall take care of Mr. Fairweather for you," she promised, and Felicity capitulated and returned to Lord Barry's tales of Yorkshire farming.

"It was very civil of you to include me in your gathering tonight, Miss McHenry," Fergus said.

She smiled. "You may change your mind within the next minute." She saw his look of surprise and explained. "I am about to intrude on your amiability by introducing you to the Coppletons. Pray don't eat me later as you shall have every right to do!"

He laughed, but was too much of a gentleman to demur, and he stood the introduction to the viscountess in good grace. He would have endured an army of relations if in the end he would be allowed to dance with Felicity.

As Fergus underwent the trials of Waldo's family, Rosalind mingled with her guests, coaxing some of the shier girls into dancing and bullying some of the gentlemen into asking for dances. She soon discovered that she liked matchmaking.

She also became aware that Felicity had won an enviable amount of attention. Lord Barry, Mr. Maxwell, and Major Winchester were as impressed as she had hoped they might be.

Since Rosalind had seated Lord Ebbing next to Felicity at dinner, he presumably had the advantage over his rivals. Indeed, Ebbing was the chief prize on Rosalind's list, as he was a well-liked, excellently featured young man with an income of well over forty thousand pounds a year. When they went into dinner, however, she discovered that someone had switched the place cards and that Felicity was now seated to the right of Mr. Fairweather.

As she took her own place, she noted the faint guilty flush on Felicity's cheeks. She was growing more and more disturbed over what lay between the earl's secretary and her niece. As she sipped her turtle soup she wondered about them, but her attention was soon claimed by Waldo's mother, who wished to know the ingredients of the soup she was drinking and whether it was the latest remedy in warding off the grippe. If only it were as effective in warding off certain ineligible suitors, Rosalind thought.

Her spoon clanked down against the bowl. What could she be thinking of? Mr. Fairweather was no suitor of Felicity's! He was going to Brussels. It would be impossible to carry on a courtship from there! Almost at once she felt better, and she chided herself for allowing her imagination to run away with her. She also decided that she would write to Mr. Osgood Fairweather suggesting he lose no time in furthering the career of so worthy a nephew.

By the time they had adjourned to the ballroom, Rosalind could even face with equanimity the sight of Felicity standing up with Mr. Fairweather. Since she also danced with Lord Barry and Mr. Maxwell, Rosalind could really find nothing to task her about.

She herself was not so inclined to dance this evening, particularly since she regarded most of the males present as more suitable for someone Felicity's age. But Waldo was not to be put off, insisting that his dear mother had expressed the desire to see them dancing together.

Rosalind was beginning to grow heartily sick of the "dear" viscountess and her whims, but one dance wouldn't hurt. She soon discovered that she was wrong. The viscount, she should have remembered, was possessed of two left feet, both of which found their way onto hers.

"Oh, I say, Rosalind, I do beg your pardon," he repeated for the third time.

"It's quite all right, Waldo," she said, yearning for the safety of a chair and wondering how anyone so amiable could be so clumsy.

"This ball of yours isn't really in your style," he said as they lurched from one side of the room to the other.

She was surprised at his acuteness. "It's for Felicity, actually," she confessed.

Waldo look puzzled. "Felicity? My word, Rosalind, I wonder that you didn't invite Eberhart. Fellow might take it the wrong way if he hears about this."

His partner smiled even as one of his feet again landed on one of hers. "I'm certain Lord Eberhart shall take it exactly the right way when he hears of it," Rosalind assured her faithful beau.

At that very moment the earl sat in the cardroom at White's, enduring the utter tedium that came from gambling when he had not a jot of interest in its outcome. He had been playing for about an hour, and the din in the room now matched the level he supposed the inmates of Bedlam must endure.

He devoutly hoped he would not be deafened by evening's end. But deafened or not, he did possess an excellent view of Mr. Gerald McHenry and his cardplaying.

Eberhart had already learned a good deal about McHenry from his banker. Gerald's credit in the City had been stretched so thin that no reputable banker would have a thing to do with him. Even the moneylenders, a hardened bunch, had despaired of ever reaping any part of the vast sums they had invested with him.

Now as he watched Gerald lose yet another hand, he began to think that Rosalind's characterization of her brother as a wastrel and profligate was on the mark.

By midnight he deemed it time to quit. He had seen more than enough. McHenry truly was the worst of gamesters, never knowing when to cut his losses. The earl rose from the table, a thoughtful expression on his face. If Rosalind had been right in her reading of her brother, could she also be right about Felicity?

Bidding adieu to his friends, the earl left White's, once again mulling over what Rosalind had told him at Somerset House that morning. Was it really possible that Felicity did not wish to marry him?

He pondered this sticky problem as he walked the few blocks that would lead back to St. James Square. Ordinarily he would have called out a carriage, but the night was clear and he felt in the need of exercise. A few minutes into his stroll he heard his name called and, turning, recognized Mr. Gideon Dankley hurrying after him.

"Not leaving so soon, my lord?" Mr. Dankley quizzed, puffing from his exertions.

"Just so, Mr. Dankley," Eberhart replied politely. He had seen the other man in the club on several occasions, but this was the first opportunity they had had to exchange words. "Your friend Mr. McHenry can still be found at the tables."

Dankley's smile glinted in the moonlight. "Our mutual friend, you mean. Poor Gerald does have the rummest luck at cards. I've told him so at least a dozen times."

"You might repeat it again," the earl said, walking on. Dankley, undaunted by this comment, fell in stride with him.

"By all rights, my lord, I should be angry with you."

The earl was astonished. "Angry? Why so?"

"Miss Felicity McHenry," Dankley said with another thin smile. "I consider myself something of a vanquished rival for her hand."

Since Dankley was rising fifty, Eberhart felt an urge to laugh. He manfully controlled this impulse.

"Do you indeed?" he asked now.

"Yes, and in truth if for any reason you do not see fit to marry Felicity, Gerald has assured me my offer will be weighed next."

"I would have thought that a man like you would desire a different sort of wife," Eberhart said as he digested this news.

"I have every hope that Miss Felicity would make me exactly the type of wife I desire."

Eberhart resumed his walking, not about to let Dankley see how disturbed he was at the idea of a man of his ilk marrying an innocent like Felicity.

"I hope you are not harboring thoughts about any wife of mine, sir," he said.

"Oh, no," Mr. Dankley said hastily. "Mere conjecture. A lovely air dream. It is amusing to think that if you did bow out of the match I would be waiting in the wings, as they say in Drury Lane!"

They had come to St. James Square, and he left Eberhart at his doorstep. The earl stood for a moment, gazing after the retreating back of the other man. He had no real acquaintance with Dankley, but knew that most considered him a Cit who had traded on his fortune for some measure of standing in society.

Could McHenry really be entertaining Dankley's suit for his daughter? The earl had heard a few rumors about Dankley's amorous dealings. He was not a monk himself, but Dankley's activities had not done credit to a man of his years.

Aware now that Hedges had been holding the front door open to him for considerable time, the earl crossed the threshold just as Mr. Fairweather stepped down from a hack, a look of utter bliss on his face.

Smiling at his secretary, the earl demanded to be told the name of the lucky female.

Mr. Fairweather was jolted out of his happy fog. "Female, sir? I assure you—"

"When a fellow looks like you do, Fergus," the earl said amiably, "there's a female behind it."

"Sir, I assure you—"

"Silent as a grave, is it?" Eberhart teased as they went into the house. "Well, I shan't plague you." He left his secretary at the foot of the stairs and went up to his bedchamber.

It was all such a coil! Marriage had seemed like a good idea two weeks ago, and yet nothing but vexation had resulted from putting that plan into action. He undid his cravat. He had no intention of marrying a female who dreaded a match with him, and yet, if he didn't, what would be her fate? To be wedded instead to the lecherous Mr. Dankley!

* * *

To add to Eberhart's trials, a new problem descended on him the next morning in the persons of his two nephews, Alec and Mark Templeton, the male issue of his sister Margaret, who had sent them down to London from her home in Cheshire to enjoy a month with their doting grandmother—the same doting grandmother who was now trying to foist them on her illustrious son.

"For I couldn't monopolize them, Alastair, when I know quite well you haven't seen them in an age."

"Several ages, I should think," he retorted, in no way pleased to have a pair of pasty-faced brats underfoot. "Mama, don't turn that innocent face to me. I have no interest in nursery brats."

"Oh, they aren't in a nursery." Lady Manning made haste to correct such a notion. "If they were, I daresay Margaret would not have been so shatterbrained as to send them down alone. At the very least she would have sent a nurse with them."

"Margaret is shatterbrained like a fox," her son replied with a snort. "She's bullied you into taking care of her brats for a month. And what does Manning say to this?"

Lady Manning colored slightly under her son's scrutiny. "He doesn't know yet."

"Mama!" the earl expostulated. "You are going to tell poor Harry, aren't you?"

"Yes, of course, Alastair. But it didn't seem necessary in the beginning. You and I know Margaret is prone to change her mind with the wind, so it was no use saying a word to Manning until the boys arrived, if they ever did."

"And have they?"

His mother nodded.

"Well, where are they?"

Lady Manning waved a distracted hand. "Hedges took them off into the small parlor. And I don't like to ask you for help, Alastair, but I do think the boys ought to get to know their uncle, don't you?"

"What I think," he replied, "is that you should pack them back to Margaret immediately!"

"I can't do that."

"Then let them stay a week and then plead fatigue or a spasm or some such thing. Nothing very major," he said as she shot him a look that as good as told him she was not so ticklish a female. "Then Margaret shall be duty bound to take her boys back."

Lady Manning shook her head. "I can't do that," she repeated. "She and Stephan are on an expedition to the Lakes. It's so pretty this time of year. And you know how Stephan fancies himself a poet."

Eberhart snorted. Margaret had always schooled herself as a bluestocking, and while he had no dislike of his brother-in-law, whom he found amiable if occasionally foolish, he considered his posturing fatiguing.

"Remember when he thought he had the consumption?" Eberhart asked his mother. "Stephan languished for days. I thought he looked overjoyed to have so tragic an end until Dr. Whaley told him it was merely a touch of the grippe and to get off the daybed!"

"Yes, I recall that," his mother said with a distinct shudder. "I also recall the words that erupted soon after between you and Margaret."

"And that precludes my taking an interest now in her offspring."

"Fiddle! The boys are quite congenial. Nothing at all like Stephan, thank heaven. They put me in mind of you, Alastair!"

The earl held up a hand. "Mama, stop. You could not say anything that would make me more determined not to see them!"

Fate, however, intervened, for as soon as these words had left his tongue an earsplitting crash erupted from the next room.

"*Devil!* What was that?" he asked, and went out into the hall, followed by Lady Manning. The crash had also summoned Mr. Fairweather from his office.

"Good God!" Eberhart ejaculated upon entering the small parlor.

A large porcelain vase that had once adorned his mantel lay in pieces on his rug. His eyes swept up from the shat-

tered remains of the Grecian vessel to the two red-faced
boys standing on either side of it.

The older and taller of the pair was blond and freckled.
That would be Alec, fourteen or fifteen, if memory served
correctly. The other Eberhart put at perhaps twelve, a red-
head. He would be Mark.

It was Mark who spoke first. "Oh, sir, we do beg your
pardon. It was an accident, truly!"

"What were you doing, Mark?" Lady Manning asked as
a maid swept in with a broom and dustpan.

"I was showing Alec how Dave McGregor knocked out
Black Bart on the heath last year," Mark replied innocently.
"He wouldn't believe that one with such a height disadvan-
tage could turn the trick. I bet him I could floor him, which
is how my elbow jostled the vase. We tried to catch it, but
that only made it worse!"

"Alastair, the boy's hurt," Lady Manning said, catching
sight of blood on her grandson's hand.

"It's only a scratch, Grandmama," Mark said stoutly.
His response cheered his uncle. At least the lad hadn't inherited Stephan's predilection to overplay his emotions.

"Scratch or not, it must be tended to," Lady Manning
said, and after calling for water and linen began to dress the
cut herself.

"I am most dreadfully sorry, Uncle Alastair," Mark said
while the injury was being tended to. "I'll pay for the
vase."

"Gudgeon," his brother spoke up. "That shows what a
cawker you are. We don't have the money between us to pay
for such an item."

"Our allowances together," Mark said naïvely.

"It would take years of your allowances to make a dent in
the cost," Lady Manning replied. "Alastair, I'm responsi-
ble and shall pay."

"Don't be absurd, Mama. The vase was a gift from
Grandaunt Mary on my come-out. I always hated it but had
to keep it on display in case she ever dropped in. The boys
have relieved me of that burden." He glanced at the two
faces in front of him. "So, you are my nephews, are you?"

"Yes, sir," Alec said. "I'm Alec and he's Mark. And I do apologize for the accident. Mark would insist it was possible to floor a taller opponent, which I couldn't see for the life of me."

"Neither could I," Eberhart agreed, "which is how I came to lose two hundred pounds that day on the heath betting on Bart."

"Oh, sir, really?" Mark exclaimed, his eyes very bright. "Did you see the mill, then?"

"Indeed I did. And a corker it was!"

"Did you also see the Greek and Tall Sam fight?" Mark asked.

The earl admitted he had, but Lady Manning brought an end to this promising topic, stating that however much addicted to sport her son and grandsons might be, she was not. And the conversation obligingly changed to what sights in London might be worth exploring. Eberhart's faint interest in his nephews had been fanned, and to his astonishment he found himself at the end of their visit agreeing to accompany them on their rounds in the city!

Chapter Ten

"Miss Rosalind, Miss Rosalind, do wake up *please*, Miss Rosalind!"

Rosalind came awake to the sound of Mrs. Withers's frantic voice. She blinked at the rays of sunlight streaming through her curtains.

"Oh, you're up, thank God!"

"What time is it?" Rosalind asked, sitting up and fighting back an enormous yawn.

"It's eleven-thirty or thereabouts," Mrs. Withers said, helping her mistress up in the bed. "And Lord Eberhart arrived in the drawing room only minutes ago, leading a horse, if you please, and Mr. Maxwell is there, too, with a huge bouquet of roses."

Still in a fog, Rosalind demanded to know just what Eberhart proposed to do with the horse in her drawing room.

"Oh, it isn't in the drawing room, Miss Rosalind," Mrs. Withers said. "John has it now, but the earl is still impatient to see Miss Felicity or you, and it must be you, Miss Rosalind, because Felicity has gone off with Anna to Hookam's."

"Good gracious, she fairly haunts that place now," Rosalind said. "I hope she doesn't become wholly addicted to lending libraries or Walter Scott. He appears to have a dubious effect on her." She turned back to her housekeeper, a slight frown knitting her brow. "Did you say the earl and Mr. Maxwell were waiting? Did they arrive together?"

"No, but they are together now, and I don't think it's a good idea for them to be together for long. Mr. Maxwell attended your ball last night. The earl did not."

"Yes, I know," Rosalind said, dressing as quickly as she could manage.

Downstairs in the crimson saloon, the two gentlemen waiting had fallen into conversation, prompted by Mr. Maxwell's bouquet of flowers.

"For Miss Felicity," Maxwell had explained, putting down the roses and mopping his brow with a handkerchief.

"You tax her strength to present such a large bouquet, Maxwell. But you shall undoubtedly be at first oars with her after such a gift."

"I thought it best to strike while the iron was hot."

The earl lifted a pinch of snuff to one nostril. "Iron?"

"Miss McHenry's ball last night," Maxwell explained. "She certainly knows how to look after her guests."

"I'm sure she makes a gracious hostess."

At that moment, the gracious hostess herself made an appearance in a day dress of lilac muslin. She greeted both her visitors with the news that Felicity was out.

"I shall tell her you called with the roses, Mr. Maxwell," she told him as he swallowed his disappointment and promised to call back in the afternoon.

"No doubt bearing another bouquet of equal proportions," Eberhart observed acidly after he was alone with Rosalind.

"I think the flowers very pretty!"

"So they are if you wish to live in a garden," he retorted. A curious smile played about his lips as he watched her arrange the bouquet. "Do you actually believe that Maxwell or any other sprig you gathered here last night shall cut me out with Miss Felicity?" he asked blandly.

She met his question without flinching. "I certainly hope so."

He couldn't help but laugh. "That's honest, at any rate!"

"I have long given over peeling eggs with you, my lord," she said tartly. "And just how did you find out about my party last night?"

"Maxwell! You can't expect me not to have asked what in thunderation he was doing carrying such a thing, can you?

Is he your favorite for Miss Felicity? A bit of a coxcomb, I would call him.''

Rosalind bristled. "I think Mr. Maxwell an extremely amiable young man.''

"If one's taste runs to dolts, but he is, of course, a wealthy dolt. No, don't get on your high ropes with me," he chided. "I shan't throw a spanner in the works if you succeed in attaching the two together.''

Rosalind was astonished. "You won't?''

"No," he said, not surprised by her reaction. In truth, his magnanimity surprised even himself. But with the two choices left to him—to offer for a chit who didn't wish to marry or to withdraw his offer, thus leaving her to Dankley—Rosalind's plan seemed preferable.

"Tell me more about Miss Felicity's suitors," he invited, settling back on the Egyptian couch. "I may be able to advise you.''

"Advise me!" Her eyes flashed. "Thank you. It's not advice I wish from you.''

His shoulders shook with laughter. "No," he agreed. "I daresay you'd rather wish me to Jericho, wouldn't you? Well, I don't mean to be disobliging, but I have a fair amount of interest in this muddle.''

Rosalind glared at him. "My housekeeper said you had brought a horse here.''

"Yes, my second hack, for Felicity. She is a prodigious rider, I understand.''

Rosalind wondered if he could be hoaxing her. Felicity had undoubtedly ridden in her life, but to call her a prodigious rider! How had the earl gotten such a maggot in his brain?

"My lord, Felicity rides only tolerably well," she said now. "I can't think how you came to any different conclusion.''

Eberhart's eyes narrowed. "I asked if she rode and the chit told me yes. Do you mean she cannot ride?''

"She rides after a fashion—''

He grimaced. "You need say no more. What about you? Do you ride?''

"Yes, of course," she replied without thinking.

"Tolerably well, like your niece?" he inquired skeptically.

She put up her chin. "More than tolerably well, sir."

He smiled. "Good. Firefly still is in need of exercise, and since you say Miss Felicity is shy of the sport as well as being absent at the moment, you can accompany me instead."

"I can?" she asked coldly.

"If you wish," he corrected himself. "It is an invitation, Miss McHenry."

Rosalind hesitated at first, wondering if he could be up to anything. But a quick glance out the window showed a clear and temperate sky, and since she had not ridden in days, she gave in to temptation.

"Made quick work of it, I see," Eberhart said approvingly fifteen minutes later when she appeared in a burgundy riding habit. "I can't tolerate a dawdling female!"

She drew on her riding gloves and threw him a skeptical look. "And I suppose, my lord, that you achieved that splendid cravat in something less than fifteen minutes."

He grinned. "Touché. Much more than fifteen minutes, if you count the three I crushed before this one fell into place."

Rosalind gave a small cry of pleasure when he led her over to the high-spirited but gentle chestnut he had brought for Felicity. Firefly responded by nuzzling her cheek.

"She is delightful," Rosalind declared after five minutes in the saddle. "Your reputation as a judge of horseflesh is certainly up to the mark."

"I'm glad to have won your approbation in something, Miss McHenry," he replied, "but dare I ask how you know of my reputation?"

"I made inquiries," she told him frankly. "Discreet ones, I assure you."

"And what were the results of these inquiries?" he drawled as their horses cantered briskly along.

She shifted position somewhat in the saddle, but did not shirk from the question. "I discovered that you do not dabble overmuch in the petticoat line, that you are a top sawyer, a member of the Four Horse Club, as impeccable in dress as the Beau himself in his prime, and a doting son.''

"Do I detect disappointment in your voice?" he asked. "Were you perhaps hoping to uncover something disreputable in my character, a predilection to drink or a by blow or two?"

Rosalind nearly dropped the reins from shock. "What a thing to say! A by blow indeed. Even if I were looking for a flaw in your character, I would not have entertained thoughts of that, I assure you!"

They had been trading these barbs as they turned into the Park entrance. Since it was not the fashionable hour, the paths were clear, which made riding a pleasure. Rosalind took a deep breath of the crisp, clean air, and a sense of peace settled on her like a soft blanket.

Their ride through the Park came to a brief halt when she caught sight of Lord Barry driving his carriage with a female who definitely did not have the look of a lady, a view substantiated by the embarrassed look Lord Barry returned to her greeting.

"Is that his *chère amie*?" she asked the earl when they had passed on.

Eberhart, who had recognized the female in Barry's company as being a high-priced cyprian who had enjoyed the favors of many gentlemen, dealt his companion a quizzing look. "I believe at the moment Mrs. Cambridge enjoys Lord Barry's patronage."

"What a pity," Rosalind said. "I thought he was ever so promising for Felicity. Now I shall have to scratch him from my list."

The earl's lips lifted in a half smile. "Just what sort of male do you wish for your niece?" he asked.

She thought a moment. "Just someone kind and sensible who would love her and cosset her to death."

"Excellent qualities in a husband."

The light of battle was back in her eye. "You are scoffing at me."

"Nonsense. I am in agreement. Do you know Lord Carlisle? The quizzes say he is hanging out for a wife. Perhaps I could arrange a meeting between you and him and, of course, Miss Felicity.''

''I do not wish to match my niece to someone like Carlisle, who must have fifty years in his dish.''

''Too charitable,'' he said, amused. ''Carlisle was sixty on his last birthday. But I suppose that females are born with a sixth sense when it comes to matchmaking that we males lack.''

''I think females are born with better sense in all things than you males,'' Rosalind offered as they completed their turn in the Park.

On their way back to Green Street she asked him if he truly meant what he had said previously about dropping his suit of Felicity.

His brow creased slightly. ''I shall not stand in her way if anyone else of your choosing offers for her,'' he told her quietly.

She was delighted. ''Splendid. Have you told Gerald?''

''Your brother is not to know,'' Eberhart said, more imperious than ever.

She was surprised. ''But why not? If you dislike telling him—fearing the fuss he shall undoubtedly raise—I shall spare you that scene and do it for you.''

''No, Miss McHenry. That would be a grave mistake.''

Her eyes hardened with suspicion. ''Why won't you let Gerald know how things stand?''

''I have my reasons,'' he said, wishing she weren't so stubborn.

''How mysterious! I believe you have been roasting me all this time. You don't intend to cry off from your understanding with Felicity, do you?''

''If you mean did I plan to tell Miss Felicity or your brother that I have no wish to offer for her, the answer must be no. But before you condemn me too harshly you must contemplate one thing.''

''Which is?'' She eyed him with unveiled dislike.

''Felicity might wind up with a worse husband than me.''

* * *

The earl continued to absorb Rosalind's thoughts in the days that passed. If he was serious about ending his engagement to Felicity, why didn't he do so? Why did he continue to dangle after her? It made not a bit of sense to Rosalind.

Vexed, she tried to banish him from her mind—an impossible task, given the frequency with which their paths seemed to cross. Besides his daily visits to Green Street, in which she was obliged to partake, she happened upon him in the City, where she had gone on business to see her solicitor. She emerged from the office in time to see the earl accompanied by two young boys bent on dragging him into St. Paul's Cathedral.

"We are going up all six hundred stairs, aren't we, Uncle Alastair?" Mark announced after Eberhart had introduced Rosalind to his young relations.

"Yes, *you* are, at least, greenhorn," Eberhart said indulgently as Mark began the climb to the dome.

"Aren't you coming, Uncle?" Alec asked.

"I'll follow after a bit. You catch up with your brother. It wouldn't do to let him break his neck."

Alec grinned and went into the cathedral while Eberhart gazed over at Rosalind. She was looking quite striking in a day dress of blue gray. "Would you like to accompany us, Miss McHenry?"

"Thank you, no. Are you showing your nephews the sights?"

He nodded. "They are a pair of rapscallions, but I have reached the opinion that they might do. At any rate, they take after my sister Meg instead of her husband. Meg used to be a great gun before she turned herself into a bluestocking."

"Indeed? And what fatal flaw does your brother-in-law boast?"

"The worst imaginable. He fancies himself a poet."

She chuckled. "A poet? And you allowed him to marry into your family? A shocking lack of foresight, my lord."

"He wasn't a poet then," Eberhart said dryly, and grinned.

"Uncle Alastair!" a voice beseeched from above them.

"Alec is in need of reinforcements, I think," the earl said, and, after another bow to Rosalind, called up to Mark not to do anything gudgeonish and took the stairs two at a time.

Eberhart's involvement with his nephews did not go unnoticed in London, since in addition to St. Paul's that first week he also accompanied them to Madame Tussaud's Waxworks and the Zoo. Two high-spirited youths could not help but attract attention to themselves and their elegant companion. Some misguided wags saw it as a sign of the earl's real affection for children, while others more cynically called it a sign of his impending senility.

One who saw it as a very good thing was the earl's mother, who confided as much to Rosalind one morning at Berkeley Square.

"Although he calls them a pair of ragmannered brats, I know he likes them. I was quite astonished that he taught Mark chess and was patiently pointing out each error. It quite shocked me."

"I would not have thought patience one of Eberhart's strong suits." Rosalind accepted a cup of Bohea from her hostess.

"Nor I! But then, you see, one never does know. I am fond of Alastair, and seeing him with the boys induces me to hope that someday he shall have a son of his own." Her face brightened. "Perhaps having Mark and Alec about will make him think of setting up his own nursery before too much longer."

Rosalind choked on a biscuit. "A nursery, ma'am?"

Lady Manning gave a trill of laughter. "I daresay it is an airdream, but I should like more grandchildren. Meg is so far away. I don't have a granddaughter, either, to fuss and dote on."

The matter of Eberhart's nursery continued to occupy the conversation. Rosalind was about to take her leave when the earl came by with his nephews. Watching them squabble over the cakes and pastries, Rosalind thought that the earl looked less austere than usual, and toward the boys his attitude was bracing but affectionate.

"If you could have seen him," she told Felicity later when she returned home. "You might not have recognized him. I must agree with Lady Manning that he does seem to dote on the boys."

"Mr. Fairweather says he calls them a pair of pasty-faced brats."

"Yes, he would!" Rosalind agreed. She took off her hat and gazed at the handkerchief Felicity had been embroidering. The design of a crescent and stars was quite distinctive. "I must confess that Lady Manning dotes on them so. If she ever gets a granddaughter the child shall be cosseted to death. And if you could have heard her plans about Eberhart setting up a nursery!" She gave in to a whoop of laughter.

She turned, hearing what she presumed to be a laugh from her niece but which on closer examination turned out to be a sob.

"My dear, what is amiss?"

"Eberhart's nursery! Aunt Rosalind, how can you say such a thing?"

Rosalind felt a moment's qualm. Felicity had been gently reared.

"I am sorry, my dear. I must have forgotten myself."

"If Eberhart plans to set up his nursery, that means he must be married. He plans. Papa—" Felicity choked on a sob.

"My dear, don't distress yourself."

Felicity shook off Rosalind's hand. "How can I help but be distressed when I think of that odious man and his children?"

Rosalind blinked. "Heavens, he doesn't have any yet!"

"And he won't, if I have anything to say about it," Felicity declared. "I don't care if he is an earl. I shan't marry him and produce those nursery brats for him."

Rosalind was shocked by her niece's vehemence.

"I hate him. Do you hear?"

"Felicity, too strong by half."

"I don't care a fig for him or his precious rank and fortune."

"Well, then, perhaps Major Winchester or Mr. Maxwell would be more to your liking," Rosalind said, trying to turn Felicity's sudden dislike of Eberhart to advantage.

"No, they would not. They are just as bad as the earl."

"Unfair, Felicity. I assure you it is a great feather in your cap to have men of such fortune and position dangling after you."

"I don't care a straw for men of such fortune!" Felicity said recklessly. "I'd rather have an impecunious man whom I might love than one with the largest fortune in the kingdom."

"That's an idiotish notion."

"No, it is not," Felicity countered, looking mulish.

The contentious note in Felicity's usually mild voice caused Rosalind to cease her soothing.

"Felicity, are you trying to tell me that you are in love with someone? I hope you have not been indiscreet, my dear."

"There is nothing indiscreet about meeting by chance in public in some congenial location."

"Such as Hookam's?" Rosalind hazarded a guess that was on the mark, judging by Felicity's flush.

"I had wondered why you were so *prodigious* a reader," Rosalind said. "You have been seeing Mr. Fairweather, haven't you?"

"Yes!" Felicity met her eyes. "I have been seeing him, Aunt Rosalind, and what's more, I am in love with him!" Having made this declaration, Felicity's courage ebbed, and she broke into a fresh torrent of tears.

Chapter Eleven

While Felicity poured the whole wretched tale of her love for Fergus into her aunt's bewildered ears, Mr. Fairweather himself was strolling down Bond Street in a brown study.

The brief hour he had spent in Felicity's company amid the books in Hookam's had tried his patience to the very core. Acutely aware of the chasm that separated them, he knew the time had come for a decision. The most he could ever hope to offer Felicity was a life in the diplomatic corps, if his uncle did come to his aid.

A brief collision with a bosomy dowager walking her dog recalled him to his senses, and he accepted her scorching rebuke and the pug's nip at his heels as his just reward for woolgathering. By the time he returned to St. James Square, all thoughts of dogs and dowagers had flown out of his mind. He had reached a decision. He would leave London and the earl's employ.

His nerves, already stretched thin, were now worn to a frazzle by the peculiar circumstances of being in love with the chosen bride of his employer. Even if the earl did turn cat in the pan with regard to matrimony, there was little likelihood that Gerald McHenry would look with favor on the suit of a penniless secretary.

It would be better for everyone, Fergus thought as he took off his hat and gloves, if he posted off to Brussels. Although he had received no assurances of assistance from his uncle, it would be better to go than to languish in London watching the woman he loved become someone else's bride. With this resolve, Mr. Fairweather sharpened a quill and began to compose his letter of resignation.

The earl was not at hand to receive the letter when Fergus had painstakingly completed it. Eberhart, Hedges informed the secretary, was out on some afternoon calls, which became evening ones. Unable to deliver his letter in person, Fergus left it on the earl's desk in the bookroom, planning to go in and bring it to Eberhart's attention the next morning.

This proved unnecessary, for as soon as the earl emerged from his bookroom the next morning he sought out his secretary.

"Resigning, Fergus?" he asked, letter in hand. "Never tell me there has been some problem here!"

"Oh, no, sir," Fergus said hastily, not wishing the earl to think he had been badly treated in his establishment. "You have always treated me splendidly, almost as a member of the family."

Apparently won over by the sincerity in the secretary's voice, the earl waited. Fergus swallowed the lump in his throat and plunged ahead.

"It's just that I can't work for you any longer."

The earl drummed his fingers lightly on the banister of the stairs. "Have you found a better position, Fergus? I promise you, I shan't hold it against you if you have!"

This query cut Mr. Fairweather to the core. "I'm not the sort that would desert you for another position," he ejaculated.

"Then what lies behind this sudden decision?" Eberhart asked amiably. "Have you been overworked? That shall stop, I promise. Or would you liefer I double your salary, or triple it?"

"Sir, it's not money," Fergus protested.

Eberhart looked at him quizzingly. "Then what, pray?"

"I suppose it's just the principle of the thing," Fergus blurted out.

The earl's face underwent a marked transformation. "Principle? Perhaps you'd better explain yourself, Fergus."

"It's not your principles, sir," Fergus said quickly. "It's mine. It's just that I can no longer work for you," he ended feebly.

"Am I such a blackguard?" the earl asked, a trace of hauteur discernible in his eyes.

"I'm sorry, sir," the secretary murmured. "I didn't mean to offend. It's just that truly I can't work for you."

"Very well," the earl said with rigid courtesy, "since you offer me that as your excuse. You shall give me time to find your replacement?"

Mr. Fairweather nodded, already wondering if he had done the right thing. He hated to offend his employer, who had always treated him more like a friend.

"I have several acquaintances who might be interested in the position," he said.

"A rather civil offer from a gentleman of your principles, Fergus," Eberhart said, betrayed into uncharacteristic anger. He moved down the hall with long strides.

He had fully expected that one day his hardworking secretary would tender his resignation, but he had never imagined the quitting to be so abrupt and without a good reason.

His irksome mood did not abate as he passed the green saloon and found his butler ushering in Rosalind and Felicity.

"Visitors, Hedges?" Eberhart asked.

The butler turned. "Yes, my lord. I was just seeing them into the drawing room."

"I shall see them in," the earl insisted. He turned to the two visitors, noticing that Felicity looked paler than ever in a blue walking dress and striped spencer. As for Rosalind, she cut a fashionable swath, in an emerald-green dress with matching kid gloves.

"Well, Miss McHenry," Eberhart asked, "to what do I owe this pleasure?"

"I fear the pleasure isn't yours, my lord," Rosalind replied politely.

"Then whose is it?"

"Mr. Fairweather's," she replied with aplomb, and noticed the look of annoyance crossing the earl's countenance. "We had just asked your butler if we might have a word with Mr. Fairweather when you descended on us much the way Attila is said to have descended on Rome."

Eberhart gave a short laugh. "So I am a Hun now, am I?

For your information, I've never been to Rome, and this is my residence!''

"Yes, to be sure. Does this mean you shan't allow poor Mr. Fairweather a few moments' conversation with us?''

"Apparently you share my secretary's low opinion of me, Miss McHenry," Eberhart replied frigidly. "But I am no jailer. Fergus shall be notified of your call. Ah, it seems that Hedges is better at discerning such things. Come in, Fergus.'' He beckoned to the secretary, who hesitated in the doorway. "Miss McHenry and Miss Felicity wish to see you.''

Rosalind stood to shake hands with the secretary, wishing heartily that the earl would vanish. He was, however, seemingly rooted to his chair, and it would have been rude to ask him to quit his own drawing room.

With the earl present, Rosalind could do little to determine the exact nature of Fergus's feelings for her niece except in the most roundabout way. So she chattered on inanely about books and bookshops, a hint coy enough to cause a guilty flush on both Felicity's and Fergus's faces. The earl, baffled at such henwitted conversation, ordered sherry brought out.

"For I shan't abide this nonsense about lending libraries without some fortification.''

"Your grace is mistaken if you think you must abide anything," Rosalind replied sweetly.

"May I remind you again, ma'am, that this is my residence?'' Eberhart asked as the sherry was produced.

"Indeed you need not," Rosalind replied, accepting a glass from the footman. "You have made that point so often I wonder you bring it up yet again. I daresay Mr. Fairweather would not bring up his place of residence so often.''

"True," the earl said sourly, taking a swallow of his sherry. "But then this shan't be his residence for much longer.''

"What do you mean?'' Felicity cried out, nearly overturning her glass. She turned tremulous eyes on Fergus, who could not bear to look away.

"Mr. Fairweather has given me his notice," Eberhart said, not appearing to see the ardent exchange of glances across the Trafalgar chairs. "Something about my dissolute way of life."

"I'm not surprised," Rosalind said. "But what do you plan to do?"

"I plan to hire another secretary," Eberhart told her.

"I was not addressing you, my lord," she said with a sigh, "but Mr. Fairweather."

Vexed that his secretary should warrant more attention than he at such a time, the earl withdrew into his sherry, leaving Fergus to announce his impending departure for Brussels.

"Brussels?" Felicity exclaimed. "Do you mean the Continent?"

"I suppose you shall be working with your uncle Osgood?" Rosalind asked.

Fergus nodded, still mesmerized by Felicity's eyes.

"I have written him on your behalf," Rosalind revealed.

"Oh, have you? That was good of you," Fergus said absently.

The earl's eyes darted from face to face. "What is all this about Brussels?" he demanded, unable to keep quiet. He fixed a baleful eye on Rosalind. "Have you been encouraging my secretary to seek employment elsewhere, Miss McHenry?"

"There is no need to get on your high ropes," Rosalind retorted. "I know Mr. Fairweather's uncle in Brussels, and when Fergus told me of his wish to secure a diplomatic post there, I was more than happy to write him a sterling recommendation."

"Aunt Rosalind, how could you do such a thing?" Felicity wailed.

Her words caught her aunt and the earl by surprise.

"I assure you, my dear, it was the merest trifle," Rosalind said, rather distracted.

"Fergus, is this what lies behind your resignation?" the earl demanded. "Good heavens, man. If you wished a diplomatic post, why didn't you apply to me? I've a score of friends.''

''Thank you, sir, but I couldn't accept your help. Indeed, I must—''

''You must not go to Brussels,'' Felicity interrupted, twisting the strings of her reticule about her fingers. ''Do tell him so, Aunt Rosalind.''

''I'm afraid that Mr. Fairweather is the only one who can decide that,'' Rosalind replied firmly. ''And apparently he thinks that going to Brussels would be the right choice for him.''

''You're only saying that because you want him out of London,'' Felicity accused.

Eberhart put down his glass, drawn into the family quarrel. ''What an addled notion. Why on earth should she wish such a thing?''

''Because of me,'' Felicity said.

''You!'' Eberhart stared at her, wondering if the poor creature had lost what few wits she possessed. But the tear-filled eyes made him less sure of his ground. His head swiveled toward Fergus, and he intercepted a yearning mooncalf look on the secretary's face. Good Jove! He turned toward Rosalind, who nodded her head.

''Merciful heaven.''

''Sir, I can explain!'' Fergus declared as Felicity began to whimper into another one of her handkerchiefs. The earl was beginning to dread seeing that embroidered border, which seemed to portend another fit of the dismals.

''There is no need for an explanation, Fergus.'' The earl held up a hand. ''It is all writ plainly on your faces.''

''But we didn't mean it, my lord,'' Felicity sniffed into her handkerchief. ''Truly, we didn't mean to fall in love!''

''They *are* in love, you must realize,'' Rosalind informed Eberhart later in the green saloon after Felicity and Fergus had been dispatched to the breakfast room, leaving the earl and Rosalind to thrash out the matter.

''You can't possibly offer for her now,'' she continued,

gazing at his profile, which looked to be chiseled out of stone for all the emotion evident.

"I know I can't offer for her now," he said, turning to catch her scrutinizing him closely. "I had no intention of ever offering. I counted on you to bring one of the sprigs like Maxwell up to snuff. But now look at the fix we are in. Fergus! What does he see in her?"

Rosalind blinked, in no way pleased by his tone of voice. "Felicity is an extremely well-behaved young lady. And her lineage is impeccable."

"Yes, I know, but Fergus!"

Rosalind failed to see any problem with Mr. Fairweather. "He is an unexceptional young man of good family." Her words were an echo of her niece's only a few hours ago.

"Don't lecture me on Fergus's virtues," the earl retorted impatiently. "I know all about his excellent family and his sterling qualities. I also know he lacks a purse, being the fifth son of an impecunious country squire. How do you think that brother of yours shall ever consent to this match?"

Rosalind herself had pointed out just this obstacle to Felicity the previous evening, but somehow having the earl point it out to her hardened her resolve that a way must be found for Felicity to marry Mr. Fairweather.

"They are in love," she said.

"Oh, pray spare me that romantic bibblebabble," the earl exclaimed.

"I shall have to tell Gerald about Fergus, I suppose," Rosalind went on. "Since Felicity's feelings are engaged, I don't think she will be happy with anyone but Fergus. They've been meeting regularly at Hookam's."

"Oh, do spare me the lending library details of their romance, Miss McHenry," Eberhart uttered in strangled accents. "I have not a jot of interest in their travails against Cupid's arrow."

She eyed him with acute dislike. "Obviously, my lord, you have never been in love yourself."

"That experience has happily escaped me," he acknowledged, "but I have observed Cupid's work in others. Take Lord Delbarton, for example. Some years ago he had his head turned by a pretty chit just out. Something like your Felicity, in the Immaculata style. And when the silly thing turned down his offer, he sailed off for the Americas. And this in the thick of the 1812 War.''

"Really?'' Rosalind asked, her curiosity aroused in spite of herself. ''What became of her?''

"She married someone else and became so fat I daresay Delbarton was well out of it. Only, of course, he couldn't know this, being in America.''

She chuckled. ''Oh, Eberhart, instead of prattling on this way do help me think of a solution to this muddle.''

"If you refer to Miss Felicity's little problem, I think it best if you left it in my hands.''

"Your hands? You don't know the slightest thing about handling Gerald!''

"And you do, I suppose?'' he asked sweetly, and was rewarded by another sigh.

"No, of course I don't.''

His smile was kinder than she had any right to expect. ''I have the uncanny notion that should you tell your brother that Felicity had chosen to marry an impecunious but highly principled young man he would think you foxed. Whereas if I did the same he might be compelled to listen.''

Much as it vexed her, Rosalind was obliged to admit the truth in this and agreed to give the earl his head in the matter. She then swept off to the breakfast room, surprising Felicity in Fergus's arms, and in a brisk undertone to Eberhart—who, accompanying her to the parlor, had witnessed the lovers embracing—remarked that the quicker he made things right with Gerald the better off they would all be, and she took her charge back to Green Street.

Chapter Twelve

Because of his propensity for frequenting the more notorious Greeking establishments on London's seamier side, Mr. Gerald McHenry did not return to his lodgings until quite late Tuesday morning. The message that Eberhart had called twice requesting an opportunity for private speech caused an immediate lightening of his dismal spirits. Eberhart's visit must mean he wished to fix the date for Felicity's wedding—and those precious settlements.

Stopping only long enough to change his cravat—for he knew that so noted a Corinthian as the earl would notice the wear on his neckcloth—he was ushered into the earl's presence an hour later.

"Ah, McHenry." Eberhart waved him to a chair in the green saloon. "I have been meaning to have a word with you about your daughter."

"I suppose it is the wedding plans that you are concerned with," Gerald said, rubbing his hands together in anticipation.

"Yes. When I spoke to you some time ago you brought up your debts. A rather staggering sum in the neighborhood of twenty thousand pounds. Correct?" the earl asked through his quizzing glass.

"Well, I don't know it to the penny. I leave that to my solicitor."

"Then we must call him in."

Gerald's pulse quickened. This could only mean the earl was ready to draw up the settlements.

"I don't think we need to bring Ratchet in on this," he said.

Eberhart smiled. "Am I to infer you have recollected the sum of your debts?"

Gerald nodded. "Twenty-seven thousand pounds." He added after a judicious pause. "I incurred a few more losses after our last talk."

"Twenty-seven thousand pounds. You are certain?"

"Yes."

The earl rose and went to his writing desk, where he pulled out a document from a drawer and offered it to his visitor.

"I had my solicitor prepare this. Everything is quite in order. I shall merely pen in the sum of twenty-seven thousand pounds. I give it to you on condition."

"Yes, yes, I know. You want to marry Felicity," Gerald said with some impatience.

"Perhaps you should read this as well," the earl said, handing over a second document.

Gerald looked up, confused by the two documents. "What is this, Eberhart?"

"Read it," the earl said.

Gerald scanned the lines quickly, his color turning almost purple by the time he reached the bottom of the page.

"Devil! This is a letter of consent giving guardianship of Felicity to Rosalind. You're trying to pull the wool over my eyes, sir!"

"If I am, it's rather expensive wool," Eberhart said affably. "Twenty thousand pounds' worth of wool, to be precise. No, I beg pardon, twenty-seven thousand pounds."

Gerald's jowls heaved. "There's something havey-cavey about this or I'll go bail! And I shan't sign it."

Eberhart picked a thread off the sleeve of his coat. "What a pity," he said, scrutinizing the thread momentarily before tossing it away. "I did so hope you would be reasonable. You see, I don't want to marry Felicity. I rather hope she shall marry Mr. Fairweather. She has her heart set on that, from what I can deduce and from what your sister tells me."

"My sister!" The mention of Rosalind brought McHenry to his feet. "I might have guessed she had a hand in this. And who the devil is Fairweather?"

"My secretary. I believe you met him the night of my dinner."

Gerald gaped. "Your *what*?"

"My secretary," Eberhart repeated. "At least, he was my secretary until a few days ago. He plans to leave me to pursue a diplomatic post in Brussels. Felicity shall make him a perfect wife. And he'll make her a better husband than I ever could. In addition, the two are in the throes of a grand passion. Spurred, or so I have been told, by Mr. Walter Scott's literary works."

"A secretary!" Gerald choked. "By Jove, can you believe I would allow my daughter to marry such a person?"

The earl's eyes glinted dangerously. "Fergus is an excellent person. And I hardly think you need scruple about your daughter's choice of husband. You might have married her off to that loose screw Dankley."

Surprised that the earl knew of this, McHenry flushed. "That's different. I never said he might marry Felicity. I just said that if anything scotched the match between you two I would consider his suit. And by Jove, that's what I shall do."

"No, you won't," the earl replied, looking bored.

"Just watch me, sir," Gerald said, moving toward the door.

"If you don't sign that document I shall call in the authorities, McHenry."

Gerald turned, letting out a crack of laughter. "What would they arrest me for? You shall be the laughingstock of the *ton*. Would they really arrest me for not wishing your secretary to marry my daughter?"

"No. They'd arrest you for not paying the considerable debts you owe to me," Eberhart said. He opened his desk drawer again and brought out a large stack of bills.

"I have spent several hours along with my good friend William Wilding, tracking down your many creditors, who were only too willing to hand over the notes you had signed with them." He clucked his tongue. "Some are shockingly overdue. This one, for instance." He plucked one out from the pile. "The sum of five thousand pounds owed to Lady

Tibbs since three years ago. And there are other debts in here nearly twice that old.''

Gerald trembled with mingled rage and fright. "You have no right!''

"I know the fashion these days is not to haul someone off to prison because of debts, but exceptions are made, particularly when the creditor is of high enough rank, and''—he gave a modest smile—"I think I have that.''

"But you can't,'' Gerald protested, paling at the thought of prison. "This is robbery, sir.''

The earl held out the pen. "Sign the document and I'll cancel the debt. That's what you want, isn't it?''

For one moment McHenry thought of refusing, but the thought of himself in the confines of a debtor's prison clinched the matter. Shuddering a little, he scrawled his signature on the form.

"This is coercion, sir,'' he complained after the deed was done.

"There is one additional matter,'' Eberhart said as he took possession of the document.

"I don't wish to hear any of your ideas. It was your notion to offer for Felicity in the first place.''

"I think it would help if you did listen. You have often expressed interest in the Americas, or so my friend Wilding tells me. I have taken the liberty of arranging your passage there. A boat leaves Bristol tonight for Boston.''

"Boston!'' Gerald looked dumbfounded. "You're queer in the cockloft if you think I wish to be buffeted across the sea!''

The earl allowed himself a smile. "Emigration is no longer as arduous as that. And America, although a trifle primitive, is alleged to be quite beautiful. To ease your pain of travel I have ordered fifteen thousand pounds to be placed at your disposal when you arrive there.''

Gerald's jaw dropped. "What did you say?''

"I am giving you fifteen thousand pounds to go to America,'' the earl replied, watching the greed mingle with suspicion on the other man's face.

"Why must I go to America?'' Gerald demanded. "If

you're willing to part with your ready, give it to me now and I shan't bother you.''

The earl stifled a yawn. ''Unfortunately, you would contrive to lose the entire sum in a week. I've no great interest in you, McHenry.'' His eyes settled on Rosalind's brother seriously for a moment. ''But because of an impulse of mine I have become embroiled with you and the affairs of your family. I wish nothing more than to sever all such ties. I shall see that Miss Felicity marries Mr. Fairweather. I shall see that your debts are canceled.'' He threw the notes into the flames in the fireplace. ''And,'' he said as he turned back to Gerald, ''I shall see that you are given a new chance for life in America. That done, I can withdraw with a clear conscience.''

Gerald sat chewing on his lip. Fifteen thousand pounds. The Americas.

''It's fifteen thousand pounds, you say?''

The earl nodded.

''I've never been to the Americas.''

''Everyone should go at least once.''

Gerald stared at the earl. ''You would have thrown me into jail, wouldn't you?''

''Without a moment's hesitation,'' Eberhart said cordially.

McHenry nodded. ''Rosalind was right about you. Felicity is well out of this match. Very well, the Americas and fifteen thousand pounds it is!''

The news that Eberhart had called brought Rosalind from the back parlor, where she had been sewing, and into the blue drawing room later that same day.

''I've just left your brother,'' Eberhart told her in a matter-of-fact way. ''This may be of middling interest to you.''

Rosalind's eyes widened as she read the document Gerald had signed.

''Gerald signed this?'' she exclaimed. ''I recognize his hand, but how in the world—''

The earl smiled. ''I have my methods, Miss McHenry,''

the earl said, enjoying the incredulous look on her face. "Rather rough and ready ones. But I'm sure that given enough time, you could have done the same."

Rosalind was not so quick to share the victory. "I could never have induced Gerald to sign anything," Rosalind said frankly. "Where is he? I must speak to him."

"That is impossible. He is on his way to Bristol."

Rosalind made no attempt to hide her amazement. "To Bristol? Why on earth?"

The earl helped himself to a healthy pinch of snuff. "There is a packet bound for Boston this evening. Mr. McHenry will be aboard it."

Rosalind shook her head as though to clear it.

"America? Gerald? I don't understand."

"It's simple enough," Eberhart told her. "He professed a great interest in travel. I brought that document to you so that in his absence you might know I speak the truth when I say Miss Felicity is free to marry Fergus. I do wish her happy, and I am safely out of things."

"Yes, but how did you get Gerald's consent?"

The earl grinned.

"I made him a proposition, Miss McHenry, one that he was persuaded to accept. And now if you will excuse me, I have to tell Fergus the good news. He was out when your brother called on me."

"Eberhart," she said quickly, feeling a trifle self-conscious, since she had taken issue with his high-handed behavior in the past. "I do thank you. And Felicity will as well!"

He smiled and flicked her on the cheek with a forefinger. "I did it for myself as much as for Felicity and Fergus, you know!"

Hard on the heels of the routing of Mr. McHenry came the start of the London Season. One of the prizes on the marriage mart, however, was not at hand to witness the festivities. As the earl confided to Mr. Wilding, after nearly sticking his neck into the noose of matrimony he wished to replenish his spirits at his country seat for several days of

ishing, desiring nothing whatever to do with fashionable young ladies.

As for Rosalind, her days and nights passed quickly with the opening of the Season. Felicity, top over tail in love and assured that nothing would stand in the way of her marriage to Fergus, flung herself wholeheartedly into her first Season.

Her aunt, however, was beset with a certain ennui as she made the rounds. She had seen the Opera and Vauxhall so often that even their amusements began to pall. She had borne with Mrs. Burrel's reproaches, the Countess Lieven's sly hints, and even Lady Sefton's platitudes too often to take either umbrage or delight in them.

"I seem to be old-cattish of late," Rosalind confided one morning to Lady Manning at Berkeley Square.

Her hostess nearly dashed the tea she was pouring down the side of a porcelain cup.

"My dear Rosalind, you will put me into whoops with such talk! And you don't know what you are saying. You are not old-cattish in the least," Lady Manning protested.

Rosalind gave a rueful smile. "I am three and twenty. Everyone in London knows I am at my last prayers!"

"No woman is ever at her last prayers," Lady Manning said authoritatively. She poured her guest a cup of tea and gazed at her, thinking that old-cattish was not the way she would have described her guest, garbed this morning in an embroidered India mull muslin.

"Can you be so tired of the Season when it is less than a fortnight old?" she asked curiously.

"It's infamous to confess to boredom, isn't it?"

"Oh, I don't know. Alastair has much the same complaint."

Rosalind hunched a shoulder. "It's different for a male."

"Yes, very true. He can take refuge at Pelhelm. But I hope he doesn't become ensconced there. I should like to have him about for some of the Season."

"Yes, that would be nice for you," Rosalind said indifferently, leading Lady Manning to complain to her spouse after her guest had left that she despaired of ever seeing Alastair and Rosalind happily matched.

"Matched?" Lord Manning put down his copy of *Gentleman's Quarterly*. "I thought you had given that over, my dear. Alastair's already had one skirmish with marriage plans. He's bound to fight shy of another."

"Oh, that wasn't a serious skirmish," Lady Manning said as her spouse returned to his magazine. "That dratted Alastair. If only he were here instead of racketing about with fish. I could throw him in Rosalind's path."

"I don't think Alastair would be thrown anywhere he didn't wish to go," her husband replied. "Best give up the notion, my dear. I know you are partial to it, but there are too many obstacles. They have met often enough while he was in London," he pointed out, "and didn't appear too fond of each other."

"Yes, I know," Lady Manning agreed. "But Rosalind did say she was attending the Sefton ball Friday evening, and Alastair did say he might be returning to London this week, so perhaps something might happen there!"

Unbeknownst to Lady Manning, her son was in fact headed back to London sooner than she thought. Confinement in the country had palled quickly, especially since news of his nuptials had preceded him and he had had to contend with the mistaken idea that he had brought a wife with him. Several awkward moments passed among the staff and neighbors in the region, capped by the morning call and effusive congratulations of the vicar and his wife, which had led Eberhart to ascend the stairs and immediately pack his bags for his return.

He departed Pelhelm that morning and at noon stopped at a small posting house for a brief luncheon of ham, beef, and a tankard of ale. Replenished by this he was about to set off again in his carriage when his attention was drawn to a female just being put off the mail coach. There was something familiar about her face. Frowning, he waited until he heard the sound of her voice arguing with the coachman and then had no difficulty in recognizing her as Isabelle Garret, with whom he had shared a dalliance back in his salad days.

She had married well, he had heard, but if so, why was she being set down so rudely by a coachman?

"Isabelle?" he asked as he approached.

The pale face glanced up and the anxiety in the shining blue eyes cleared at once. A look of rosy good humor lit up her eyes.

"As I live and breathe, is it you, Alastair?" she demanded.

"The one and the same," he said, shaking hands. But she was not to be put off by so pallid a greeting and kissed him soundly on the cheeks. Isabelle, he remembered, always was the affectionate sort.

"What are you doing in the wilds of the Cotswolds?" he asked.

"I could ask you the same thing," she retorted playfully.

Despite the few lines that age had etched about her mouth, the years had been kind to Isabelle. She had been in her late twenties when he had fallen under her spell, and she had taken pity on his youth and had, he realized only later, taught him a good deal about females. She would now be, he supposed, at least thirty.

"I was visiting Pelhelm," he told her as he led her toward the posting house. "I'm on my way back to London and stopped for a bite to eat. Confess, were you trying to flirt with a passenger and so enraged the coachman?"

She trilled with laughter. "Don't be absurd, you dear boy!" Her hand flew to her mouth. "But you aren't a boy, are you, Alastair? I vow, how time has flown. And I have more than one gray hair to hide under this hat!"

"Nonsense," he retorted. "You look not a day over twenty-one."

"Always the gallant. I did like you for that."

"Not enough to stay with me when Ozwald beckoned," he retorted.

"Ah, Ozwald." A nostalgic look crept into her eyes. "Did I really leave you for the likes of him?"

"Indeed you did. I cried my eyes out!"

Her laugh at this outrageous whisker sealed their mood, and he bustled her into the inn for a plate of food, insisting that she tell him all that had happened to her in the years.

"Well," she said as she polished off a chicken leg, "I did go to Ozwald. It was nothing but a hum. He promised me diamonds and rubies, and while I know men in love are prone to overstate such things, he was terribly purse-pinched. And he gambled!"

"We all gamble."

"Yes, but he lost!" Isabelle said naïvely. "It's all well and good to gamble when one wins, but when one loses, it's idiotish."

"Did you tell Ozzie this?"

"Heavens no. I'm not such a ninnyhammer. What I did was find a new patron. Ozwald didn't mind. He couldn't afford to keep me. So I went to Olaf Jergsen. Do you know him?"

"Vaguely. German, wasn't he? Some sort of count."

"Actually he was a Dane. Or do I mean a Swede? I can't really tell the difference. He was quite taken with me."

"We all were," Eberhart said indulgently. "Then what happened? I heard you had married. Was it the Dane?"

"No." She shook her head. "He lasted only a year. Then what must happen but he broke his neck in a carriage accident, leaving me quite distraught." She saw the earl's quizzing look. "It's not mere flourishing, Alastair. I quite liked him. He left me a little money."

"Sounds like a good fellow."

"He was. And then I had the misfortune to fall in with Mr. Sedgewick Hubbel, who proposed marriage to me. And I foolishly accepted. Pray don't ask why. I must have been mad. I suppose I was tired of being considered a bit of muslin."

"Bosh. You were no such thing."

"Yes, I was," she said realistically. Having finished one chicken leg, she methodically started on another. "Oh, I don't repine. As long as the gentlemen *were* gentlemen. And some, like you, I was genuinely fond of."

"And your husband?"

Isabelle made a face. "That was a hideous mistake. He married me for the money I had inherited from Olaf. He went through that quickly. His own estates were mortgaged, which I did not know at the time. The secrets you gentlemen will keep when it comes to marriage!"

The earl laughed. "And are you still married to him? Or have I interrupted a runaway?"

"Well, I did think of running away, but that wouldn't answer, for I'd be quite penniless then, wouldn't I? Actually, two months ago I received a letter saying that Hubbel had died in Bristol. So I am widowed and penniless."

He made a sympathetic murmur. "And what are you doing here?"

"Well," she answered, her tone turning brisk, "I thought I'd do some respectable work for a change. I decided to try my hand at the theater. After all, I couldn't see myself a governess."

"Not while there was a male in the household," he agreed.

She laughed, not displeased. "And I was doing quite well, Alastair, touring in France, and then last week I fell into a frightful row with another actress. She was jealous of me. Anyway, she prevailed on the director to give me my notice. And we were just to begin a new play in London. I was trying to get to London on the mail coach, but the coachman would try to get fresh with me. I don't stand for that from the lower classes."

"No, of course not," he soothed.

"And that's how I wound up here. And now you! I read about you constantly in the pages of the *Morning Post*. You are quite a top sawyer these days!"

"Don't pitch that gammon at me, Isabelle. We know each other too well."

"Indeed we do," she said with a speculative look. "Are you married yet?"

"No. I nearly put my foot in Parson's Mousetrap, but it didn't come off."

"Ah, well. I'm sorry for it if *you* are. You always did

seem the marriageable type. What happened to sour the plans?''

''She chose my secretary over me,'' he said, and was rewarded with her sudden choking on a bone.

''Anyway, it wouldn't have worked. She was a schoolroom miss.''

''Ah.'' Isabelle gave an understanding nod. ''Such girls always have their heads stuffed with nonsense.''

''If you wish it, Isabelle, I can have the landlord reserve a room for you for the night.''

''Actually, Alastair, if you are in the mood to grant a favor, it's not a room I could use—it's your carriage.''

He looked at her in surprise. ''My carriage?''

She dabbed at her mouth with a napkin, having finished her meal. ''Yes, or if you will, a ride into London. I was going there.''

''I don't know.''

''Are you ashamed of me?'' she asked. ''Don't be embarrassed if you are. There's been a lot of water under the bridge.''

''Don't be so nonsensical. You were my friend, Isabelle. I'm not about to turn my back on you. I merely hesitated because I am frightfully late. I shall be obliged to drive at a devilish pace.''

''All the better. Shall we set off now?''

Rejecting the notion that she ride inside where she would not be in danger of flying off with every turn, Mrs. Hubbel climbed into the seat next to the driver's, commenting now and then on his vast improvement in handling the reins since their last drive together.

''I was a cawker, wasn't I?'' He grinned.

''No, just green, which everyone is in the beginning. But the years have been kind to you. I'm bound to think it must be Providence that sent us once again on the same path.''

''How is that?''

''Well, haven't you been telling me tales of marriage-minded females setting their caps at you?''

''Yes.''

"You don't wish to be importuned by them during the rest of the Season, do you?"

"No," he said, shooting her a quick look. "But the only way to stop it is to wed one of them, which I won't."

"Then here's what I propose. You need to be spoken for by some woman, to be taken out of the swim. So you'll fall under my spell again."

He laughed. "You weave a powerful charm, Isabelle."

"It's all sham, of course. You set me up in some house. I presume you still hold a lease or two?"

He frowned. "No, but I can find one. Am I to lavish gifts on you?"

"Just the use of a carriage. Then people shall say that with a *chère amie* in London you don't have the time to do the pretty to a respectable female."

Her scheme had some allure. "And what of you?" he asked. "Will you gain anything from such a proposal?"

"The roof over my head, for one," she said sensibly. "You see, I am serious about my work in the theater. A producer might take me on. I'll look for work in London. But even the most unscrupulous will not try anything if they know you are my patron." She went on as he fell silent. "It is a good deal to ask of you, Alastair, but we needn't keep it up for long. Just long enough for the Season to end with you safely unmarried and with me making my debut on the stage."

The earl knew that there was more for her in the bargain than for him, but he did not hesitate for long. The scheme had some merits. It would be enjoyable to see Isabelle. And if he could help her get a start on the London stage, so much the better.

"Well, Alastair?" she asked.

He nodded. "Very well. I'll do it!"

She gave an impetuous squeal and hugged him, which had the effect of nearly sending them both into a ditch. With Isabelle back in his life, he thought as he struggled to right his team, life certainly was not going to be boring in London!

Chapter Thirteen

Lady Maria Sefton was one of Society's premier hostesses, and her ball Friday evening was *de rigueur* for anyone in good standing. No one would have dreamed of missing it, except perhaps Eberhart, who returned to London after his fortnight of fishing to declare that he was well out of the chase for a bride and hence would not even attend the glittering affair. And nothing his mother might say would change his mind.

Rosalind shared the earl's dim view of the Friday-evening gala. She was herself heartily bored with the prospect of yet another night of dancing. To add to her discomfort, Waldo was sure to attend. He had been attaching himself to her so obviously that even Lady Jersey had teasingly inquired when the announcement was due to appear in the *Gazette*.

Felicity, however, had been looking forward to the ball, and Rosalind, in an apple-green satin, soon found herself in the midst of yet another ballroom, watching Felicity dance off with Mr. Fairweather.

Waldo, as she had feared, clung to her side, but she managed to fob him off on one of the ladies passing by. As she congratulated herself on this tactic, she met the twinkling eye of Mr. Wilding.

"A nice trick, Miss McHenry."

She laughed. "Well, Miss Evans was eager to dance and no one had asked her, so I thought Waldo—"

"Yes, of course you did," he said with another smile as he handed her a glass of champagne.

"I'm surprised to see you here. I thought such activities weren't in your line of things."

"They aren't, usually," he acknowledged with a sheepish grin. "But one of my mother's bosom bows just happens to have a daughter, Miss Collingsworth, making her come-out this year. And they would have us meet."

Rosalind gave a sympathetic chuckle. "I hadn't realized that gentlemen could be bullied just as badly as ladies when it came to romantic dealings."

His grin widened. "Actually, she's not a bad sort at all, although a trifle young and shy." He nodded toward the corner where Miss Collingsworth, a pretty little thing in a blue ball gown, sat.

Rosalind raised mischievous eyes to her companion. "When may I wish you happy?" she inquired.

Rigid shock suffused Mr. Wilding's amiable face. "Miss McHenry! There is no thought of that, I assure you. Someone might overhear you and blab it all over the town. I'm not saying she's not pretty, for she is." He glanced again at Miss Collingsworth, frowning slightly. "That's Mr. Dankley with her. I shouldn't have thought Lady Sefton would invite him here. I don't like him talking to Miss Collingsworth!"

Curious, Rosalind followed his disapproving gaze. Mr. Dankley had indeed sidled up to the young lady, only to be briskly sent about his business by her chaperon.

Wilding released his breath. "Her mama's no fool, thank heaven. A bit of an ugly customer, Mr. Dankley is, no matter how fat his purse. I wonder why Lady Sefton invited him. And I do hope he doesn't cause any mischief for you and Miss Felicity!"

Rosalind felt a moment's confusion. "Trouble for me and Felicity?" she murmured, puzzled. "Pray why should he trouble us, Mr. Wilding?"

Wilding looked sheepish. "Oh, good Jupiter! I shouldn't have said that. I promised Alastair I wouldn't. He'll kill me if he finds I've been prattling on about his concerns."

His concerns? Rosalind was more and more intrigued and determined to get to the bottom of things.

"Mr. Wilding, what has the earl to do with Mr. Dankley, my niece, or myself?"

"Nothing, really," came Wilding's nervous reply. "More to do with your brother, I should say, but then again you mustn't press me."

"I fear I must," Rosalind insisted, not about to let the matter drop so quickly. "Unless you prefer that I put the issue to Mr. Dankley directly."

"Good heavens, don't do that," Mr. Wilding cried out. There's no telling what he might do." He put down his champagne glass and glanced over one shoulder, making certain no one could overhear them.

"If you must know, Miss McHenry, your brother had an understanding with Dankley that should anything happen to scotch the match between Eberhart and Felicity, Dankley would be next."

"Next for what?"

"For Felicity," Mr. Wilding said, embarrassed. "Dankley's offer would be accepted if Eberhart's fell through."

For a moment Rosalind thought that the music in the ballroom had affected her hearing. "But that's absurd," she protested. "Gerald couldn't do that. Mr. Dankley is at least fifty."

"I didn't believe it myself, despite Alastair telling me so himself," Wilding admitted, "but then I chanced to overhear Dankley boast of it one day at the club. That's why the earl was so reluctant to cry off straight out. He knew Miss Felicity would only become betrothed to Dankley. The fat would have been in the fire then!"

"Indeed it would have," Rosalind agreed, stricken at the very notion of her niece wed to someone like Dankley. She knew his reputation as a rake.

"Mr. Wilding," she said, "do you know how my brother was persuaded to give me approval over whomever Felicity might marry?"

"Alastair forced his hand," Wilding revealed. "He and I had gone about the City buying up your brother's gaming debts. Alastair threatened to have him put into a debtor's prison if he didn't cooperate and sign the document." He noticed her sharp reaction and added hastily, "A drastic threat, I know, Miss McHenry, but the situation was desperate.''

"Go on," she said, determined to hear everything.

"Once Gerald signed, Eberhart threw the gaming notes into the fire, cancelling the debt. And the amount was considerable.''

Her forehead knitted. "How considerable?"

"Twenty-seven thousand pounds. He also paid McHenry's passage to America and promised a sum of fifteen thousand pounds to be waiting for him on arrival.''

Rosalind was astounded. She had never expected this from Eberhart. What could lie behind such generosity?

"He wanted his freedom from Felicity, I suppose," Mr. Wilding said when the question was put to him.

"But he wasn't obliged to go to such extremes," she told him.

"He felt he was. And to someone as stubborn as Alastair, that's all that matters. Look at it from his point of view. He couldn't bow out and leave the girl to her misery. Another man might have, but not Alastair. The only way he could see to settle the affair was to cancel your brother's debts, secure his consent to Felicity's marriage to Mr. Fairweather by giving you guardianship, and obtain his own freedom. His plan worked, too, for everyone except Dankley, who was none too pleased at being outfoxed by Alastair." Mr. Wilding paused. "I don't think he'll trouble with Alastair. He might be angry, but he's not a fool. But if I were you, Miss McHenry, I would stay out of his way.''

"Our paths rarely cross," Rosalind assured him, an abstracted look on her face. "But I do thank you for your advice. You have been very helpful.''

The evening passed in a blur. Instinctively she chatted, sipped champagne, and nibbled on lobster patties, but her mind whirled like a catherine wheel. Had Eberhart's freedom meant so much to him that he would willingly part with forty-two thousand pounds?

Late Tuesday morning as Waldo descended his stairs, intending to partake of breakfast before joining his cronies at Manton's, he was handed an urgent message from Rosalind.

Jolted by such an event—never before had Rosalind so much as hinted that she even knew where he resided—he scanned the note, a request to present himself at Green Street at his earliest convenience.

The viscount did not boast a sterling intellect, but he was an obedient fellow, and he drove over to Green Street, where he found Rosalind not prostrate with grief as he had imagined but seated at her library desk, briskly reviewing the sheaf of papers in front of her.

She glanced up as he approached.

"Oh, Waldo. It was so good of you to come."

"You did say the matter was urgent," he reminded her, taking off his hat. "I thought there might have been a mishap."

She looked up with a slight frown. "Nothing of the sort. I merely need to settle something and need your assistance."

"Well, then I'm always happy to oblige," he said, his ruffled feathers soothed by the idea of her seeking his advice. He settled in the Trafalgar chair. "Pray what is the problem, my dear?"

For a moment Rosalind toyed with the lace ruffle on the left sleeve of her yellow day dress, hesitating to put into words the scheme she had hatched the night before.

"Is it the matter of the underfootman?" he asked.

"What underfootman?" She looked confused.

"You told me he was a trifle foxed."

Rosalind's brow cleared. "Oh, yes, that underfootman. Yes, he was foxed. And Mrs. Withers was going to fire him, but during his talk with her she discovered he was languishing after Betty, a downstairs maid, and that she, Betty, was equally enamored of him. And now they are engaged and he is no longer foxed."

"Well, I'm glad to hear that," Waldo said. "But if it's not a household matter, what is it?"

Rosalind saw no way but to take the plunge. "Waldo," she said, pressing her hands tightly on top of the desk, "do you still wish to marry me?"

"Eh, what?" the viscount asked, startled by such a query.

"I said, do you still wish to marry me," she said impatiently. "You have asked me every Season since my come-out," she reminded him. "And the last occasion was only a fortnight ago."

"Yes, I recall," Waldo said. "But you've always refused me before."

"Well, I shan't now, if you still wish to marry me. Do you?" She looked at him with all seriousness. He was fiddling with his snuffbox.

"Oh, do forget all about it, Waldo," she said brusquely, wondering what on earth had possessed her to think of such a thing. "It was an idiotish notion."

"No, no," he protested immediately, shutting his snuffbox and nearly snaring his thumb in the process. "I was just taken by surprise, that's all. I most certainly do wish to marry you," he said manfully.

She smiled, pleased. "Good. Then we can consider ourselves betrothed."

"I shall have to write to my mother," Waldo said, still feeling a bit overcome by the swiftly unfolding events.

"Yes," Rosalind agreed. "But before you tell dear Mama the tidings, there is a favor I must ask of you."

"Ask away," Waldo said indulgently.

"I don't know how you shall take it. But I'd like to borrow ten thousand pounds."

The indulgent smile on the viscount's face faded. "Ten thousand pounds?"

"It's on a personal matter," she continued hastily, "so I know you shan't press me for details, since I can't tell you. And I would hate to lie to you, and I wouldn't ask if it weren't urgent. And," she went on, "I shall pay you back every penny. Although that does sound stupid, since we shall be married so shortly. Let me just promise never to waste the ready in so cavalier a fashion again. Of course," she said, seeing his hesitation, "if you dislike lending it to me—"

"No," Waldo said, roused to speech. "Ten thousand

pounds is a simple enough matter. You're going to be my wife. Do you wish it in cash or a check?"

"A check shall be fine," she said with a smile. "You'll deposit it into my bank?"

He nodded.

"Good." She picked up the papers lying on her desk. "Now, Waldo, I do thank you for coming, and I think I shall let you go, for I'm sure you have many pressing activities."

"Nothing important," he demurred, showing no eagerness to leave his chair, "merely a meeting of the fellows at Manton's."

"Ah, then you must join them. They will wonder where you have gone to."

"I don't wish to join them," Waldo said huskily.

Rosalind lifted an eyebrow. She knew that tone of voice only too well.

"But you do wish to tell your mama about our engagement, don't you?" she asked swiftly. "I think you should send her a letter express."

"I suppose you are right," Waldo said, giving in to the call of filial duty.

It wasn't until the viscount was back at his own residence that he realized that although he had just been accepted in marriage he had not offered so much as a chaste salute on his beloved's cheek.

At Green Street Rosalind wrestled with her conscience. She had spent the previous few days reviewing with her banker just how much money she could hope to raise. She was determined to pay Eberhart the full forty-two thousand pounds he had spent on Gerald. Her fortune, however, was not large enough for such an endeavor. She was ten thousand pounds short.

Her first impulse was to tell Fergus what had happened, but then Fergus, being an honorable sort, would undoubtedly feel the debt his and bankrupt himself to pay Eberhart back. A life of genteel poverty for Felicity was not what she wished.

Nor was genteel poverty what she wanted for herself,

which was how Waldo came to mind. She could marry him, ask for the necessary ten thousand pounds to repay Eberhart, and live comfortably ever after with an amiable and doting husband.

It was the perfect solution. Even so, a voice inside her could not be quieted. Marriage to Waldo might be the answer to her financial problems, but it was not the answer to her dreams. But then, she reminded herself sternly, she was no romantic schoolroom miss. All she wanted in a husband was kindness and amiability, which Waldo boasted aplenty. It was just a pity that he was also completely devoid of spirit and wit!

Chapter Fourteen

Although Eberhart had declared himself well out of all the festivities he was not above accompanying his mother on a short drive to Richmond Park one sunny morning.

"Not that I ever knew you to be that enamored of Richmond Park," he mentioned as he helped her into the high-perched phaeton. She would not dream of appearing in anything so stuffy as a barouche with her son at the reins.

"Actually, it is not the destination so much as my companion," she retorted with a saucy smile. In her cream-colored morning dress with a matching hat set at a particularly rakish angle she looked absurdly youthful.

Laughing, he picked up the reins and sternly told her not to offer him Spanish coin.

"How can you say that! It adds enormously to my prestige to even be seen with you," she replied. "Everyone knows you are such a top sawyer with a whip."

"Mama, do try for a little conduct. Top sawyer indeed. I shall become so high in the instep there shall be no tolerating me."

She laughed and settled back against the velvet squabs to enjoy the drive. The earl had anticipated a serene drive to the Park but had reckoned without encountering several of his mother's acquaintances along the way. By necessity he was forced to pull up to allow Lady Manning some minutes' conversation with each of these intimates.

These encounters were so frequent and so taxing to his patience that it was well past the noon hour when they tooled past the entrance of Richmond Park.

"Dearest, you know how I hate to pinch at you," Lady Manning said as he helped her down. "But you could have been a trifle more civil to Lady Finchwilliam just now."

"I thought I was civil," Eberhart said, astonished. "She invited me to her dreary dinner party. And I declined with every sense of cheerful good will."

"But that's just it," his mother responded, tapping him with the sunshade she had just unfurled. "Too cheerful by half. The civil thing would have been to act as though you were sorely disappointed that you could not make it, even though," she said with a sigh, "you are right that it shall be tedious."

"It's too late to be prostrate with grief over Lady Finchwilliam's party," Eberhart pointed out. "But I shall keep your words in mind if any of your other bosom bows try to entice me into the Seasonal offerings. And I am surprised she did invite me. Perhaps she doesn't know about Mrs. Hubbel."

His mother shot him a look of mild reproof. "Alastair, you are incorrigible. And I have been meaning to ask if you have lost your heart to her yet again."

"Mama, the idea—"

She twirled her sunshade. "You were linked to her once."

"Isabelle is a friend in need," he explained. "I am assisting her. I'm speaking the truth," he said as she looked doubtful. "She wants to embark on a career on the stage. I'm helping her."

"You know nothing about the stage," his mother replied.

"Yes, well, that's true," he said, a trifle discomposed. "But still I could find out which theater troupe might need an actress, and—"

"Can she sing?" Lady Manning interrupted.

"I presume so. Why?"

"Because I overheard my cousin Gertrude say that the Italian Company was in dire need of a singer."

"Really?" The earl absorbed this tidbit of information soberly. "Would that be Signor Orsini, the director?"

"Yes, that's the one."

"I shall have to tell Isabelle that. And now shall we stroll or sit?"

Accepting her son's change of topic, Lady Manning rejected strenuously the notion of merely sitting in such pretty gardens. Together they walked down one of the promenades.

"If you didn't mean to attend parties in London, Alastair, I wonder that you bothered to return. You could have stayed on in the country."

"I suppose so, Mama. Only it wasn't quite comfortable there."

Lady Manning's eyes widened at such a declaration. His country seat, with which she was intimately acquainted, had always boasted the latest in creature comforts.

"I suppose you found it insufferably boring at Pelhelm?"

"That wasn't it, Mama. I felt in need of solitude and I had plenty of that, only. . ."

Lady Manning's sunshade dipped precariously over her pretty head, almost striking her son in the eye. "Only," she prompted.

"Only a bit of a muddle ensued," he said, taking the sunshade away and holding it for her. "It seems that the servants had gotten wind that I was taking a leg shackle and thought I'd be bringing her with me. When I arrived I found all manner of arrangements had been made for the bride, including"—he grimaced—"the preparations for her room."

"Oh, Alastair, how *awkward* for you," his mother sympathized.

"That's not the half of it, Mama," he said with a rueful smile. "Just when I had convinced everyone, including Milkes—and you know what an old martinet he can be—that I hadn't married anyone, the vicar came calling with his wife, ready to do the pretty to me and my bride. Before I could say anything they were prattling on about how a wife was the very thing the parish needed!"

Lady Manning let out an involuntary gurgle of amusement.

"I didn't mean to laugh, truly. I can just see them now,

the Reverend Carter and his wife. I do hope you didn't give them a set-down."

"No," he said. "They meant well. And they were quite embarrassed when I told them I didn't have a bride and had no intention of taking one. Shall we see the maze?" he asked as they came to a stop on the promenade.

"No, what use would I have with a stupid maze?" she asked. "And do give me that!" She took possession of her sunshade again. "I'm not in my dotage yet."

"You will never be in your dotage, Mama," he said fondly, and she rewarded him with a peck on the cheek.

"Alastair, what you said a few minutes ago can't be true, can it?"

"I assure you, Mama, most visitors do wish to see the maze!"

"I am not talking about the stupid maze," his mother exclaimed. "I am talking of your future without a bride."

"I know your disappointment must be considerable, Mama," he said soberly. "But do you blame me for feeling this way after the bumblebroth with Miss Felicity?"

"Not in the slightest," his mother replied at once, stooping to sniff a rose. "But I must own," she said as she straightened, "that I never saw the rhyme nor reason for your choice of a schoolroom miss as a bride. A pretty child, yes, and well-behaved, but scarcely out of a nursery."

"Which is the perfect complement to my being in my dotage."

"Oh, don't talk fustian rubbish," his mother implored. "I'm convinced that you could easily choose a new bride from the beauties available this season."

He kicked a loose pebble on the path with the toe of his boot. "Perhaps. But I'm not interested in the new crop of beauties. Besides"—he grinned—"what female will have me? I have been bested by my own secretary! Poor Mama. I must be a sore disappointment to you. Did you have the announcement of my betrothal all ready to pop into the *Gazette*?"

"No," she said truculently. "And I am of the mind that such announcements are ofttimes premature. One has only to think of the weddings that never came off and then the embarrassment to the bride or groom.''

"My intentions toward Felicity were honorable," he assured her. "I would have married her."

Lady Manning waved a dismissive hand. "You just thought you would," she said. "After so many years of bachelorhood you had the notion to marry much in the way that Mr. Wilding has taken the notion."

Eberhart was riveted by this remark. "What? Has Wilding taken the plunge?"

"Not yet," Lady Manning said as she ascended a small stone stairway. "But his mama is most hopeful that something will come to pass with Miss Collingsworth. It is the first time that he seemed to think any female worthy of as much thought as his choice of snuff."

"William is deuced particular," Eberhart drawled. "I must wish him happy the next time I see him."

His mother quickly scotched such an idea.

"You have only to utter a word, and he will be scared off. And that will never do."

"I shall be as silent as a grave," he promised. "I just had no thought of William as the marrying sort."

"He is not the only one ready to tie the knot," Lady Manning confided. "Rumor has it that Viscount Coppleton has been successful in attaching Miss McHenry."

The earl came to a dead stop, his brow knit in a furious frown.

"Does Fergus know?"

Lady Manning was thrown back by such a question. "Fergus has nothing to do with it."

"I thought you said Waldo was marrying Felicity."

His mother heaved a despairing sigh. "Alastair, don't be a nodcock. Waldo is courting Rosalind McHenry, not Felicity. And why you insist on thinking so often of that chit I shall never know!" She gave him a poke in the ribs with a gloved finger. "Have you nothing to say about Miss McHenry's attachment?"

He shrugged. "What is there to say, Mama? I knew Waldo to be very particular in his attentions. But she showed not the 'slightest sign of partiality, treating him much like a dog allowed to run tame in her household.''

''Whatever her method of treatment in the past, in the future he will be treated as her husband,'' Lady Manning said with a searching look at her son's handsome face.

''Poor Waldo,'' Eberhart mused. ''She shall lead him a cat-and-dog life, if I am right.''

His mother had reached the end of her patience. ''You are not right,'' she said trenchantly. ''Miss McHenry is an extremely amiable and remarkable young lady. And I wish to know why you have taken her in such dislike.''

''Too harsh, Mama. I merely prefer females that are a trifle less high-handed and opinionated.''

This view, Lady Manning quickly informed him, was the most addled she had ever heard him utter. The earl bore with the litany of praises that she proceeded to rain down on his head with some discomfort, wondering why his mother would champion her cause so strenuously.

It was not until they were driving back to London that Lady Manning recollected a certain message from the same high-handed female her son held in such scorn.

''A message from Miss McHenry?'' The earl took his eyes off the road to look at her.

''Yes, you are to call on a Mr. Fogarty in the City whenever it is convenient. He is a solicitor, I believe.''

The earl frowned. ''Why didn't she send word of this herself?''

''Because she wasn't certain whether you were back, and when I called on her yesterday and told her I was coming here with you, she charged me with the message.''

The earl could not fathom what Miss McHenry's solicitor could want with him.

''It probably has something to do with that odious brother of hers,'' Lady Manning said.

''Perhaps,'' he agreed automatically, but he was not fully convinced. When Miss McHenry took a hand in things events were seldom as simple as they seemed.

Eberhart felt in no hurry to do Rosalind's bidding, particularly when her bidding had been relayed to him second-hand, so it was not until several days after his excursion to Richmond Park that he found himself on a round of errands in the City and remembered to pay a call on Mr. Fogarty, the solicitor.

"Now then, Lord Eberhart," Mr. Fogarty, a funereal-looking man, said as he led the earl toward a most uncomfortable-looking chair. "What may I do for you?"

"I was instructed to present myself here by one of your clients, a Miss Rosalind McHenry," the earl told him.

"Miss McHenry, ah, yes." Mr. Fogarty nodded, steepling his bony fingers. "A most charming young lady. As it happens I have just what she ordered right here." He opened a desk drawer. "Here it is, all nice and proper. Rather out of the ordinary, if I do say so, but Miss McHenry insisted."

Eberhart took the proffered document and scanned the few lines with an indolent eye. But his face froze as he came to the bottom of the page.

"What is this?" he demanded.

"I thought that was self-explanatory, sir," Mr. Fogarty said with a nervous titter. "Miss McHenry is repaying you the sum of forty-two thousand pounds, thirty-two thousand of which has already been deposited with your banker—Baverstock, is it not? And ten thousand additional pounds will be deposited by the end of the fortnight; of that you can be assured."

"And you may be assured, my good fellow, that I would never accept such a besotted bequest!" The earl rose and stalked out of the solicitor's office, wondering what new game that dratted female was running.

Rosalind this Wednesday morning was engaged in nothing more alarming than surveying the delights available at Messrs. Rundell and Bridges along with her doting fiancé. The excursion had been Waldo's idea. He had insisted that he had an obligation to purchase a little trinket for his bride-to-be.

Although touched by the sentiment, Rosalind was reluctant to take any gift from him and was in no mood to peruse the trays of bracelets, necklaces, and brooches Rundell held out for her inspection.

Indeed, the tray of India sapphires might as well have been Peruvian emeralds for all the difference she could deduce today. But since Waldo seemed prepared to exhaust all the clerks and view every bauble in the store until she selected something, she acquiesced finally in the purchase of a modest topaz bracelet.

Beaming happily from his morning's work, Waldo was just assisting her into his barouche when a carriage swooping past came to a violent halt a few yards away. It was Eberhart, performing the trickiest turnaround the viscount had ever witnessed. The earl climbed down from his vehicle and approached them.

"Good day, Miss McHenry, Waldo."

"Eberhart," the viscount said. "By Jove, that was a nice piece of work. Beyond me, I must confess."

"I'm glad you liked it," the earl said distractedly. He turned to Waldo's companion. "I must speak with you, Miss McHenry."

"Unfortunately, my lord," Rosalind replied, calmly drawing on her gloves, "that is impossible. As you can see, we are already holding up the traffic. I'm certain the disposition of the coachmen behind us will be rendered testy if we dally any longer."

"I don't care if they become testy," Eberhart snapped. "I insist on speaking with you. I've just been to see Fogarty."

"Waldo," Rosalind urged. "We must press on."

The viscount climbed into the carriage beside her.

"I would be obliged for a few minutes of your time, Miss McHenry," Eberhart called up. "Perhaps back at Green Street?"

"That is impossible. I am quite busy today."

"With wedding plans, I daresay?" Eberhart inquired politely and noted the sharp look she sent him. "I heard of that happy event from my mother. I wish you happy, Waldo."

"That's deuced nice of you, Alastair," the viscount said, beaming.

"Busy though you are at such a time," the earl said, returning to Rosalind, "I do beg a few moments of your time."

Beg indeed! He was wholly intractable, but she finally gave in. "Tomorrow at eleven I shall contrive to be home if you should call," she said curtly.

So curtly that the viscount felt obliged to point out that she had come perilously close to offending a peer of the realm.

"That wasn't too civil of you, dismissing Eberhart that way, my dear," he said back at Green Street.

She cast off her gloves. "I didn't want his company, did you?"

Waldo thought the matter over. "I suppose not. The bracelet, my dear. Do you like it?"

"Oh, yes, of course, Waldo," she said absently, wondering if she should offer him some sherry.

"You must wear it, then," he said, taking it out of its case and clasping it around her slender wrist. "It looks lovely, just as you do, Rosalind," he said huskily. He stared at her so ardently that Rosalind felt a flicker of alarm.

In the days since she had accepted Waldo, he had not once kissed her. But there could be no denying that this seemed his intention now. For a minute Rosalind thought of fending him off, then decided that it would be better to get the deed over and done with. Waldo, unaware of the thoughts churning in her head, planted his mouth firmly on hers. She suffered a momentary shock as he drew away a few moments later. It was not so terrible as she had imagined, and not as grand, either. It was rather like being kissed by a very wet puppy.

Chapter Fifteen

So absorbed had Fergus been in the blossoming of his love for Felicity that he had nearly forgotten his uncle Osgood in Brussels. A letter from this gentleman soon sent him scurrying to find the earl.

"It seems that, far from thinking my writing to him an impertinence, Uncle Osgood believes I can be of great help to him on several current projects."

"Splendid, Fergus," Eberhart said. He stretched his legs out in front of his library fire. "When do you leave?"

"I suppose it shall have to be soon, sir," Fergus said. "I've already gone through a list of candidates for my post and have selected a few for you to interview."

"I'll interview them later," Eberhart said, waving the list away. "Now, what of you? Do you have enough funds for the trip for you and Felicity?"

"Oh, yes, sir. You've been more than generous to me through the years. And I've saved a tidy sum. But the thing that is on my mind, sir, is—well—when do you think I should marry Felicity? Do you think I should marry her first and bring her over with me to Brussels or go on to Brussels alone and then return here and marry her?"

"I think of the two plans you propose the former is more suitable. You can rest easier having her with you."

"Yes. I hadn't looked forward to a separation."

The earl smiled. "Spoken like a man thoroughly in love."

"We shall have to post the banns soon."

"Either that or elope," the earl advised.

Mr. Fairweather recoiled at such a notion. "I'd never

think of such a thing," he said. "Besides, Felicity would never consent to such a scheme."

"You would be surprised at just how many females do consent to such schemes, Fergus," Eberhart retorted. "But I daresay Felicity is not of their league." He gazed steadily at his secretary. "When will you be leaving for Brussels?"

"Oh, I thought in about a month, if it's agreeable to you."

The earl found nothing to quarrel with in this time schedule. "That will give you enough time to post the banns, arrange the wedding, and still enjoy a brief honeymoon on the Continent. My mama can fill you in on all the romantic spots there."

The evening progressed, and the earl, to his mild astonishment, found his advice sought with regard to the wedding preparations and the trip. As the hours went by his amusement gave way to a slight envy. Would Cupid never reward him with a suitable mate? But then almost instantly he banished such a thought. It was just being privy to Fergus's plans that preoccupied him with thoughts of love.

The following morning he and Fergus drove to Green Street together. Mr. Fairweather intended to take Felicity out on a morning drive while the earl conducted his tête-à-tête with Rosalind.

"Well, my lord, you came," Rosalind said, strolling into the blue drawing room after Fergus and Felicity had departed.

"Yes," he agreed, taking note of those violet eyes, which looked more magnificent than ever. "It was *too* good of you to allow me a few moments' conversation with you."

She bit back a gurgle of laughter. "Oh, sit down, do." She pointed to a chair. "I don't even know what it is you wish to speak to me about."

"Don't you?" he asked cordially, seating himself. "I suppose any number of topics might suffice. We could start off with the weather, but I daresay there are forty-two thousand *other* things that might come to mind."

"There is nothing to discuss," Rosalind said, throwing

all pretense to the wind. "I am in your debt. And I mean to pay you back."

"Bah!" he scowled. "You owe me nothing."

"Gerald does. I suppose marrying into my family was so horrid that forty-two thousand pounds seemed a paltry amount to part with?"

"I shall not dignify that idiotish statement with a reply," he said coldly. "You've never seen fit to repay your brother's debts before. Why the sudden compulsion now?"

She frowned. "I dislike being beholden to you."

"You shall have to grow accustomed to it," he replied, not unkindly. "I shan't take any of your money. And even though Baverstock has informed me that you settled the sums in my account, I am ordering that they be returned to your account."

"I will refuse to take them back," she countered mulishly.

"Then we are at an impasse," he pointed out, dipping two fingers into his snuffbox. "Perhaps a third opinion would help in unraveling this coil. Shall we ask your fiancé for assistance?"

"My fiancé?"

"Yes." Eberhart gazed at her blandly. "Have you forgotten Waldo so quickly? I was under the impression that the two of you would shortly be pursuing a life of wedded bliss."

"Oh, *that*!" she said distractedly.

"I don't suppose Waldo knows about this, or does he?" the earl inquired.

"No, and he is not to know," she commanded. "This is none of his affair. I don't want him dragged into it. I forbid you to say a word to him."

The earl blinked. "You *forbid* me?"

She lifted her chin. "Yes!"

For a moment he was tempted to unleash a thundering setdown, but her flagrant disregard for his rank tickled his sense of the ridiculous.

"Where did you get the money?" he asked mildly.

"That is none of your affair. It is perfectly legitimate, I assure you."

"I was not accusing you of counterfeiting, Miss McHenry," he said, wondering why she must take issue with each of his statements. A sudden light dawned. "You applied to Waldo for the loan, didn't you? That's why you're marrying him. My dear girl. I would never allow such martyrdom."

"I am not a martyr," she said, flinching from the pity and alarm she spied in his eyes. "Heavens! And you accuse *me* of being melodramatic, sir. Viscount Coppleton and I have been acquainted for years, and when he offered for me last week I decided to accept him."

"I'd sooner accept a Hindu," the earl muttered as he put his snuffbox back in his pocket.

Rosalind's eyes flashed. "My lord, I did not invite you here to listen to you cast aspersions on the gentleman to whom I shall shortly be wed."

"If I don't cast them, you might actually wed him," Eberhart retorted. "And really, there is no need for such self-sacrifice. I'm not saying Waldo isn't a good soul, for he is. But there's not much in his old cockloft, is there?"

"Waldo's cockloft is my concern, Eberhart, not yours!" Rosalind replied, coloring furiously. "And if I say he suits me, that is that."

"Is this storm of protest meant to convince me or yourself?" he asked delicately.

"Oh, you are impossible!"

"I suppose Waldo is cast in alt by the wedding. When is the great day? Fergus is planning his wedding. Perhaps you could make it a double wedding."

Rosalind held her temper in check with a Herculean effort. "I don't know when the wedding will be, sir, but you won't be invited."

"That's deuced uncivil of you," he protested. "I've just finished wishing you happy."

"You have done nothing of the sort. You've been asking the most impertinent questions on matters that do not concern you."

"Oh, they haven't been that impertinent," he said. "Had I really wanted to act in a coming way, I should have asked if you love Waldo, but that is one question I'm sure you would not dare to answer truthfully!"

A half hour later Rosalind sat jabbing a needle into her embroidery, wishing that her tambour frame were Eberhart's skin. His parting words still rang in her ears. Love Waldo? She wasn't prepared to go that far. But there was no law that said marriages must be for love. If such a law were enacted, half the married people in the kingdom would undoubtedly be rendered single again!

She wasn't in love with Waldo, but she did admire him. No, admire wasn't the right word. She tried again. She did like him. He was kind, as a rule, patient to a fault, and always did exactly as she commanded. He would make her the perfect husband.

These thoughts, which should have reassured her, fell sadly short of banishing her qualms. She pushed aside her stitchery, finding it wholly impossible to concentrate. Eberhart was the most autocratic, high-handed, overbearing man she had ever met. And that's what made Gerald's debt to him so difficult for her to countenance. She would *not* be beholden to him. And her marriage to Waldo would be a happy one if she killed them both trying to prove it!

Unaware of the dire plans Rosalind was sketching for them, Viscount Coppleton stood in the midst of Davidson's shop, tolerating the usually protracted fitting that would occupy his morning.

"By the by, Davidson," he said as the tailor tucked and pinned, "I shall be needing a wedding suit in the near future. I leave the matter in your hands. Something simple and yet elegant."

"Of course, my lord, of course," the tailor murmured. "Might I be among the first to wish you happy?"

Waldo's face creased in a vacuous smile. "Why, thank you, Davidson. That's devilishly civil of you."

The tailor laid down his measuring stick. "Might I inquire who the lucky lady is?"

"Miss Rosalind McHenry," Waldo said, gazing at his profile in the mirror and feeling rather satisfied with the reflection. He might not be a Corinthian, but his cravat was the equal of any gentleman's.

"Miss Rosalind McHenry." The tailor continued to sit back on his heels. "An unexceptional choice! But if you plan to marry, you will need more than just a wedding suit, my lord. Permit me to show you a few of my sketches."

After a half hour spent approving several of Davidson's designs for the newly married gentleman, it was no surprise that when Waldo emerged from his tailor looking bang up to the nines, thoughts of his wedding were fixed in his brain. As he strolled along Bond Street, he felt himself the luckiest of men, having won the lady he had pursued for years and earning for his efforts the congratulations of several elderly gentlemen at White's. And several of the younger sprigs at the club had asked him to divulge just what strategy he had used in winning Rosalind's hand at last.

An honest soul, Waldo had endeavored as best he could to answer the question, but he didn't know exactly how he had won her over. One moment she was laughing off all his entreaties to marry him. And the very next she was seizing him, metaphorically speaking, to her bosom.

Of course, females were a peculiar sex. It was not in Waldo's nature to question his luck. Rosalind had accepted him. And if only she would set a date for their nuptials he would be totally satisfied. But each time he had broached the topic she brushed it aside. Perhaps today they would settle the matter once and for all when he drove her in the Park.

Rosalind herself noticed that Waldo was even more garrulous than usual during their carriage ride. Even before she had been fully settled in the vehicle he had begun an exhaustive recital of his morning with Davidson. Without pausing to take a breath he had next dwelled at length on his evening ahead at White's.

"I shall probably lose at whist," he said philosophically,

"but you know that old saying: unlucky in cards, lucky in love!"

"I have heard of it," Rosalind said, adjusting the chip hat she wore. "But all the same, Waldo, I should hate for you to be too unlucky in cards."

"I never play for more than is comfortable," he told her as they turned into the Park, which was already thronged with carriages and riders. "I say, isn't that Eberhart riding by himself?"

"Where?" Rosalind asked, then caught sight of the earl cantering on horseback. He stopped every now and then to pay his compliments to several ladies out enjoying the fashionable hour. The exchanges so gracefully given and so coyly accepted irritated Rosalind beyond belief.

"What did he want with you?" Waldo asked.

She looked up, momentarily flustered. "With me?"

"Yes." He seemed puzzled. "Didn't he mean to speak with you today? He said so yesterday outside of Rundell's."

"Oh, that," Rosalind put in hastily. "That was nothing important. Do go on about your visit to Davidson."

"I told you most of it," Waldo said, falling in agreeably with this opening. "I wanted him to fix me up right and proper for our wedding. And that reminds me, I've written up the announcement to be sent to the *Gazette*. I know you are too busy to see to the matter. Shall I send it in to be published?"

Rosalind opened her mouth in automatic protest, then closed it. "Certainly, if you wish it, Waldo. But perhaps your mother would lodge an objection."

Waldo frowned. "How could she? She's back in Kent."

"Exactly my point," Rosalind said, improvising feverishly. "She might wish to send the announcement in herself. Some mothers do, particularly those with only sons."

"I hadn't thought of that," Waldo admitted, turning the carriage around the Serpentine.

"And," Rosalind went on, "we must not allow ourselves to be premature."

"Premature?!" Waldo pouted. "Dash it all, Rosalind, we are getting married, aren't we?"

"Yes, yes, of course," she soothed. "It's just that we ought to wait until your mama tells us how she wishes the announcement handled and other things," she finished lamely.

He conceded the point, none too graciously. "I don't see why Mama must settle the month for us. It's already April. Is May too soon? Do you prefer June?"

"Waldo," Rosalind pleaded. "Of course we shall settle on a date for our wedding. But need we do so now? This very second?"

"No, I suppose not. But we shall have to decide soon enough," he said in a cheerful tone that quite inexplicably cast his companion into the fiercest gloom.

Although Rosalind and Waldo's engagement had not been formally announced, word of what was afoot had reached Waldo's aunt, Lady Bonham, who demanded to meet the prospective bride. Lady Bonham was the elder sister of Lady Coppleton, and she wielded enormous power within the family. So on Friday evening, at approximately the same time that Mrs. Hubbel was making her debut with the Italian Company across town, Waldo accompanied Rosalind to the Bonham residence on Hill Street.

Dreading the inevitable encounter—what rational female would look forward to being interrogated by a tartar?—Rosalind was even more discomfited to find the drawing room filled with Waldo's relations.

"Waldo," she hissed as she took in the numerous cousins, aunts, and uncles, "did you know they were going to be here?"

"No, 'pon rep," he protested. "Aunt Gertrude said not a word to me. But there's no harm done. You would have met most of them at our wedding."

Rosalind paled slightly as she smoothed a fold of her silver-colored silk. Hitherto she had thought of marrying Waldo as a civil arrangement, but seeing his relations gathered under one roof she was aware of the finality of such a step.

"Waldo, my dear," a plump matron in a vivid blue turban said as she advanced their way.

"Cousin Winifred, how do you do?" Waldo said, kissing her on the cheek. "May I present Miss McHenry?"

Rosalind shook hands with the other woman.

"Waldo and I are cousins," Winifred explained. "Naturally when my grandmother told me he was thinking of marrying, I was in a pelter to meet his bride-to-be. And when I finally won her permission to come tonight, Celia, my sister, decided that she must be here, too."

"That explains why everyone is here," Waldo said.

"Not everyone!" Winifred corrected. "Uncle Harry and Aunt Mildred live in Yorkshire, and a few others couldn't make it this evening. But Grandmama is a little cross about us all being underfoot. She vows that she didn't undertake to feed an army of relations. None of us are allowed to consume as much as one lobster patty."

"Winifred, what are you babbling about?" Another matron joined their group. "I'm Celia," she said, drawing Rosalind aside as Winifred went off. "Waldo, you mustn't let Winnie bore your friend to death."

"Oh, she wasn't doing that!" Rosalind protested.

Celia made a face. "Civil of you to say that, but I know different. I'm her sister, after all. She's been boring me to tears since the day she was born. I daresay you must feel as though you've been set upon by Huns."

"No, actually—"

"Don't bother to peel eggs with me. Waldo will help you sort us out. Not that there's much to distinguish us. Rather ordinary family. Just don't call me Winifred and we'll get along. There's Bertie and George with Abner and Hiram. And that's Pamela's youngest. She'll be out next Season. Don't worry," she told an increasingly bewildered Rosalind. "We shan't eat you. That's Grandmama's privilege."

With a snort of laughter she led Rosalind to a figure seated in the corner. Lady Bonham dressed in stiff, starched black bore an alarming similarity to Lady Coppleton and Waldo.

"Waldo will make the introductions," Celia said cheerfully, departing for the refreshment table.

"You took your time bringing Miss McHenry to me, Waldo," Lady Bonham said.

"I beg pardon, Aunt Gertrude. We were speaking with Winifred and Celia."

"Winifred is a goosecap, and so's Celia, for that matter," Lady Bonham said trenchantly. She pounded her cane into the rug, then pointed to a chair. "Sit there."

Waldo obeyed instantly. His aunt cracked him across the knee with the cane.

"Not you, dolt. Your friend."

"Oh, beg pardon." With some confusion and a certain amount of pain he exchanged places with Rosalind, then looked uncertainly at his aunt. "What should I do, Aunt Gertrude?"

"Go eat a lobster patty," she ordered. "But mind, not too many of them or you'll wind up with gout and dyspepsia like me."

Looking suitably chastened by the thought of such a future, Waldo sped off, leaving Rosalind to inquire if Lady Bonham did indeed suffer from both gout and dyspepsia.

"One I could see, but two seems an intolerable burden."

This won a bark of laughter from her hostess. "You won't like the lobster patties," she confided. "My chef is notoriously temperamental."

Rosalind's initial uneasiness faded into amusement. Lady Bonham was still daunting, with a heavily rouged face and a mop of tight little curls, but the blue eyes burned bright with curiosity and not malice, and Rosalind found herself intrigued at matching wits with her.

"Gerald McHenry is your brother, I'm told."

"That's right," Rosalind said, surprised by this opening.

"A wastrel and a profligate," the old woman said, with a challenge in her eyes.

"I've told him the same thing many times."

Lady Bonham grunted. "He was set to match his daughter with Eberhart, I have heard."

"Yes, that was the initial plan, but they decided they wouldn't suit."

Lady Bonham nodded. "He'd have led her a sorry dance. Oh, there's nothing wrong with Alastair. But he doesn't need a schoolroom miss for a wife. He needs a strong woman. I've told his mother so. She agrees. She may look like a frivolous widgeon, but she's not." She cackled.

"Took us all by surprise when she landed Manning, which just goes to show one is never at one's last prayers!"

"Lady Manning seems very happy with Lord Manning."

"Have you met Waldo's mother?"

"Briefly, ma'am. She was in London earlier, and Waldo arranged a meeting." She searched desperately for something she could say in praise of Lady Bonham's sister. "She seems devoted to her children."

Lady Bonham cackled again. "She's a quack. She wasn't always like that, mind. Waldo's father encouraged her. It gave her something to do while he was out gadding about. And after her children came she transferred her imaginary ailments to them. Does she know about you and Waldo?"

"Waldo wrote a letter, I believe."

"And she'll probably receive a letter from the likes of them." Lady Bonham bobbed her head at the cluster of her female relations. "Bunch of hens. A pity they are all so ordinary-looking."

"I think them very pleasant," Rosalind protested.

"Pleasant, yes: good-looking, no," Lady Bonham said bluntly. "I give you the word with no bark on it, Miss McHenry. Our family was never famed for its looks. Maybe Waldo had the right notion to marry someone with your beauty. New blood might be what it takes. Lord knows, the family could do with some handsomeness." She shook her head. "Just don't be too surprised if your children take after Waldo instead of you. Won't matter with sons, of course, but daughters . . ."

Rosalind was torn between amusement and dismay. Indeed, she had not gone so far as to picture herself mother to anyone. And yet Lady Bonham's comment was not too far off the mark, judging by the faces surrounding her. They all bore an alarming resemblance to Waldo.

"Why are you marrying Waldo?" Lady Bonham asked bluntly.

Rosalind looked up in surprise. "He made me the offer."

"But why Waldo? Surely you've had other offers. You ain't a Homely Joan."

Rosalind shrugged, wondering what to say to Waldo's aunt. "It seemed like a congenial arrangement," she said finally.

"Love him?"

She felt her cheeks flush. Whatever she had expected of the interview, it was not to be asked such intimate questions. Lady Bonham clucked her tongue.

"Don't need to say another syllable, my dear. I can see you don't. You didn't strike me as a wet goose. Nothing about Waldo that a female like you could love!"

"Really, Lady Bonham," Rosalind exclaimed. "You misjudge my feelings for Waldo. He's warm and so eager to please."

"So's a puppy. Would you marry one?"

There was no sensible reply to such a question.

"You think I'm poking my nose into what doesn't concern me, don't you?" Lady Bonham asked, her voice surprisingly gentle.

"Well, yes."

The face of the old woman softened momentarily. "Marriage does strange things to a female, Miss McHenry. It changes her for good or ill. Just look at me. I wasn't always such a bag of bones. Be careful whom you marry, that's what I say. His habits have a way of rubbing off on you."

"Lady Bonham, do you disapprove of my marrying into your family?"

"God's sake, girl, of course not. I'm no fool. I just think you'd be wiser not to marry Waldo. You probably know that yourself." Their eyes locked momentarily, and Rosalind was silent.

"Didn't mean to get on my high horse," Lady Bonham said briskly. "You'll do as you think best, of course. Now you'd better grab a lobster patty before my relations devour them all. I should be upstairs myself with a bowl of gruel."

This Rosalind accurately took to be a dismissal, and she went off to the refreshment room, mulling over the curious talk with Lady Bonham. It had disturbed her almost as much as the idea of giving birth to children who all looked exactly like Waldo!

Chapter Sixteen

Miss Rosalind McHenry announces with pleasure the impending wedding of her beloved niece, Felicity, to Mr. Fergus Fairweather.

The announcement in Monday's *Gazette* was short and to the point, but not short enough to suit Mr. Gideon Dankley. The lines of print jumped back and forth as he read the announcement through a second time, growing even more infuriated. By all rights the *Gazette* should have been announcing Felicity's impending marriage to him and not to some secretary!

Brooding over what might have been had it not been for the interference of Eberhart, Dankley tossed the newspaper aside and uncorked a bottle of claret. The earl might accept the ignominy of being bested by a secretary, but not so Mr. Dankley.

He had thought himself close to securing a position worthy of himself. Hitherto all he had to boast about was a small niche amid the lower strata of Society. He had tried for years to improve that position through marriage, but while gentlemen might accept funds from him when hard pressed and enjoy his conversation over whist they refused to entertain the possibility of his marrying any of their daughters. His reputation as a rake hadn't helped matters, either.

Except when it came to McHenry, who was too far in debt to quibble over the niceties. Unfortunately Eberhart had stolen a march on him by broaching the matter of marriage with Felicity to Gerald first.

Mr. Dankley turned his wineglass over in his hand. Although some men might have married Felicity for her youthful beauty and sweet nature, Dankley did not care about these virtues. Youth and beauty soon faded, as he knew well after a lifetime in the muslin company. He was after her position in the *ton*. Her lineage was impeccable, and it was that which Dankley craved.

Now all that had been snatched out of his grasp. Finishing his first bottle of claret, he started on a second. Damn Eberhart! If he hadn't wanted the chit he should have bowed out, not pushed his secretary forward. Dankley's lips twisted again. Bested by a secretary.

Everyone was probably reading the betrothal notice and laughing at him behind his back. That notion, mingled with the wine he had consumed, fouled his temper even more. By the time the second bottle was down to its dregs he had reached his Rubicon. He would show the entire family and that precious earl just whom they had slighted. But how? That was the crux of the problem he contemplated through the haze of drink. It would not be wise to plot against Eberhart openly. Mr. Dankley flung his wine bottle into the fireplace. But, by Jove, he would think of a way.

While Mr. Dankley sat preoccupied with malevolent thoughts, Eberhart was pondering anew the mulish nature of Rosalind McHenry. She had indeed made micefeet out of his attempt to return her money. On any given morning he would order Baverstock to transfer the funds to her account, but by noon she would have commissioned it back to him.

"Why doesn't she just let the matter rest?" he complained to his mother.

Lady Manning had heard with delight the story behind her son and Miss McHenry's strange banking impasse from Mr. Baverstock, with whom she was long acquainted. She glanced over at the lanky figure of her son, sprawled on her crocodile-legged couch.

"I suspect, Alastair, that she is just as stubborn as you!"

"Stubborn!" A protest registered in the earl's voice. "This isn't mere stubbornness, Mama. You wouldn't wish me to accept money from a lady, now, would you?"

Lady Manning patted a few wispy curls from her brow.

"Accept money? Of course not. But I can understand how she considers it a debt of honor that must be repaid."

"It's nothing of the sort," Eberhart said, rising irritably and striding the length of the room, nearly crashing into a Chinese screen his stepfather had just purchased. "She doesn't owe me a groat. It's that brother of hers who owes it, and he shan't pay it for I cancelled it. Why does she insist now on shouldering that burden?"

"Perhaps because you are the one he is indebted to," Lady Manning said wisely, wincing as she watched the black Hessians treading on her precious Wilton.

"Speak to her, Mama," the earl implored. "You are such friends with her. She must be induced to let the matter rest! I feel like such a nodcock when I go to the bank and discover the funds have been transferred back to me. That idiot Baverstock sits grinning at me."

Lady Manning, who had shared several of the banker's personal opinions on the peculiar situation he found himself in, hid a smile.

"You are not the first gentleman to feel idiotish at the hands of a lady, Alastair."

"No. And I'm not the only one that Miss McHenry has made a fool of," he said, stopping in mid-stride an inch in front of the screen.

"Will you sit down?" his mother pleaded. "Who else has Miss McHenry made foolish?"

"Waldo," the earl answered, sinking down again on the couch. "I'll wager a monkey she bamboozled him into lending her part of the money to repay me. She doesn't have the entire amount. That's why she agreed to marry Coppleton."

Lady Manning fiddled with her stitchery. "Perhaps not. Waldo is a very congenial soul."

Her son stared at her as though at a phantom. "Mama. He's a bore. A very civil bore, I grant you, but a bore nevertheless. And so lacking in wit—"

"He is pleasant-looking."

"So is a horse," Eberhart scoffed.

His mother fixed a quelling eye on her son. "A lady might do worse than Viscount Coppleton, Alastair."

"Mama, you can't honestly believe that Rosalind boasts a *tendre* for Waldo."

"Perhaps not a *tendre*," Lady Manning admitted. "But she seems fond of him."

Thinking it wisest to be off and allow the seed she had just planted to bear fruit, she then excused herself, pleading some morning calls of her own to be made.

The earl was dotingly fond of his mother, but on this matter he thought she was mistaken. He judged Miss McHenry's affection for Waldo as temperate at best, though of course she'd sooner perish than admit that to anyone. And perhaps death might be preferable to marrying Waldo!

Back at St. James Square he withdrew into his bookroom. Rosalind would never bow out of the match with Coppleton willingly. She'd go to St. George's, grim and determined to marry the viscount, and it would be on his conscience.

Eberhart gave a disgusted sigh. What, pray, was it about the McHenry females that made him feel guilty at the marriages they concocted for themselves? He certainly had had no part in Rosalind's betrothal to Waldo.

It would be hellish for her, all the same, to be saddled with a bore like Waldo for the rest of her days. But what the devil could he do about it? Advice was futile. She had never listened to a word he said. But could he just stand idly by and allow her to go to her doom?

He poured himself a sherry and pondered the dilemma. Rosalind would never break the engagement, but perhaps Waldo might, given the proper encouragement. Eberhart turned this promising notion over in his mind. In no time at all he was chuckling to himself.

He was still chuckling when he strolled into Lady Jersey's ballroom Saturday evening.

The Patroness, swathed in an exquisite sky-blue satin, exclaimed as she caught sight of him and clapped one hand to her bosom. "Eberhart, do my eyes deceive me? Is it really you?"

"Yes, Sally," he assured her. "This is Saturday the fifteenth, is it not? And you did dispatch a card to me."

"So I did, but with nary a hope of seeing you here," she

said, holding his extended hand to her heaving bosom. "My dear, the other hostesses in London shall be ready to kill me. I am in transports that you chose to make your reappearance at my ball. How comes it that so noted a recluse has decided to take part in the festivities?"

"Call it a whim," he said sweetly, reclaiming his hand and passing down the line.

He made his way to the ballroom after negotiating obstacles in the form of marriage-minded matrons with daughters to launch. He smiled civilly and even withstood introductions to several simpering misses, but ultimately he pressed on to the ballroom, where he hoped to find Waldo and Rosalind. He had it on the very best authority possible—his own mother!—that they would be in attendance this evening.

"And Mama is never wrong," he murmured, finally catching sight of a familiar figure in a beguiling green satin gauze. Her raven hair, done up in ringlets, fell to her shoulders and made her look more youthful than before. He made his way leisurely toward her, a move noted avidly by Lady Jersey, Lady Manning, and Rosalind herself.

"Good evening, Miss McHenry," he greeted her with a bow.

"Good evening, Lord Eberhart," Rosalind replied, wondering why he was smiling so complacently.

"Waldo." The earl bowed politely to the viscount.

"Hallo, Eberhart."

"Would you allow me the honor of a waltz, Miss McHenry? I hope I am not too late to beg one from you."

Her lip twitched slightly. "Beg, my lord?"

His eyes met hers. "That is the proper term when a gentleman desires a dance, is it not?" he quizzed.

"I suppose so," she conceded. "And I do owe you a waltz from before."

They glided off, conscious of the bemused glances of several of the Patronesses.

"What are you up to, Eberhart?" Rosalind asked.

"Is it so astonishing that I should wish to waltz? As you reminded me, I did ask you for one some time ago."

"But why tonight?" she said with a tiny frown. "You haven't attended a soiree in a fortnight."

She found the gleam in his eyes disconcerting. "I had no idea you were so intimately acquainted with my activities," he drawled.

She blushed. "I am not intimately acquainted with your activities, but it is well known that ever since your return from the country you have been avoiding the balls as though we all had the plague."

"No fear of the plague, ma'am," he replied, moving her adroitly away from the lummoxlike Major Winchester dancing inches away. "Merely a dislike of being bored. Suffice to say that the life of a hermit began to bore me. You waltz divinely."

"I am delighted to have won your approbation, sir," she said demurely.

He laughed. "Minx."

She smiled reluctantly.

"Are you spoken for for supper?" he asked as he twirled her breathlessly toward the opposite end of the room.

"Naturally I had assumed I would sup with Waldo," she said, rather out of breath from the last dizzying set of spins.

"If he hasn't asked you, then he is too late," the earl declared. "I shall take you in."

"Eberhart!" she exclaimed, intrigued at his audacity. "You have been out of the swim too long. That is not the way you invite a lady to sup, although I'm sure you meant it as a compliment."

He glanced down at her upturned nose, which shone slightly with perspiration. "A compliment, Miss McHenry? Any other female after a waltz and invitation to supper would be busily ordering her trousseau!"

"Fustian!"

He lifted a brow. "Fustian? Permit me to say I have met more marriage-minded females than you. I know I am right. And it is not all fustian rubbish. You are a charming lady when you aren't flying into the boughs with me. And, if I may boast a trifle, I am alleged to possess a modicum of charm. So it would not be too preposterous for the two of us to meet and become besotted with each other.''

"Except,'' she said, cordially interrupting this scenario, "that we have met and, far from being besotted with each other, we took each other in a hearty dislike.''

"A mistake easily mended. Supper, then?''

"Lord Eberhart, why are you flirting with me in so outrageous a fashion? You forget yourself. I am practically betrothed to Viscount Coppleton.''

"Yes, and doubtless you are counting the days until your exchange of vows?'' he asked, and was rewarded by her choke of laughter.

"You are incorrigible. And you are forgetting Waldo is watching us.''

"You are wrong there,'' he said mildly. "I haven't forgotten old Waldo, even though he might have slipped *your* mind on occasion.''

"He has not,'' she denied vehemently. "He is an excellent person, and I shan't listen to you say a word against him.''

"Don't get on your high ropes,'' he said dampeningly. "You aren't married to him yet.''

After the waltz he led her back toward a chair. It had been fun to pretend to flirt with her. Now if only Waldo had been paying attention. When he found the viscount, Eberhart fully expected to be taken to task for flirting openly with Rosalind: instead, Waldo insisted that Eberhart be the final judge of the snuff he and Wilding were sampling.

It would take more than one flirtatious episode to get Waldo's dander up enough to break his engagement to Rosalind, the earl decided as Wilding and Coppleton debated the merits of dry versus wet snuff.

He made no further attempt to waltz with Rosalind, nor did he stand up with anyone else. After his supper, which he took in the company of his mother and stepfather, he left for White's, leaving behind the prattle boxes to indulge freely in speculation about why he had come to Lady Jersey's ball if only to dance one dance with Rosalind McHenry!

Chapter Seventeen

The next morning Rosalind, accompanied by John, her stalwart groom, approached the entrance to the Park just as a mounted figure stepped out from the shadows.

"You are late, Miss McHenry," Eberhart called out. "I suppose you stayed rather late at Lady Jersey's affair?"

"I was home by one, my lord," she said, soothing her frightened mare. "And what do you mean by frightening me like that? And how do you know I'm late?" she demanded. "Have you been spying on me?"

His smile broadened. "Nothing so cloak-and-dagger, I do assure you. And nothing to fly into a pet about. Will you ride this way or that?"

She pointed her crop toward her preferred route, and they set out together, trailed at a discreet distance by John. The pace she set was a brisk one, and Eberhart, riding smoothly next to her, approved of her obvious ease with the rein.

"A nice mare," he commented as they paused to watch children sailing their boats across the lake.

"It was a gift from Waldo."

"A wedding gift?"

Instead of answering, she shrugged a shoulder, preferring not to dwell on her impending marriage to the viscount. She rode on, and the earl, smiling to himself, followed.

Although it was early by town standards, they were not the only riders in the Park, and several curious glances came their way. Some were so quizzing that Rosalind peeked over her shoulder for John, who had unfortunately dawdled behind in the mistaken notion that his mistress desired privacy.

"Are the Runners after you, Miss McHenry?" Eberhart drawled.

"John is trailing so far behind."

"I would consider that an excellent trait in a groom," he said dryly.

"Ordinarily I might agree, but you do see the awkwardness."

"No, I don't," he said, thinking that her burgundy riding habit brought out the unusual color of her eyes.

"Don't be blockish, Eberhart," she said with some exasperation. "I shouldn't have to spell it out for you. There are people who might see us together, and since their minds and intellects are not large—"

"Are you perchance speaking of your illustrious fiancé?" he asked, admiring the flash of color in her cheeks from the morning wind.

"I am not!" Her tone was scorching, and two spots of color mounted in her cheeks. "I refer to those who might have seen us. They can leap to unpleasant conclusions, particularly since John insists on loitering behind us."

"But that's absurd," he said. "You are in the habit of riding alone with your groom far behind. I recall as much from seeing you in the past. Today I merely happened to intercept you. I assure you, I am not about to seduce you in broad daylight."

She choked on a laugh. "I know that. But do think of my situation. I am practically betrothed to Waldo."

"You keep reminding me of that. But practically betrothed ain't the same as married for better or for worse." He paused to let his words sink in. "Odd that you dispatched the announcement about Felicity to the *Gazette* and did not include your own."

"Eberhart, I wish you would stop commenting on my marriage."

"Guilty conscience?"

"Nothing of the sort." She glared at him. "What is there for me to be guilty about?"

He flicked a speck of dust from the coat of his velvet riding habit. "Females are a romantic lot. Perhaps you feel guilty marrying Waldo, since you don't have much of a *tendre* for him. Or are you now going to tell me you are nursing a grand passion for him?''

"My *tendres* are my own affair, Eberhart,'' Rosalind said, her eyes slanting dangerously.

"I didn't mean to set your back up,'' he said cheerfully and not quite truthfully. "Strange how my mentioning Waldo always makes you skittish. I shan't say another word about him. Shall we simply enjoy what is left of our morning ride?''

After his ride with Rosalind ended, Eberhart paid an impromptu call on Isabelle. He was not the least surprised to find her entertaining several callers. Nonetheless she flitted over to bestow a peck on his cheek.

"You didn't stay long Friday night,'' she chided. "And on the night of my triumph, too. I should be vexed with you, Alastair!''

"The house was overly full with your well-wishers,'' he said, kissing her hand. "I would have only gotten in the way. Besides, I didn't wish to be trampled by the horde.''

Her laughter bubbled up quickly. "And,'' he added as he flicked her cheek with a forefinger, "you didn't miss me, I daresay.'' He glanced about him, nodding to a half dozen acquaintances before finding a pair of stormy eyes staring daggers at him. He struggled to place the downy face.

"Isabelle, who is that mooncalf you have roped?'' he asked.

She repressed a chuckle. "That is Lord Michael Hastings, Eberhart, a most estimable young man.''

"Is he, now? Well, someone ought to tell him not to glower at his elders. I suppose he is top over tail in love with you! Bit wet behind the ears for your tastes, I would have thought.''

"He is just as old as you were when we first met,'' she replied calmly. "In fact, he reminds me strongly of you.''

The earl recoiled. "Isabelle, do spare my blushes. Enough of such nonsense. Tell me, has Orsini signed you to a long contract?''

"No.''

"What?" Eberhart could not fully mask his dismay. He would have wagered anything that Orsini would have tried to get Isabelle into his company.

"Oh, he tried to get me to sign a contract right in the middle of the celebration. Can you imagine anything more gauche? But I'm biding my time. I've had two other offers from theaters."

"Well, well, first rate. It's what you were after, wasn't it?"

"It's beyond that. And I owe it all to you, Alastair," she said, gazing at him fondly.

"Fiddle. I merely gave you a ride to London. You were the one who took the stage by storm."

"There is just one small thing, Alastair," she said, gazing at him intently. "It's Lord Michael. He's asked me, implored me, actually, to move out of this house and into a larger residence that he owns. I told him I was perfectly comfortable here, but he is quite insistent. So, if you think it would be all right, I should like to accept. He even gave me this." She showed off the necklace around her throat, a dazzling array of sapphires and emeralds.

"Very pretty."

"Yes, isn't it?" she said naïvely. "I don't think I've ever seen anything half so pretty, not even from you or Olaf."

"It has the look of an heirloom," he said, examining it more closely with his quizzing glass.

She giggled. "Yes, I know. His mother is furious with him."

It was impossible not to laugh along with her. If young Hastings was bestowing heirlooms on Isabelle he was truly besotted. And perhaps Isabelle, whose heart was the good sort, might wind up married once more, and to a peer this time. If so, he could not stand in her way.

"So you are leaving me again, and for a green one like Hastings."

She gave him a quick look of concern. "If you don't like the notion, Alastair, I'll stay on here. I owe you so much."

"You owe me nothing," he said, kissing her hand. "There. That ought to inflame your beau. Go to him before he calls me out, and," he could not resist adding, "do invite me to the wedding."

He left Isabelle's, satisfied with the way things had turned out. She would make Hastings a capable wife. Now, if only he could contrive as agreeable an ending for Miss McHenry!

Eberhart's campaign to prove to Rosalind how ill-fated the match between herself and Waldo was led him to a small fair outside London one afternoon later that week. He had it on the excellent authority of his mother that Miss McHenry would be in attendance with Waldo, having given that as her excuse when she declined Lady Manning's invitation to tea.

As he strolled about the grounds, children dashed in between the roving clowns, jugglers, and gypsies. It was a pity Alec and Mark weren't with him, he thought, surprised by a pang of genuine regret. They were an impudent pair of pups, but all the same he did enjoy them. He bought an ice and nibbled it absently, wondering where Waldo and Rosalind could be.

At the precise moment that Lord Eberhart was finishing up the remains of his strawberry ice, Rosalind and Waldo could be found under a striped tent surveying the vials and potions spread out on a table.

"Dr. Franklin's Magic Elixir," the seller said eagerly. "Drunk, it cleanses the blood and purges the liver, rubbed on the temples it will cure the headache, and on the chest it wards off the grippe. Now, how many bottles, Miss?"

"None," Rosalind said, peering up from under a straw bonnet. "I'd rather have the ailments than such a cure, wouldn't you, Waldo?" She turned toward her companion, who was examining the elixir with great interest.

"Oh, I don't know, Rosalind," Waldo said. "If it can do all he says then it's certainly worth the cost. Wonder what it does for the gout."

"Cures it, my lord," the seller declared instantly.

"Waldo," Rosalind chided. "You can't be seriously considering purchasing such a thing."

"Not for myself," he said at once, coloring under her incredulous stare, "but for my mama. I daresay she hasn't heard of this elixir yet. It shall be a splendid treat for her. And I'll buy another bottle for my sister, Mary, and perhaps just one extra in case Mama should wish to share it with a friend.''

"That would be three bottles." The seller, quick to compute the sale, had already plucked the three bottles off his table. "There you are, my lord, three bottles for three pounds. Thank you very much.''

While the purchase was being completed, Rosalind wandered to another table. If Waldo should see these new vials, she mused, how many would he buy? She had the giddy image of the two of them laden with bottles as they made their return to London. Lady Bonham's words flitted into mind. Was Waldo fated to turn into as determined a quack as his mother?

"Is Miss interested in this?"

Rosalind looked up at a friendly gypsy woman. "No, thank you. I have not the slightest interest in tonics and medications.''

"Ah, but this one is different." The woman held out a vial. "A love potion, Miss.''

In spite of herself, Rosalind was intrigued. "Are they still making such things?" she asked. She took out the cork and inhaled a whiff. Her nose wrinkled.

"Oh, yes, and it works!''

"I think it unfair to induce love in such a fashion.''

"Oh no, Miss. This potion cures lovesickness. One never knows when someone will fall in love with the wrong man.''

"What do you have there?" Waldo peered over Rosalind's shoulder.

"A love potion.''

His face broke out in a smile. "By Jove, I wonder if it works.''

"It won't, Waldo.''

"Yes, but wouldn't it be something if it did?''

"It only costs a pound, my lord," the gypsy said.

"I'll buy it," Waldo said, fumbling with his purse and trying to keep from dropping the three bottles of elixir. Rosalind finally held them for him. "Mama can use the potion for Mary," he explained. "She fears that Mary will fall in love with someone ineligible. This will give her the means to right such a wrong."

"Waldo, I fear it's a sad waste of money," Rosalind said when they left the tent.

"Oh, you can't say that for certain," he countered. "It just might work."

"If so, I should have had it some weeks ago. I could have detached Felicity from her infatuation with Mr. Fairweather, and I wouldn't now be beholden to Eberhart."

"Beholden to Eberhart?" Waldo quizzed. "How are you beholden to him?"

Rosalind flushed, realizing her slip.

"Do you mean beholden because he cried off and Felicity is able to marry his secretary?" Waldo asked.

"Yes, yes, of course," she said, for once grateful for his obtuseness.

They continued to explore the fair, laughing at the clowns, marveling at the skill of the acrobats, and even taking in the tattooed man. That done, Waldo led Rosalind over toward a field where an archery contest was in progress.

"Don't they all look like Robin Hood?" he drawled.

One of the archers with his back to them caught Rosalind's eye. Tall and fair, with his coat off, he let fly arrow after arrow. So skillfully did he ply the bow that all were amazed. Rosalind joined in the applause until he turned around, and she recognized Eberhart.

"It's Alastair," Waldo said unnecessarily.

"Good afternoon, Miss McHenry," Eberhart said, wiping his damp forehead with a handkerchief. "Enjoying the fair in good company, I see."

"Very much," Rosalind replied.

"We've come across the best elixir known to man," Waldo told the earl. "And a love potion."

Eberhart raised one of his eyebrows in the daunting manner that always made Rosalind yearn to box his ears. "A love potion? Not content with one lovely lady, Waldo? Are you planning to put more females under your spell?"

"What?" Waldo looked dumbfounded.

"Eberhart is roasting you," Rosalind intervened. "The potion cures lovesickness rather than induces it."

"In which case," Eberhart murmured when Waldo strolled off to have a few words with some of the other archers, "I should advise you to take a healthy dose yourself, Miss McHenry."

"You are insufferable."

"Yes, I know," he said affably. "Perhaps we ought to peruse the fair and find a potion that cures a fever of the brain, for that is what you shall have if you marry such a bag pudding."

"Lord Eberhart!" Rosalind had no opportunity to unleash her outrage, for he had strolled off to challenge Waldo to a friendly contest of archery.

Well aware of the earl's superiority in sport, the viscount fought shy of the challenge until Eberhart offered to shoot left-handed.

"You can't ask for a better chance than that, Waldo."

"I suppose not," Waldo replied. "Very well." He turned to Rosalind, who had tried to dissuade him. "Just a little sport, my dear. Hold my coat and parcels, won't you?"

She had no choice but to acquiesce as he thrust these burdens upon her.

"Holding Waldo's coat, Miss McHenry?" the earl drawled as Waldo took some practice shots. "Quite in the chivalrous mode of old. Perhaps you have a scarf or glove he could carry with him."

"Do be quiet, Eberhart," she fumed.

He moved off, hiding a smile.

"Have you had sufficient practice, Waldo?" he asked after five minutes.

"I think so. Bow feels a trifle stiff."

"It shall feel more comfortable during the contest. Shall we say the best of five shots?"

"Done!"

As Waldo prepared to let fly the first arrow, Rosalind became aware of the interest the contest had aroused in several fairgoers. Wagers were being placed within plain sight of the competitors, and several unflattering remarks were heard as Waldo's first arrow landed well short of the target. Eberhart's first arrow was a bull's-eye, as were each of his next four. Waldo could do no better than to have one land on the target, the previous four having found the dirt.

By the time the competition ended Rosalind was beside herself with rage. How dared Eberhart subject Waldo to such a humiliation? Her mortification for Waldo was absolute, but the viscount himself took his thrashing in good humor.

"Next time I accept a challenge from you, it shall have to be with you blindfolded," he told Eberhart as he took his coat from Rosalind. "Sorry I couldn't win the match for you, my dear."

"You needn't repine," Rosalind replied. "You have more important things to attend to than some others who do nothing but indulge in stupid games of sport."

Her words startled the viscount and the earl. Still puzzled, Waldo acceded to Rosalind's request that he buy another bottle of Dr. Franklin's Elixir. This errand removed him from the vicinity while she gave Eberhart the set-down he deserved.

"Did you enjoy the contest, Miss McHenry?" the earl asked, unaware of her seething indignation.

"I did not," she snapped.

"Well, Waldo was never much with an arrow. Nor, now that I think of it, is he much with a pistol or sword. And we have discussed his poor seat before."

"Leave Waldo's poor seat alone," she exclaimed. "I know his talents and deficiencies. And now I know yours as well."

He gave her a modest smile. "Well, I vow, I am rather good with a bow. Of course, humility forbids me to speak of what I can do with a pistol or sword."

"Humility!" She gave a hoot of laughter. "How dare you speak of any such thing? There is not a modest bone in your body, my lord. You knew you would best Waldo, and in the most lowering fashion. I can't think that you possess an ounce of consideration for what he must be feeling."

The earl was taken aback. He had meant the match to prove to her what a poor specimen Waldo was. But he had not anticipated that it would drive her to his defense. Was there no understanding the female mind?

"Anyone with a pair of eyes can see how superior you are to Waldo. You needn't flaunt your advantages like an April squire."

"April squire, am I?" Eberhart looked black. "I at least am not a pea goose like you. Actually, I don't know why I concern myself with your stupid affairs. I should just let you marry that slow top."

"Oh, you are insufferable," Rosalind said, and she stormed away, almost bowling over Waldo and his fourth bottle of the magic elixir.

Eberhart watched them leave, the muscles of his jaw clenched with repressed anger. Much as he hated to acknowledge it, her reproaches had stung. While he had intended to win, he hadn't expected to knock the stuffing out of old Waldo. He certainly anticipated that Waldo could land his arrows on the target and hit more than one bull's-eye. At the same time, he knew he had foisted the contest on Coppleton.

The devil of it was that Rosalind herself knew what a bag pudding Waldo was, and it didn't seem to matter. She just leapt more to his defense. Such misguided loyalty amazed him, and yet, he was bound to admit with shock as he mulled over the matter, he was a trifle envious of old Waldo for having her loyalty, even undeserved.

Word of the archery match reached the ears of Coppleton's friends and Eberhart's. The earl, recalling Rosalind's strictures, went to considerable pains to dismiss the contest, stressing Waldo's unfamiliarity with the bow and arrow. By the end of a week he made it appear that Waldo had acquitted himself ably enough during the match.

Despite such protestations, however, it did appear to the more acute that Eberhart was trying to cut Waldo out with the McHenry chit.

"Not that it would be difficult," William Wilding quizzed as he strolled toward White's with Eberhart one evening. "Waldo ain't the nonpareil you are. But why the McHenry chit? I thought you were at dagger points with her."

"I was," Eberhart said, a look of mild abstraction on his face. "But within the past few days I've corrected my previous opinion of her."

Mr. Wilding stabbed his ivory-handled cane at the ground. "Then she ain't the most vexatious, high-handed, arrogant female you've ever laid eyes on?"

"Oh, she is, she is," the earl countered. "But she is also the most enchanting, charming creature."

Stunned by such words from a friend who was notoriously close-mouthed on the topic of female charms, Mr. Wilding could be excused for pushing back his high-crowned beaver felt and demanding to know if his friend was hoaxing him. And no one could blame him as he perused White's betting book later to determine if Alastair's courtship was prompted by a wager.

Eberhart, a fair man, did not blame Wilding for his incredulity. He was himself a trifle stunned by the tide of his own emotions and behavior. He had intended from the first only the mildest flirtation, aimed at cutting Waldo out and proving to Rosalind how ill-mated she and the viscount were. But as time went by, the flirtation ceased to be a game, and he had grown to anticipate seeing her and talking to her.

In plain truth the unthinkable had happened. Eberhart had fallen in love and with Rosalind McHenry, the female he had previously scorned. He who had blithely assumed a schoolroom miss would make the best wife now discovered that the only wife who would suit him was Rosalind, whom he had once stigmatized as opinionated, high-handed, and interfering. She was all that, but she was also high-spirited, keen of wit, graceful, and lovely—and, dash it all, still practically betrothed to Waldo!

Just as perplexed as Wilding on the matter of Eberhart's behavior was his beloved mother, who had discussed the issue at greath length with her husband, offering many diverse opinons and interpretations.

"It could be just a freakish whim," she said one morning. "I daresay Alastair could be prone to whim, but why doesn't he hit upon some other female? Why must it be dear Rosalind? Oh, Harry, I do hope he doesn't mean to raise expectations and then dash them."

Lord Manning glanced up from his copy of the *Racing News*. "I thought the chit was betrothed to another. Alastair wouldn't be raising expectations then, would he?"

"I suppose not," Lady Manning said, after mulling over this point. "But then why is he doing this when he knows quite well that Rosalind and Waldo are within an ames-ace of marching down St. George's, Hanover Square together?"

"Perhaps he doesn't know," Lord Manning replied, trying to return to his reading.

"He does! I told him so myself!"

At this news he lowered his magazine and gazed at her curiously. A pretty blush suffused her cheeks.

"Was there some particular reason you told Alastair such a thing?"

"I thought he should know," Lady Manning said defensively. "But I didn't suspect that he would begin a flirtation, for he seldom flirts with any female." She wrung her hands. "Oh, what is he up to? He abhors the Assemblies and claims to hate the Season. And yet he has appeared just to dance with Rosalind. Can it be?" She came to a sudden halt, her mouth rounded in amazement. "Can it be possible that he's fallen in love with her?"

Lord Manning fingered the ends of his mustache. "You're his mother. Ask him."

"I can't do any such thing!" she protested. "He's bound to cut up stiff at the merest mention of it. But that may be what has been ailing him," she chuckled. "Alastair in love. I should have known. It's the perfect match."

So flown into alt was she by the prospect of her son finally seeing the light that it was several minutes before Lord Manning could point out the only flaw in the scene she had sketched. Like it or not, Rosalind was still practically engaged at the moment—and to Waldo, not Alastair!

Chapter Eighteen

If Waldo had temporarily slipped Lady Manning's mind, he had not slipped Rosalind's. With each passing day she found herself dwelling more frequently on the viscount, particularly when she thought of Eberhart. Her annoyance with Eberhart for besting Waldo at archery had faded, especially after she learned how he had plumped up Waldo's role in the competition.

Of her own feelings for the earl it was difficult to speak. He had certainly aroused in her breast a veritable torrent of emotions from the first second she had clapped eyes on him. That had not changed a whit.

Not that she was impervious to his considerable charm. She knew that in the minds of several in the *ton*, including Waldo's aunt, Lady Bonham, the earl was attempting to fix an interest in her. He certainly seemed bent on flirting with her whenever their paths crossed. She neither encouraged it—for she did not wish to be stigmatized a hussy for encouraging one gentleman while practically betrothed to another—nor discouraged it, for she thought at times she glimpsed a warmer, less mocking glint in his gray eyes when they spoke. And yet what did it all mean?

Odious though it was to compare him to Waldo, it was wholly impossible not to, at times. On the one hand there was the viscount: civil, eager to please, prone to agree with everything she uttered, and, she could not help admitting, a hopeless bore. Then there was Eberhart: opinionated, frank, quick to antagonize her, and yet she had a growing propensity to like him.

Of course, that was folly, she told herself strictly as she

sat in her sitting room struggling vainly to concentrate on Felicity's copy of *Pride and Prejudice*. Nothing would come from nursing a *tendre* for Eberhart. He had all but declared his intention of thrusting a spoke in the wheel of her impending marriage to Waldo. A self-sacrifice, he had termed it weeks ago, and she wryly admitted as she laid aside Miss Austen's novel that he might not be wholly in the wrong there.

Yet despite what Lady Bonham had said of his having the unmistakable look of a man in love, she knew different. Eberhart was not dangling after her out of any real affection or—she was obliged to swallow a large lump in her throat— love, but as a means of getting her or a scandalized Waldo to cry off the match. It was another of his high-handed methods of forcing her to admit that he was right and she was wrong. When she had done so, he would probably retire from the scene.

She blinked back a sudden rush of tears. If only his attentions had been motivated differently. But there was not a jot of sense in indulging in such an airdream. Rosalind had always prided herself on having a practical mind, and however much she would have liked to delude herself into thinking she was the true object of the earl's interest, her mind insisted she not be such a wet goose.

Forcing herself to face this unpleasant truth, she decided that she would not allow him to make her the object of any more spurious flirtation.

At their very next encounter, at Almack's on Wednesday night, she turned him a cold shoulder, fobbing him off on a cluster of girls newly emerged from their schoolrooms.

"What was the meaning of that little charade?" he demanded later, after he had escaped from them.

"I thought you might wish to meet them, my lord," she said, fanning herself with a Chinese lacquered fan.

"If I desire to meet nursery brats, I can find them myself," he retorted. "Are you spoken for for this waltz?"

"Yes," she said, meeting his eyes defiantly. "Colonel Fitzgerald asked me earlier in the evening."

The earl stroked his chin. "Rather odd. Fitzgerald avows

a strong aversion to dancing. You can't fool me, Miss Mc-
Henry.''

''I don't wish to fool you or dance with you,'' she said
hotly.

''Do lower your voice,'' he advised. ''Three Patronesses
have their six eyes on us!''

''If they do it's because you have made me the target of
on dits.''

He was unprepared for this charge and for the tremulous
look in her eyes.

''My dear,'' he protested, fighting a real compunction to
take her in his arms, Patronesses or no Patronesses.

''I am not your dear,'' she railed. ''And I do wish you
would stop plaguing me. Go off, why don't you, and plague
your friend, Isabelle Hubbel!'' she blurted out, then paled at
the stony expression that overcame his face.

''I say, Rosalind, is anything amiss?'' Waldo asked,
sauntering over with a smile on his face.

''Merely a slight altercation,'' Eberhart answered for her.
''Miss McHenry was explaining to me that she infinitely
preferred you as a partner for this dance to myself.''

''Oh? Always happy to oblige, my dear,'' Waldo said.

Mutely Rosalind took the viscount's hand, conscious of
Eberhart's mocking gaze. Why did he stare so? And why
had he bullied Waldo into dancing with her? And, good
heavens, why had she flung Mrs. Hubbel in his teeth? No
lady should even acknowledge the existence of a gentleman's *chère amie*. By the time the waltz ended she found
herself with a throbbing migraine, necessitating an early exit
from the Assembly rooms.

''Is your head any better?'' Waldo asked as they drove off
in his barouche. He pressed his hand damply on hers in what
she took to be a comforting gesture. ''Pity I don't have a
bottle of Dr. Franklin's Elixir with me now.''

''Pray, don't concern yourself. My head already feels
better,'' she said. This was not entirely true. The rattle of
the carriage wheels on the cobblestones promised to bring
on the throbbing all over again. But that would be bearable
compared to the quizzing eyes of the earl.

Waldo, wondering how best to cheer her up, remembered the letter he had received that day from his mother and immediately told her its contents.

"Mama has no objection whatever to our marriage. She told me to send in the announcement to the *Gazette* at once. Isn't that splendid?"

"Quite the best news I've heard all day," Rosalind agreed with a sigh.

"I'll be sending the announcement in tomorrow," he told her.

"Whatever you say, Waldo," she replied, and lapsed into a silence that lasted until he put her down at Green Street. After saying good night she fairly flew up the stairs to her bedchamber.

The viscount was himself rather nonplussed. She had not reacted the way he had anticipated to his happy news. Indeed, reviewing the matter as he returned to his barouche, it seemed that ever since she had accepted his offer, Rosalind had turned more skittish than usual. And he wasn't quite sure if he liked her that way!

Daunted by the prospect of an early evening alone, he ventured on to White's, where agreeable companionship could always be found, and in short order he found himself fortified by copious glasses of claret and was soon pouring out his troubles to a new friend, Gideon Dankley.

Mr. Dankley had not strayed a jot from his original intention of revenging himself on the family McHenry, and when the viscount had stepped into the club, Dankley had felt his patience at last rewarded. Word had reached his ears of Coppleton's impending engagement to Miss McHenry, and he judged the viscount to be the weakest link in the chain that included not only Rosalind and Felicity but the earl and his secretary.

Without attracting much notice he placed himself at the viscount's elbow during the consumption of a first bottle of claret, and by the time they had started on a second their friendship was firmly established. It only became a matter of time as the night wore on till Waldo confided his romantic woes to Dankley.

"Women are behind all manner of disturbances of the male," Dankley agreed.

"Aye, but this one's different. She's a lady and one would think she doesn't wish to marry me," Waldo said, flushed from the drink.

"Impossible!" Mr. Dankley clapped him on the back. "Fine fellow. Known you just a few hours but I can see that plain enough."

The viscount smiled through a happy haze. "Why, that's devilishly good of you. Didn't catch your name."

"Dankley," Mr. Dankley supplied helpfully. "Now then, why don't you tell me more about your troubles? I don't mean to poke my nose into what doesn't concern me, but a man doesn't reach my years without some measure of experience in dealing with females. I may be able to counsel you on your problem."

"Oh, it ain't a problem really," Waldo said with a sigh. "But she ain't that interested in our wedding. Every time I bring up the matter of settling a date she fights shy of it. And tonight when I told her I would send in the announcement to the *Gazette*, damn me if she didn't practically burst into tears."

"Perhaps she has some aversion to the *Gazette*," Dankley said, refilling the viscount's glass. "Or perhaps," he added as he settled back in the leather armchair, "someone else has been vying for her attention."

Waldo's brows shot up. "Another man? As a matter of fact, there is one who has driven her about and danced with her. But I don't consider him a rival. She loathes him."

"It is the one you don't consider a serious rival whom you should watch most carefully," Mr. Dankley informed him. "Tell me, what do you and your lady do these days?"

Waldo stiffened. "Sir, I am a gentleman, and she is a lady."

"Yes, yes." Mr. Dankley hastened to sooth the viscount's ruffled feathers. "I didn't mean to imply you weren't. I merely meant what have you done for courtship's sake? You may have won her hand, young man, but some ladies are of an incurably romantic disposition. She might want the ardor of your courtship rekindled.''

"I don't think Rosalind's that sort," Waldo said. "And I do my share of dangling. I call every day and bring flowers. I take her for drives in the Park. And I bought her a trinket from Rundell and Bridges. What more could a female want?''

Mr. Dankley clucked his tongue and wagged a finger even as an idea began to take root in his feverish brain.

"My dear fellow, you have much to learn about women. What they crave most is romance and adventure. Don't you think by now your Miss Rosalind has gotten bored with flowers and drives about the Park?''

"But I thought every female likes that!" Waldo protested.

"Up to a point," Mr. Dankley declared authoritatively. "After that, ennui sets in. You must make her see that you still possess dash, adventure, and romance.''

"Perhaps I could compose a poem to her," Waldo said, reflecting a moment. His face fell. "No, that won't serve. I always was a notoriously bad hand at poetry.''

"You don't need poems," Mr. Dankley said. "Nor the announcement in the *Gazette* about your engagement.''

Waldo looked utterly befogged. "I don't?''

Mr. Dankley leaned over with a conspiratorial air. "A wedding must be adventurous as well as romantic, something a woman shall remember for the rest of her life. Don't you agree?''

"Well, yes," Waldo acknowledged. "I suppose so, and yet . . .''

"You must give Miss McHenry that type of wedding.''

"I plan to," Waldo said stoutly. "St. George's, Hanover Square, whenever she says the word.''

Mr. Dankley issued a quick contradiction.

"Not St. George's, but Gretna Green—and not when she says the word, but when *you* say it shall happen!''

At the mention of the Border, Waldo spilled his claret down his frilled shirt. "Good Jupiter," he exclaimed, rising. "You must be foxed. Are you suggesting an elopement?"

Mr. Dankley nodded, busily wiping the viscount with a handkerchief. He pushed him back into his chair.

"An elopement will answer her desire for romance. Only consider for a moment how romantic a figure you shall cut as you sweep her off to the Border in your carriage. What female would fail to be moved by such a spectacle?"

"I suppose so," Waldo said, looking doubtful.

"It's done quite often," Mr. Dankley went on. "And you say you both wish to marry, unless the family frowns on the wedding."

Waldo shook his head. "No, her family's dead, those that count anyway. And my mama approves the match."

Mr. Dankley spread his hands wide. "Then nothing stands in your way."

"I suppose not, but the propriety," Waldo said with a shake of his head. "It seems drastic to resort to an elopement."

"If it's propriety you're after, you might as well hand her over to that other fellow," Mr. Dankley said. "Come, man, there can be no real scandal to concern yourself with. She is of age?"

"Oh, yes, to be sure. Still . . ." He paused.

"You mean to marry anyway," Mr. Dankley went on in his most persuasive tone. "What harm will ensue?"

Waldo screwed up his nose in thought. "Do you really think it will serve?"

"Positive! What you must do is show your lady that you are still the dashing, romantic man who won her heart in the first place!"

"By Jove, you're right!" Waldo said, much taken with this image of himself. "Gretna it shall be!"

Chapter Nineteen

Eberhart, standing in front of his mirror applying the last turn to his *Trone d'Amour*, was mildly perturbed by a knock on his dressing room door. His entire household knew his dressing room was sacrosanct at this hour of the morning. His valet, even more conscious of this fact, hurried to the door, ready to unleash a blistering set-down of the perpetrator. The miscreant, as it turned out, was Fergus.

"I do beg your pardon, sir," he said to the earl.

"What is it, Fergus?" the earl asked, frowning in concentration as he gazed into the mirror.

"I have an urgent message from your mother. It just arrived."

"My mother?" The earl slid his long arms into the coat sleeves and nodded his dismissal of his valet. Then with a quizzical look he took the note Fergus handed him and broke the seal. Lady Manning was never one to waste words.

"Alastair," the note read in her hasty scrawl, "come immediately."

Frowning even more, he picked up his gloves and made the trip to Berkeley Square in record time, wondering what could have prompted so unprecedented a summons. His mother did not usually demand he dance attendance on her, and since she was quite adept at handling her own affairs—he had been about the last to know that she had accepted Manning's offer!—she did not usually hang on his sleeve for assistance. Then, too, since her marriage to Manning she would undoubtedly turn to him for advice. So what could be amiss?

He found out as soon as he entered her blue drawing room. Lady Manning, in trailing orange drapery, sat comforting another female on the Egyptian couch.

"Alastair, thank heavens," she ejaculated, drawing away and allowing him to recognize the tearstained face of the other female as that of his sister, Margaret.

"Alastair, my *rescuer*!" Margaret, having quitted Lady Manning's bosom, showed an affinity for attaching herself now to her brother's.

"Hallo, Meg," Eberhart said, holding her off none too successfully, for she laid her teary face on his coat, which would no doubt enrage James, his valet.

"It's good to see you," he said, not quite truthfully. "How is Stephan?"

This, he realized too late, was not the thing to say as his mother shot him a quick warning look. Meg began to cry once more, nearly crushing his cravat in the process.

"Meg—" he implored, striving to loosen her grip on his throat. "Mama, *please*."

Lady Manning had as much distaste as her son for emotional scenes; nonetheless, she rose to the occasion now and plucked her daughter from Eberhart's bosom, taking her over to a Windsor chair and offering her a fresh handkerchief and a glass of sherry.

"Mama!" Meg accepted the handkerchief and wiped her eyes but waved off the glass. "You know I never touch sherry."

"Well, perhaps you should," her mother declared.

"Will one of you tell me what is going on?" the earl demanded, one boot tapping impatiently against the rug.

"Stephan's left me," Meg wailed, and she burst into tears again.

"Oh, Alastair, stop doing that!" Lady Manning commanded.

"Doing *what*?" he demanded in outraged innocence.

"Stop asking questions," she said crossly. "It only distresses poor Meg."

Eberhart cast a sympathetic eye on his sister, who was not

in her best looks this morning, her eyes rimmed red with tears.

"Has he really left you?" Eberhart asked. He was not overly fond of his brother-in-law, but Stephan had been Meg's husband for considerable time.

"Yes," Meg said emphatically, her dark head still bent over her handkerchief. Her words came between sobs. "Last week at the Lakes. We were going to paint the Lakes the way all the painters do. But he fell in with a poetess. Miss Yolanda Burgess. Have you ever heard a name more insipid? He fell madly in love with her."

"Bosh! Mere poetic inspiration," her brother said encouragingly. "These artistic types are prone to that."

"That's what I said!" Lady Manning nodded her quick agreement. "It's goose to guineas that given enough time Stephan will come to his senses."

"You don't know Stephan!" Meg said, her eyes now dry but no less distressed. "I couldn't bear the sight of them cavorting together so I came here. And you don't know the worst of it. He's asked for a divorce so he can marry his wretched poetess!"

At the word divorce Eberhart raised his brows, and even Lady Manning was taken aback. A divorce, while not unheard of in polite society—Grafton, a duke, had divorced his duchess sometime earlier and she had turned around and married an earl—was still frowned upon.

"Surely the situation won't come to that," Eberhart said, sitting down next to Meg.

"It will. It has," Meg said emphatically.

"Where is Stephan?"

"With his stupid poetess," Meg said, practically spitting the words out. "She is such an odious creature, Mama. So frail and weak, but she is quick with a couplet. Try as I could, I could never get the things to rhyme."

Lady Manning patted her hand. "There, there, love. You are worlds better at painting."

Meg rallied slightly. "Yes, I am. Stephan always did say my brushwork was superb. But he's too dazzled now to pay me any mind. Oh, I hate him. I vow I could kill him! Alastair," she said as she turned to her brother, "you must avenge my honor!"

The earl, trying to keep abreast of his sister's emotions, which seemed to shift with every minute, was stunned by such an addled command.

"Your *honor*, Meg?" he asked uncertainly. She had been married for almost sixteen years.

"Yes. You are my nearest male relation."

"Yes," he conceded, "but that's no reason to foist a duel on me. Stephan's a notoriously bad hand with a pistol, I recall. I wouldn't feel right about it. Talk to Stephan; there's the answer."

"He won't listen to me," Meg said mournfully. "He called me a shrew compared to that poetess, who does naught but smile and chirp at him." She fell into a fresh deluge of tears at this thought.

Lady Manning drew her son to one side of the room. "Alastair, do you think you might speak to Stephan on Meg's behalf? Man to man, as it were."

"Mama!"

"I'd ask Manning, but he'd fight shy of such a scene."

"And with good reason," the earl declared. "Really, Mama, I've never liked Stephan overly much. How will it look if I plead with him to stay on?"

"Not half as bad as it will look when Meg sinks into a decline."

"She's not so poor a creature," he said.

His mother was not so certain.

"She has an artistic temperament, and you know what that means. Please, Alastair, I don't like to ask it of you, but it alarms me to see her so unhappy. And what of the boys? Fortunately Harry took them on a visit to Tattersall's this morning, and we shall contrive some story to tell them about their mother's visit. But what of their future? They deserve a father, too, no matter how much a skittlebrain!"

This won a reluctant smile, and he agreed to speak to his brother-in-law on the delicate matter. That would mean that his own plans to pursue a more open and ardent courtship of

Rosalind despite her engagement to Waldo must perforce wait.

"Where did you see Stephan last?" he asked his sister.

"In Scarborough."

His eyes widened. "Scarborough! That means a journey of at least two days."

"Yes, he was on his way to Chardwiche's. He is a cousin to that odious poetess."

Eberhart felt on firmer ground, having a passing acquaintance with Lord Chardwiche. "All right. I'll go and find Stephan and recall him to his duties as a husband, Meg."

His lighthearted words left his sister unmoved.

"He won't wish to recall his duties as a husband," she warned bitterly.

"Then perhaps he'll remember he's a father as well. The boys are worth some measure of consideration."

"I shouldn't wish him to stay with me merely on their account, Alastair," Meg said, turning mulish.

Eberhart felt on the verge of losing his temper. "Meg, what do you want?" he exclaimed. "I vow, you try the patience of a saint, which we all know I am not! First you want Stephan back at any cost, then you wish me to fight a duel with him, and now you want me to find him but not to bring him back to you!"

"I want him to return because he loves me, not merely on account of the boys," Meg said, close to tears once again.

"Now, my dears, pray don't fight," Lady Manning interceded as she did when they were children squabbling over toys. "Meg, you are fagged to death. Let's go and leave it all to Alastair. You know he shall contrive something to make things turn out all right."

About this Eberhart was not as confident as his mother. But he went off to spend his first day on the road, and by the afternoon of the second day's travel, when he finally reached Scarborough, he was hot, tired, and hungry. He could not call on Chardwiche in all his dirt, especially since he had not prepared any sensible reason for such a visit. He took a hearty dinner at a nearby inn and tried to think what might make a convincing tale to allow for his presence in

Scarborough, a town that had little to recommend itself to him.

He fell asleep with the answer still unsolved, but sleep brought a solution. Scarborough was famed for its sea bathing, and he decided to abandon his robust good health and contrive a faint but persistent cough that necessitated his taking the waters on the coast.

Prepared in this fashion, he set off for Kendle, Lord Chardwiche's estate, and his host, a genial-looking gentleman a decade older than Eberhart, was most sympathetic at hearing of the earl's cough.

"Coughs are a nuisance," he said. "I know that well. And your physician might be right. Some claim the saltwater revives their health. I don't know whether that's true or not, but it's worth a try."

"Indeed, yes. And since I was in the vicinity I thought to call on you."

"I'm glad you did so," Chardwiche said gruffly. "Don't get too many visitors. Do you feel up to a walk?"

"I think I can manage that," Eberhart agreed.

"There's something I wish to show you. I'm building a grotto."

Chardwiche led Eberhart across the grounds, which several gardeners were in the act of transforming.

"That lake didn't used to be here," he said, pointing. "Used to be a mound of dirt."

The earl murmured an appreciative sound. "You follow Mr. Capability Brown's code, then, sir? Creating lakes and leveling mountains?"

Chardwiche grunted. "Brown has a point, not that I care overmuch for that other fellow, Chambers. Chinese pagodas. Fancy fishing pavilions. Stuff and nonsense, that's what I say. The simpler the better. Ah, here we have the grotto."

The earl took a tour of the grotto and found it not unexpectedly damp, dark, and muddy.

"It is that," Chardwiche agreed. "But it shall rival Shaftesbury's when it's done. Have you seen Shaftesbury's?"

"No."

"It's a beauty. Pearls stuck to the walls along with the oyster shells. It's said to have cost a pretty penny. I don't mean to go that far. I'll have marble and crystals, though—that goes without saying—and perhaps a few stalactites."

"It sounds delightful," Eberhart said, blinking as they emerged into the sudden light. "By the by, Chardwiche," he asked as they strolled back toward the house, "did you have occasion to see my brother-in-law, Templeton? I heard he had visited you."

Chardwiche grimaced. "Aye, Templeton," he snorted. "What a jackanapes he is, and I don't care if he is your brother-in-law."

"I share your opinion," the earl told him.

"He came by with that idiotish cousin of mine, Yolanda Burgess."

"Is he still about? I'd like a private word with him."

"Sorry, Eberhart. The pair had a frightful row over some ode or sonnet or some such, and he went off in high dudgeon. I wasn't sorry to see him go, either!"

Eberhart frowned.

"Yolanda's still here," Chardwiche went on, "if you want to talk to her. Not that she'll be of much use. A featherbrain if there ever was. Fancies herself a poetess. Come along." He led the way into the house. "Oh, botheration! You can't see her just yet. I've forgotten."

"Is she still asleep?" The hour was nearly noon.

"She's communing with her Muse." Chardwiche made a face. "Difficult having a poetess in the family, Eberhart. But stay on and have some luncheon with us. She's bound to emerge soon. Even poets must eat."

The meal Lord Chardwiche provided was hearty country fare: poached salmon, roast chickens, and mincemeat pies. Eberhart enjoyed his visit with the peer, whose conversation seemed fixed on his grotto and his plans to improve his entire estate.

How would Pelhelm look with a grotto? Eberhart wondered, then dismissed the whole idea as an absurdity. His country seat suited him as it was. While the two men were finishing up a bowl of strawberries, the poetess made her appearance. She was thin and blonde and pale, not at all the sultry temptress Eberhart had imagined.

"Well, Yolanda, and about time!" said her cousin. "This is Eberhart, brother-in-law to that fellow Templeton you had here earlier."

"Cousin Jonathon, I pray you, do not utter that man's name again in my presence." Miss Burgess thrust out her lower lip in a pout.

"Am I to take it that Stephan is in your black books, ma'am?" the earl inquired.

"He lied to me!"

Wondering whether Stephan had pretended he was not married in an effort to entice Miss Burgess, Eberhart was at first uncertain how to proceed.

"He told me he was a poet," Miss Burgess explained.

"So he is. I can count any number of verses he's written over the years. Far too many, if you want my opinion," he confided to Chardwiche, who let out a bellow of laughter.

Miss Burgess sniffed. "I've read his verse and," she declared authoritatively, "it's not half as good as Mr. Bentley's or Sir Jack Sprague's."

"Did you tell him this?" the earl asked.

"Yes, of course," Miss Burgess said forthrightly. "I believe in speaking plainly. I thought he might need to know so he could try and improve. But all that happened was that he was put into a flame and called me the most horrid names possible. He was in a frightful mood when he left."

The quarrel was a relief to Eberhart. At least he wouldn't have to pry Stephan from his poetess's bosom, a specter that had filled him with dread.

"When did he leave?" he asked.

"Yesterday, or was it the day before?"

"Day before, I think," Lord Chardwiche said.

"Do you know where he was bound?"

Miss Burgess shrugged. "He can't have gotten far. He didn't have a carriage. And he didn't think to borrow a horse from Cousin Jonathon."

"He might have caught a coach in town," Chardwiche said. "Looking for him, are you?"

"Yes. There is a family matter that needs discussion."

"You might try Sheffield. The coach from here goes that way."

Eberhart nodded his thanks for the information and the lunch and made a swift adieu. Now that Stephan was no longer in the clutches of his poetess, the path toward reuniting him with Meg seemed clearer. With any luck he could bully Stephan into returning to London. The sooner he was done with that the better. He still had Rosalind to woo and win.

He thought of Rosalind as he rode to Sheffield, cursing the poor condition of the roads. Arriving there, he found an ostler who remembered his brother-in-law.

"All done up in pink and lavender he was." The ostler grinned at the memory. "And in a rage. Claimed someone lifted his purse while he was having a pint of ale. Some say that just to keep from paying for the ale. It's an old trick we're wise to."

"Do you know where he might be?"

The ostler caught the coin the earl tossed him and grinned. "Mrs. Michelby who works in the kitchen took pity on him. I hear she sent him over to her mother's farm. She lets folks work for their keep. They get to sleep in the barn."

An involuntary smile flashed across Eberhart's face as he tried to imagine his fastidious brother-in-law sleeping on straw. In due course he found his direction to Mrs. Michelby, who furnished him with the directions to her mother's farm. This, as it turned out, was not nearly as squalid as some others the earl had seen in his time.

"Stop, do stop. Here chickie, chickie," a voice in the yard pleaded.

The earl's arrival had gone unnoticed, and he dismounted and was treated to the sight of Stephan chasing a chicken about the farmyard. His laughter rolled unchecked down from his eyes, and he held his aching ribs.

Finally, he strolled over. "Hallo, Stephan!"

At the sound of his name, Stephan turned and reeled. "Alastair, is it really you?"

"Indeed yes, but more to the point, is that you?"

Mr. Templeton had the grace to blush. "I know I look hellish. I've had some rum luck. I had my purse pinched and not a sou left to me. I thought I'd earn my passage to London on the coach. Mrs. Grantham, the farmwife here, said she'd keep me a week. That would give me enough for a fare."

"What were you trying to do with the chicken?" Eberhart asked curiously.

Stephan threw down the bag of feed he had been holding. "She wants it for supper. I'm supposed to wring its neck."

"Good heavens!" The earl made a face.

"Yes, I know. It's nauseating, and I really don't think I could do such a thing—if I ever caught it, which I don't seem to be doing. But that means I won't have the fare to London." He looked so mournful that Eberhart was forced to remind him that his own purse was full.

"Rather than bear the discomforts of a cheap fare on the coach, you might come back with me. I'll hire another horse at the inn. You do ride?"

"Yes, of course. And it is good of you, Alastair. But perhaps you won't want to help me when I tell you. Meg and I are getting a divorce."

"Are you, now?" The earl's steely eyes met Stephan's.

Mr. Templeton nodded. "She's probably seen her solicitor by now. Not that I blame her. I've acted like such a cake. I've had my head turned by flattery. Never trust a poetess, Alastair," he said darkly.

"I shall keep that in mind," the earl said gravely. "Buck up, Stephan. I'll put in a good word for you with Meg. I'm sure the breach can be healed."

"Devilishly good of you, but I don't know if she'll listen. I've treated her abominably."

"She'll listen," Eberhart promised. "And if she doubts your penitence, I'll tell her of your travails. Wringing chicken necks, indeed! Knowing Meg, she'll make you crawl before forgiving you," he warned.

"Oh, I don't mind that," Stephan said cheerfully, and

went off to tell Mrs. Grantham that he would not after all be staying the week. Eberhart took him up on the back of his horse and the two returned to the inn, where Stephan was soon enjoying the soothing benefits of a hot bath, fresh clothes, and a meal, although nothing would induce him to try a piece of the roast chicken!

Chapter Twenty

On Saturday Viscount Coppleton set out with Rosalind on an excursion to Lord Kitteredge's summer home for a view of that gentleman's famous orchid collection. Rosalind had no real love of flowers, but Waldo had been so insistent about the outing that she had finally consented, thinking that she might as well get accustomed to his habits since they were shortly to wed.

For two days she had searched the pages of the *Gazette* for the dreaded announcement, only to come up empty-handed. She had made a similar search of the columns of the *Morning Post*, thinking it just like Waldo to have said one journal when he meant the other. But here, too, her hunt proved futile. She didn't know whether to be entirely pleased or not about its continued absence.

No such qualms afflicted the viscount, who was rendered giddy at the prospect of spiriting Rosalind away to the Border this spring morning. Meticulously he had prepared for the jaunt, aided by Mr. Dankley's counsel. Remembering Dankley's words on the importance of not giving away the game too early, Waldo controlled his impulse to dash off and drove at a sedate pace toward the North Road. Rosalind wanted adventure, dash, and romance, did she? She would soon find them in abundance.

At the precise moment when the carriage carried Rosalind and Waldo toward the North Road, a footman entered the breakfast parlor at Green Street, extending to its sole occupant a small note on a silver tray.

Curious as to who might be sending her a message, Felicity broke open the seal and scanned the scribbled lines.

"My dear Felicity, meet me at the White Elephant Inn as soon as possible. Papa."

"Papa is in London," she murmured to herself. How odd. He was supposed to be on his way to the Americas. Her first impulse was to seek help from her beloved Fergus, but she soon remembered that he was engrossed in legal matters having to do with their removal to Brussels.

Her next confidante would have been her aunt, but a swift consultation with Mrs. Withers revealed that Rosalind had set out for a day's journey with Waldo, and they would be returning quite late.

Deep in thought, Felicity mounted the stairs toward her bedchamber. Long aware of the mutual hostilities between her father and aunt, she was not surprised that he had written to her for help instead of to Rosalind. She was even flattered in a way. Previously, he had treated her like a scruffy schoolgirl.

Knowing that her father would be in need of funds, she stuffed a hundred-pound note into her reticule. That was supposed to go toward the cost of her trousseau. But of course she knew one hundred pounds would be practically nothing to a man of her father's notorious habits. Had Rosalind been present she would have contrived some excuse to ask for additional funds. Her aunt was usually generous on such matters. But in her absence, Felicity was loath to break into the strongbox, even though she suspected her father would have no such scruples.

Wondering what might have brought Gerald back from his sea voyage, she went out the door, thinking how best to get to the inn. Fortunately an empty hack passed and she directed the driver to the address her father had given.

Lost in thought over the morning's events, Felicity was at first oblivious to the hack carrying her further and further from the polite sections of London and into its more unsavory environs. When she chanced to glance about she was dumbfounded to see how dirty the streets were, not to mention the dilapidated buildings. Surely her father would never summon her to such a place. The driver must be in error.

"No, Miss," said the driver in answer to her question.

"This is the route to the inn. Course, if you be having second thoughts, which I dinna blame you for having, I'd be pleased to take you back where I found you."

"No, that's all right," she said, pushing aside her qualms. "I must go on." Indeed, it was imperative that she find out what her father wanted.

Felicity, mild and gentle-hearted, had long nursed modest hopes that her two nearest relations, namely her father and her aunt, might somehow be reconciled. Not informed of the whole truth regarding Mr. McHenry's removal to the Americas, Rosalind had merely told her that Gerald had left, giving her Felicity's guardianship; the younger woman was inclined to view his return now as the perfect opportunity to bring about the longed-for reunion.

And yet nothing in her young life had prepared her to enter such a hovel when the driver finally stopped. She swallowed her misgivings, paid the driver, and, squaring her shoulders, entered the inn. Her courage nearly deserted her as several men approached. She sidestepped them quickly, holding her breath against the foul odors of rum and whisky, and walked toward the counter, where a bearded proprietor swatted flies lazily.

"McHenry, is it?" the proprietor said when Felicity asked after her father. He jerked his head to the left. "You'll find him in the parlor."

Gladdened by this reply, she went immediately to the parlor, but instead of her father, Mr. Dankley sat alone by the fire. At the sound of her footsteps he turned.

"Why, Miss McHenry!" He rose and greeted her with a pleased smile.

Felicity had seen Dankley before in her father's company and, although surprised to see him here, she was relieved at recognizing a familiar face.

"Mr. Dankley. Where is Papa?"

"Do come in where we can talk in private," he invited, drawing her toward a chair and closing the door.

As Felicity bent toward the fire to warm her hands, he quickly locked and secured the door.

"Gerald has been unavoidably detained," Mr. Dankley

said. "He asked me to meet you here lest you wait in such a place alone."

"That was good of you," Felicity said naïvely. Mr. Dankley sank into the chair next to hers. "How is it that Papa has returned? Aunt Rosalind said he was bent on emigrating."

"I daresay he can explain that better than I," Mr. Dankley replied. He held up a pitcher. "Would you care for some lemonade, my dear? I ordered it especially for you. I'm afraid a place like this doesn't carry ratafia."

She accepted the glass he poured for her with thanks. She was rather thirsty. His duty as a host done, Mr. Dankley sat back, an odd glint in his eyes. Felicity sipped the lemonade and made a face. This refreshment was sourer even than Almack's!

Mr. Dankley swallowed some of his brandy. "You are looking quite lovely, Miss Felicity. Do you know, I can recall the first time I saw you with your papa."

His voice sent in involuntary chill the length of Felicity's spine. Although carefully schooled, she intuitively recognized the change that drink occasioned in a man. She took another sip of her lemonade, shook her head at its tartness, and put the glass down. She had erred badly in coming to such a place.

"Mr. Dankley, I am returning to Green Street. Kindly tell Papa when he arrives to see me there. Aunt Rosalind is gone on a day trip, so he need have no fear of a horrid scene arising with her."

"But you are already here," Mr. Dankley exclaimed. "I'm sure Gerald will be stepping through the door at any moment. Do stay."

"I must not," she said, feeling lightheaded. She put that down to the peculiar smells wafting about the inn.

"I'm leaving," she repeated.

"As you wish it, Miss McHenry." Dankley shrugged indifferently.

She moved toward the door, repressing a feeling of triumph. But her victory was short-lived. She had taken only two steps when the room began to spin alarmingly and, dizzy, she collapsed on the floor.

With surprising complacence Mr. Dankley surveyed the sprawled figure on the parlor floor. He remained seated, tossing off the remains of his brandy. Only then did he bestir himself to stoop over her with an audible creaking of his bones.

He checked her wrist to assure himself that, while the laudanum had done its job, her pulse continued to beat. As he let her hand drop, he ran the other hand down the hollow of her throat. As though in protest of the caress she did not desire, Felicity stirred. Dankley gave an odd smile.

"You'll be mine soon enough, my pretty," he murmured.

Straightening, he scooped her into his arms and flung her over one shoulder, then stalked out of the room. The bearded proprietor stood waiting in the hall. He winked.

"Everything satisfactory, guv'nor?" he asked with a leer.

Dankley had no time to waste. "Help me with the back door," he grunted.

"Right you are," the innkeeper said, preceding him down the hall and opening the door for him. Outside, Dankley's carriage waited.

"Not a word about this, mind," Dankley said as he pushed Felicity into the carriage and tossed a bag of coins to the other man.

"Mum's the word, guv'nor," the innkeeper said, shaking out one of the coins and biting it. "Be happy to oblige you again whenever you wish," he cackled.

Dankley ignored him and settled himself more comfortably in the seat while Felicity slumbered against his shoulder.

"To Swindon, then, Alfred," he called up to his groom.

The two gentlemen riding hard on the London-bound road appeared to be somewhat fatigued from their days of travel. Eberhart and Stephan had made good time, and by sunset the earl fervently hoped he could deposit his brother-in-law with his sister and wash his hands of the whole affair.

Stephan's spirits had been restored to normal, and he was beginning to grate on the earl's nerves. If there was one thing Eberhart didn't relish, it was listening to a litany of praise of his sister, Meg.

As their horses neared Cambridge, however, Stephan fell oddly quiet, and before too long he begged the earl to stop at a nearby posting house to hoist a tankard of ale.

"It will prepare me for seeing Meg," he explained with a sheepish look.

The earl, knowing full well the peal that Meg would ring over Stephan, pulled in willingly enough at the inn, and while Stephan drank his ale, keeping a close hand on his purse all the while, Eberhart took a turn in the yard, stretching his legs, which had been cramped from his day in the saddle.

As he walked he heard voices raised in argument and, intrigued as to what might be happening, he gazed around the corner and saw Gideon Dankley arguing with one of the ostlers.

"That can't be the best horse here!" Mr. Dankley exclaimed, looking out of patience.

"Sorry, sir, but it is. If you'll wait until tomorrow we'll have some others."

Dankley gave a snort of disgust. "I can't wait. One of my team pulled up lame. But I vow, if I don't make Swindon by nightfall I'll have your hide."

"Shall I hitch the horse, sir?"

"No, my groom will do it," Dankley said.

"There's ale in the inn if you like it, sir."

"I don't," Dankley said, preferring to stand where he could be sure no one would approach the carriage and could see the still-slumbering Felicity. Of all the ill luck to come his way! His horse *would* have to pull up lame.

Eberhart, watching the horse being hitched, was about to turn back toward the inn when his eyes met Dankley's. Their relationship was far from cordial, and yet there was no reason that he could deduce for Dankley turning chalk-white. Within seconds the man was demanding that his groom hurry it up.

More and more intrigued as to why his mere presence should spark Dankley's sudden desire to be quit of the vicinity, he sauntered over. Dankley met him halfway across the yard, lest he come too close to the carriage.

"How now, my lord Eberhart. Pleasant day, isn't it?"

"Most pleasant," Eberhart agreed. "But bad luck for you."

Dankley licked his lips. "What do you mean?" he croaked.

"Your horse," the earl said gently. "It pulled up lame. I overheard you speaking to the ostler."

"Oh, yes. That it has," Dankley said, letting out his breath.

"On your way to Swindon, your estate?"

"Yes. As soon as the horse is hitched," Dankley said, looking over his shoulder at his carriage. Two little urchins were playing near the carriage wheel.

"Get away from there!" he shouted.

The two boys ignored his order, and Dankley strode over, plucked them up by the backs of their necks, and shook them.

"Wawww!" one yelled.

The other aimed a kick directly at Mr. Dankley's shin and connected. With a muffled oath, Dankley dropped them both. The earl chuckled.

"Brats!" Dankley cursed and made a vain grab for a pair of chubby legs running past.

The boy, skirting Dankley's outstretched arms, dashed for the only safe spot he could see—the carriage. He yanked the door opened and climbed in.

With a curse, Dankley went after him into the carriage, shutting the door quickly. He picked the boy up by the scruff of the neck and threw him out. The earl, catching a glimpse of blond hair and a dress, curled his lip. So Dankley was up to his womanizing, was he? No wonder he was nervous being seen by the earl.

"Alastair!" Stephan had come out of the inn. "Are we off, then?"

"Just about," the earl agreed. He walked with his brother-in-law toward their horses.

"Nyah, nyah!" The two boys stuck their tongues out at Dankley who was seated at the window of his carriage. One waved a lady's handkerchief that he had taken from the carriage.

Eberhart laughed until his eyes fell on the embroidered crescent and stars. Felicity's handkerchief! He had seen it innumerable times. His eyes hardened.

"Stephan," he said in an undertone, "how are you at diversions?"

"Eh, what?"

"I haven't time to explain, but I suspect that something or someone is in danger in that carriage. I shall approach it from this end and try to get the attention of Mr. Dankley. While I do so you approach from the other end and help the young lady out."

"A young lady? In distress, Alastair?"

"I suspect so."

Stephan beamed. "First rate. I've always wanted to rescue a lady in distress."

"Quickly," Eberhart told his brother-in-law, "around the back you go."

Stephan, smiling, waved a hand and sauntered off. Eberhart made his approach. Dankley's groom had just finished hitching up the horses, and Mr. Dankley, seeing the earl's approach, came out of the carriage once again to forestall him.

"Mr. Dankley, I wonder if I might have your assistance in a matter."

"Er, yes, of course, my lord. The thing is, I am frightfully late."

"Yes, but this shall only take a minute. Those two urchins who were in the carriage. They've turned up with a purse. It wouldn't be yours, by any chance, would it?"

Mr. Dankley made a quick search of his pockets, finding his purse secure.

"I have mine," he said with some satisfaction as Stephan Templeton gave a shout from behind.

"Ho! Ho! Alastair, you were right!" Stephan called out.

Too late Mr. Dankley whirled around. The earl had already taken two quick steps around the carriage as Stephen carried out the prone form of Felicity McHenry.

Mr. Dankley, muttering a choked oath, turned as though to flee, but he found his way blocked by the earl, who pushed him back against the carriage.

"She's been drugged, I think," Stephan said.

"What did you give her?" Eberhart demanded.

"Just some laudanum," he muttered. "It should wear off soon."

"Pretty little thing," Stephan said, gazing down at Felicity. At the sound of his voice, Felicity stirred.

"I told you it would wear off," Dankley said as Felicity's eyes fluttered open. "But it's too late for you and her," he said with a leer.

Felicity blinked at the rush of sunlight and drew away as she noticed she was in Stephan's arms.

"Who are you? Put me down!"

"Easy, my dear." Eberhart came to the rescue, helping her to her feet.

"Lord Eberhart!" Felicity said. "Oh, how my head aches. Oh!" She caught sight of Dankley and shrank back against Eberhart. "Now I remember. Papa's note, and you were at that disagreeable inn. You tricked me."

"Yes," Dankley admitted. "And it was a disagreeable inn, was it not? And we were alone there for considerable time!"

The earl's jaw tightened as Felicity gasped. "Not that long a time!" she protested.

"Long enough to cause certain disagreeable comments to arise about your reputation, should I care to make them."

"Which you won't," the earl said.

Mr. Dankley smiled thinly. "I am not in the habit of doing favors for you, my lord."

"No," Eberhart agreed. "But I would advise you not to say a word about the trick you played on Miss Felicity."

"I think it makes a good story," Dankley said. "Whom shall I tell first? Perhaps your Mr. Fairweather. He always struck me as deplorably strait-laced. What will he say when he hears you have been compromised?"

"I wasn't!" Felicity protested.

"You may rest easy," the earl comforted her as he grabbed Dankley by the throat. "For if I hear one syllable against Miss Felicity from whatever source I will take the greatest pleasure in putting a sword through you."

"Swords are so messy, Alastair!" Stephan volunteered. "Why don't we just break a few bones? We could start with his ankle and work our way up."

"Take your hands off me," Dankley snarled as Stephan ran a gloved hand over his boot.

"Your suggestion has merit," the earl agreed. He stared at Dankley for a moment. "Which will it be, sword or broken bones? The choice is yours."

Dankley broke free of Stephan's grasp. "You'll hear not a word from me," he muttered.

"Good. I always knew you were a reasonable man," Eberhart said. "Come, Felicity, allow me to escort you back to your aunt. By the by, this is my brother-in-law, Stephan Templeton, whose talents I've sorely underestimated." He handed Felicity up into the saddle of his horse. "Broken bones indeed, Stephan," he said with a chuckle.

"We are going home, aren't we?" Felicity asked anxiously.

"That we are," the earl answered, giving his horse a slight nudge forward. "The whole business won't be over until we get you to Berkeley Square."

"Berkeley Square? I thought you were taking me to Aunt Rosalind's!"

"I am taking you to my mother until we think how best to mend the damage the day has done to your reputation. I don't trust Dankley, and he may or may not keep a civil tongue in his head. And until then I don't wish to face your aunt with her questions and no answers to them. And while I don't mean to scold you, for I'm sure you had a devilish time of it, what possessed you to fall for such a trick?"

Felicity had endured a long and arduous day. Her nerves had been stretched to the breaking point, and she answered the earl's mild rebuke by succumbing to a vigorous attack of the vapors.

Upon recovering she voiced the opinion that, having been ruined, she could not foist herself on Fergus and must now retreat into a nunnery, an opinion she continued to cling to up to their arrival in London, which caused Eberhart as he rang the bell to his mother's residence to wonder how he had ever entertained the idea of marriage to such a baconbrained chit.

Chapter Twenty-one

"Waldo, where are we going?" Rosalind's query ended Viscount Coppleton's peaceful reverie. "We should have been at Lord Kitteredge's by now," she said, surveying the landscape they were traversing, which bore little evidence of Lord Kitteredge's prized exotica.

"Yes, I know." Waldo gave her hand a little pat. "In point of fact, my dear, we aren't bound for the orchids. It's a surprise."

Rosalind repressed a sigh. "Waldo, I'm not in the mood for one of your larks."

The viscount looked aggrieved. "This ain't a lark. And you'll see where we are headed soon enough." He could not avoid one tiny hint. "You ought to feel right at home, for you do have Scottish blood!"

Rosalind stared incredulously at Waldo's beaming face. It wasn't possible. Not even Waldo would consider a flight to the Border.

"Waldo," she commanded now. "I pray you, be serious and turn this vehicle around. An expedition to Kitteredge's is all well and good, but I have plans for Drury Lane this evening."

"I'm sorry, Rosalind. You won't be able to keep that engagement. We'll be spending our night at the Border. Quite a cozy little hotel there, they say. We'll be married first," he said to assure her. "You needn't fear any scandal."

"You are right about that, at least!" she said, an ominous ring to her voice. "For there shan't be any Border escapade. Waldo, turn this carriage at once."

The viscount shook his head. "Sorry, my dear. I can't."

"Waldo!" Rosalind stamped her foot, nearly startling him into dropping the reins. "Do as I say. Your jest is no longer amusing."

"It ain't a jest," he said testily. "Man plans an elopement, and you take it for a joke. What sort of female are you?"

"The sort who doesn't relish being carried off in broad daylight."

"Oh, it ain't that bad," he coaxed. "And I don't see the harm, for you do plan to marry me eventually."

"That doesn't mean I wish to marry at the Border."

He frowned. "But Dankley told me—"

Rosalind froze. "Dankley? Pray, what does he have to do with this? I didn't even know the two of you were acquainted."

"We weren't, but we are now. And he's quite an amiable fellow. Full of good sense."

"And did the good sense include a trip to the Border?" she demanded. "My God, Waldo. Don't be a paperskull! I would never consent to such a ramshackle notion. Turn the horses about!"

"Dash it all, Rosalind, you are spoiling everything," Waldo retorted. "Any other female would be swooning from the sheer excitement of it, or clapping her hands, or crying!"

"I'm sorry if my reactions fall short of the mark, but what made you think I would agree to so preposterous a plan?"

He made a face. "You've been so silent about our wedding plans. I thought a little adventure might remind you of the man who offered for you."

"I need no such reminder," Rosalind replied truthfully. "I know exactly the type of fellow you are. And now, unless you want me to throw myself down from this carriage and risk a broken neck, please let's get back to London!"

Grudgingly Waldo turned the carriage around, feeling much abused. As for Rosalind, she could not help recalling Mr. Wilding's warning about Dankley. Had Waldo been an unwitting dupe for Dankley's mischief? And just what sort of mischief had he in mind?

"Can't we go any faster?" she urged when they were half an hour from town.

"I'm going as fast as I can," Waldo said, struggling with his reins. "Ain't the easiest thing in the world."

The viscount's sense of ill usage had not diminished. Whoever heard of a bridegroom turning back with the bride in the midst of an elopement? It just wasn't done. He found himself glancing at Rosalind out of the corner of one eye. Did he really wish to marry such an unromantic female?

Rosalind's own thoughts were not on the elopement, which she put down to just one of Waldo's freakish whims. A hunch that something might be brewing back in Green Street had taken root and grew stronger with each mile. Another plea to Waldo to go faster elicited the acid comment that she could try to take the reins if she wished, and he was shocked into silence when she wrenched them from his hands.

His feathers were still ruffled when he escorted her through the door of Green Street, intending to take a particularly cold farewell. He was precluded from doing so by the baleful eye of Eberhart.

"Well, it's about time, Miss McHenry," the earl said acidly as he descended the stairs. "How, pray, were the orchids?"

"We didn't see any," Rosalind replied distractedly.

"What? An absence of more than four hours and not one glimpse of orchids?" He glanced over at Waldo and was rewarded by the viscount's coloring up.

"What are you doing here, Eberhart?" Rosalind asked, realizing that it was her staircase he was descending.

"Trying to keep from going crazy," he said succinctly. "I have had a devil of a day and see no need to prolong it."

"Where is Felicity?" Rosalind asked.

"Upstairs, preparing for her wedding."

Rosalind had been climbing the stairs, but she came to a halt on the step just below the earl. "Her *what*?"

"Her wedding," the earl said, with a paternal smile. "That's a ceremony usually performed when a man and lady wish to marry. Usually it is conducted by a minister.

And one of that calling is upstairs in your blue saloon partaking of nourishment from a goodly amount of refreshment that Mrs. Withers insisted on supplying him with. The result will be that he will be too full to do much but groan through the ceremony. And what were you two doing for four hours, if not looking at Kitteredge's orchids?'' he asked absentmindedly.

Neither Rosalind nor Waldo wished to answer. Eberhart looked from one to the other. ''Perhaps you lost your way?'' he inquired gently.

This shot in the dark caused Waldo to flush to the roots of his red hair.

''Lord Kitteredge's orchids are of no interest to us, my lord,'' Rosalind said.

''Oh, I quite agree,'' Eberhart answered. ''Rather strange-looking flowers, all in all. But why if you had no interest in them did you go to see them?''

''We didn't. And do stop talking about them!''

''Alastair, why are you standing on the stairs?'' Lady Manning asked, coming down in a flutter of blue silk.

''I don't know, Mama,'' her son replied. ''Should we stand in the hall instead?''

Rosalind turned to the other woman. ''Where is Felicity?''

''In her bedchamber with Anna.'' Lady Manning furnished this reassuring news. ''But you are not to see her yet,'' she said as Rosalind picked up her skirts. ''Anna will bring Felicity to the blue saloon, where the wedding will be held.'' She gave Rosalind a peck on the cheek. ''I'm so glad you could make it, my dear. Alastair threatened to hold the ceremony without you if you hadn't returned within the hour. And he looked peevish enough to do just that, which would have been unconscionable, since it is your residence.''

She bestowed a forgiving smile on her son. ''But all in all he has had a harrowing morning, what with rescuing Felicity from that horrid Mr. Dankley and bringing her to me in the midst of a hysterical fit. Felicity, I mean, not Alastair. Although *he* did appear ready to throw a fit himself.

And when I would ask them to speak sensibly—for who could understand a word with her weeping and his roaring?—Felicity sobered and said she had no future left except as a nun or governess. And what with Alastair dashing home to bring Mr. Fairweather here and persuading her that she didn't wish to be any such thing and then going off to find a bishop who would grant a special license, you can see that we have been at sixes and sevens.''

"What has Mr. Dankley to do with this?" Rosalind asked.

Lady Manning cast a stern eye on her son. "Haven't you explained things to Rosalind yet?"

"We seem to have wandered off on a tangent adorned with orchids, Mama."

"Well, do hurry," she urged, "for that minister is devouring everything in sight. I don't think they feed him enough in his parish." With this solicitous thought she picked up her skirts and returned to the blue saloon.

"Eberhart, will you tell me what has happened here before I scream?" Rosalind threatened.

"Gladly. In as few words as possible, your niece was the victim of a cruel hoax. Dankley sent her a note pretending to be your brother asking her to meet him at a particularly disreputable inn on the other side of town."

"And she went?" Rosalind asked.

"If she hadn't I wouldn't be here now," he said acidly. "But she came to no harm," he said in a softer voice as he realized her concern. "Stephan, my brother-in-law, and I happened upon Dankley at an inn while he was exchanging horses. We managed an effective rescue, and after hearing what had happened I thought it best if she marry Fergus at once. It took nearly all this time to get Felicity to agree that she'd much rather marry Fergus than become a nun or governess. And you might have driven faster, Waldo. We have been waiting for you to arrive."

"I didn't do the driving," Waldo said. "She did."

Eberhart had no chance to further investigate this point, which intrigued him greatly, for Lady Manning appeared to shoo them all into the blue saloon.

"The reverend has finally finished his refreshments and is ready to start the ceremony," she explained.

Within minutes Rosalind was standing next to a beatific Felicity, radiant in a gown of Valenciennes lace. On the other side, Fergus appeared happy but nervous while Lady and Lord Manning looked on indulgently.

Rosalind shifted her head slightly and found the earl's eyes on her. Why did he stare? Shaking her head, she returned her attention to the ceremony. Her eyes filled when Felicity and Fergus exchanged rings. It was not the wedding she had dreamed of giving her niece, but what dream ever approached reality? Involuntarily her eyes moved to Waldo, who was watching the event with a slightly petulant frown. The earl, still watching Rosalind, knitted his brow ever so slightly.

"I now pronounce you man and wife."

As Fergus bent to kiss Felicity, Rosalind's eyes overflowed.

"Tears of happiness," she assured a worried Felicity minutes later as she hugged her tightly. "My dear child, I do wish you happy."

"I know you do, Aunt Rosalind," Felicity choked on her own tears. "And I do thank you for everything."

An air of conviviality soon surrounded those in the room, augmented by Lord Manning's foresight in bringing over several bottles of his finest champagne.

"Sir," Eberhart told his stepfather after a judicious sip, "you are as excellent a judge of champagne as you are of claret and sherry."

Manning beamed. "Thank you, my boy. Good of you to say so."

"If that inn in Dijon can produce champagne, sherry, and claret of this quality, I must brave the Channel," the earl went on. "And speaking of the Channel," he said as he turned to his secretary, "you shall precede me there, Fergus. I know the impulse to dawdle, but the sooner your wedding trip commences the sooner I shall rest easy."

"You are right, sir," Fergus agreed, laying aside his glass.

"But Felicity's clothes," Rosalind protested. "Madame Fanchon has not yet completed all her dresses."

"You can send them on to her in Brussels," the earl pointed out. "Fergus, you can have the carriage to the coast for the crossing."

"Oh, Lord Eberhart." Felicity hugged him. "How shall we ever thank you?"

Eberhart, fearing that she would succumb to another attack of vapors, sent a supplicating look to Fergus, who with a grin led her away. But before they left the room, Felicity turned and bestowed her bouquet—a charming collection of yellow and red roses—on Rosalind.

Chapter Twenty-two

"Strange how one wedding inevitably leads to thoughts of another," Eberhart drawled, bending to take a sniff of the bouquet Rosalind held in her hands. "Pity they aren't orchids."

"What did you mean about a second wedding, Alastair?" his mother demanded.

He turned toward her with a smile. "Rosalind's wedding to Waldo, Mama. Don't tell me you've forgotten. Now that we have a minister present we can have another ceremony. I took the liberty of procuring another special license, for one never can find a bishop to issue the blasted things when one has need of them." He observed Rosalind's whitening face. "You and Waldo could take the plunge now, if you wish." He paused. "You appear to be struck dumb, Miss McHenry, but don't fall into a pelter: a simple 'I do' a few moments from now is all that will be required of you."

Rosalind choked. "Lord Eberhart, you are without question the most autocratic, high-handed, interfering gentleman I've ever known. What gives you the right to procure a special license for me?"

"Would you care to examine it?" Eberhart asked, producing the document with a flourish.

"No, I would not." She crossed her arms and turned her back to him.

"Then what about you, Waldo?" the earl asked, holding it out toward the viscount. Waldo, floored at so unprecedented an action, looked from Eberhart to Rosalind.

"Point is, Eberhart, I must be returning home," he stated, and he bolted out of the room.

"Waldo always was a man of action," Eberhart remarked when the viscount had left. "Funny how the merest mention of marriage to you, Miss McHenry, should put him in a quake."

"Alastair," his mother objected, "you are being most provoking to Miss McHenry. I can't think what has gotten into you today."

"Oh, today is no different from any other day, ma'am," Rosalind said. "He has always been provoking to me."

"Today, actually, is different," the earl contradicted. "It's not every day I get married."

Lady Manning was betrayed into a shriek, while Lord Manning suspected his hearing had gone bad.

"Married?" Lady Manning exclaimed when she could speak.

"You can't get married," Lord Manning said after a large swallow of champagne restored his wits. "You need a bride. You've got the minister right enough, and the special license, but no bride."

"As usual, sir, you have the uncanny knack of hitting the nail on the head. But I do hope that if you allow me a few moments alone with Miss McHenry the role of bride might be filled."

"Alastair." His mother beamed. "You have seen the light at last. Didn't I say so all along, Harry?"

Rosalind rose in splendid fury. "What are you saying, Eberhart? This is the most audacious thing I've heard you utter yet."

"You'd best sit down and listen to me," he told her calmly. "Mama, would you leave us alone?"

Lady Manning, curbing her real desire to see how things turned out, marshaled her forces and led the exodus from the blue saloon.

"I know it sounds strange," she said to Rosalind as she passed, "but Alastair has always had sound reasons for his actions, peculiar though they might seem."

"I know the reasons well enough," Rosalind said to the earl when they were alone at last. "You dote on humiliating me."

"Don't be missish and do sit down! I shan't eat you!"

In no way mollified by his tone, she sat in a chair, arms still crossed on her chest.

"Here." He thrust the special license at her.

She waved it off. "I don't want it."

"Look at it," he commanded.

Fixing a glare on him, she snatched it up and turned it over with a puzzled frown. She had no experience with such documents, but what she held between her fingers did not look like a license, but like a bill. And one from a chandler, at that.

Her eyes flew up to meet his. "Eberhart, this isn't—"

"Yes, I know."

"But then why did you say it was?"

"To force Waldo to bolt," he explained, raking his fingers through his hair. "I had to do something to break up that match, or you would have gone to the grave married to him. I could see he didn't much wish to marry you, but he would have been duty-bound to go through with it."

"What a coming thing to say!"

He smiled at her, and she felt suddenly nervous. "Pray forgive me for the indelicacy of causing your betrothed to bolt, but the situation appeared to warrant desperate measures. You see"—he took possession of her hands—"I have grown a trifle tired waiting for you to notice how superior I am to old Waldo and to give him his congé."

"Is that what I was supposed to do?" Rosalind asked, feeling suddenly and uncharacteristically shy.

"Yes," the earl said with an emphatic nod. "So I did the deed for you."

"You seem rather sure of yourself, my lord. I might have viewed the bolting of Waldo in a different light."

"Yes. You might have been prostrate with grief."

"Odious, odious man," Rosalind said, her shoulders quaking.

"I knew you wouldn't be annoyed," he went on happily. "You think Waldo a bore and a coxcomb, too."

"When did I ever say so?"

"Each time you gazed at him. I, on the other hand, while

aggravating and opinionated, am not a bore or a coxcomb."
To prove his point his strong arms swept around her shoulders and his mouth descended to plant a resounding kiss on her lips.

Caught by surprise, Rosalind felt herself responding to the embrace with a fervor that left them both breathless. It was, she thought as they drew reluctantly apart, nothing at all like kissing Waldo.

"You see?" Eberhart gave her a little squeeze.

"Do you always conduct your flirtations in so brazen a manner?" she asked.

He held her off a moment. "Flirtation? My good woman, I am making you a declaration, if you would but notice. And how dare you ignore me these last few days when I was dangling after you in full view of the *ton*?"

"Is that what you were doing?" she teased. "I thought you had a new liking for Society."

He dropped a kiss on the top of her head. "What I had, minx, was a liking for you. And it was not mere liking, either. I was top over tail in love with you."

"And what about Isabelle Hubbel?" she asked curiously.

He met her eyes solemnly. "Isabelle is a friend, and she is enjoying the protection of Lord Michael Hastings, as I recall. She is no threat to you, my dear," he said, and he kissed her again.

Fully satisfied on that score, she sank back against his shoulder, nestling happily against his coat of Bath blue superfine.

"I thought you'd never see the light and send Waldo packing," he murmured. "Any other female would have dragged me to the altar by now."

"But I am not any other female," she pointed out.

"No," he acknowledged. "You are just Rosalind, whom I love and can't bear to live without. Now what is the problem?" he asked as she bolted out of his arms.

"Waldo!"

"You can't have a sudden attack of conscience over him now," he protested.

"Not him, but his ten thousand pounds. I borrowed it to pay you back."

He chuckled. "You may simply deposit that amount to Waldo's account whenever you wish from our account with Baverstock. And that is the last I wish to ever hear of Gerald's debts or Waldo's loan. Now, then, Miss McHenry, I believe we were discussing a marriage to come with myself as groom and yourself as bride."

"Indeed we were, my lord," Rosalind said with a happy sigh as he drew her back into his arms. "Indeed we were."

10.88
6.52 *.05* *6.96* *.45*

True romance
is <u>not</u> hard to find...
you need only look
as far as
FAWCETT BOOKS